EYE-AWAY

Rolf-Olav

Order this book online at www.trafford.com
or email orders@trafford.com

Most Trafford titles are also available at major online book retailers.

Note for Librarians: A cataloguing record for this book is available from Library
and Archives Canada at www.collectionscanada.ca/amicus/index-e.html

Printed in the United States of America.

ISBN: 978-1-4269-0924-5 (sc)
ISBN: 978-1-4269-1050-0 (hc)

Our mission is to efficiently provide the world's finest, most comprehensive book
publishing service, enabling every author to experience success. To find out how to publish
your book, your way, and have it available worldwide, visit us online at www.trafford.com

Trafford rev. 11/20/2010

 www.trafford.com

North America & international
toll-free: 1 888 232 4444 (USA & Canada)
phone: 250 383 6864 ♦ fax: 812 355 4082

SYNOPSIS

SETTING: A Norwegian homestead in Western Wisconsin
TIME: 1935
THE TITLE: "Eye-Away" means, as explained in the telling, "look-and-run," a code created by the boys; it is also the local pronunciation of IOWA.

Bored with grade school and routine farm life, a timid little Johannes seeks refuge in a fantasy world inspired by his Uncle Snorri's annual recitations of romanticized Indian lore. Obsessed with this, Johannes dreams of exploring the forbidden bluff on their land for the secret cave where the ghosts of Indian braves allegedly gather, healers who wipe away the fears and weaknesses of anybody who recognizes them. Also he wants to prove to his Uncle that these ghosts are real, that they may have shapes, even faces.

His protective mother, troubled by her only living child's preoccupations, encourages a recent, but older, welfare boy in the community to become the playmate (and possible role model) that Johannes has never had. Although opposites in temperament and personality, the boys bond instantly, and soon create strategies for getting to and from the bluff undiscovered, each with his own goal in their summertime search for that secret cave: for Johannes, to have possible chance encounters with the healers, which will make him strong and free; for Buddy, to find a place to hide from his dysfunctional family before he can run away (again) to a sympathetic aunt in Iowa.

When the boys locate a cave, Buddy takes over the cleaning and housekeeping, while Johannes is relegated to stand on guard for calls or signs of danger from home. Later, when evidence points to similarities between their cave and the one in Uncle Snorri's tales, Johannes waits in vain for the ghosts to be felt, while Buddy finalizes plans to go down the rivers to Iowa (as also happened in Uncle Snorri's accounts). Johannes idolizes his friend for making the cave real, and he reluctantly accepts the plan to accompany him when that time comes, fearing that if Buddy goes to Iowa by himself, he'll never return. Departure rests on word from the tolerant aunt.

On the last Saturday of summer vacation, their only chance to sneak away before school starts, Johannes is kept from going to town with Dad because he failed to make-up his left-over schoolwork. Dreading their take-off because of Uncle Snorri's impending visit, and desperate for news and directions from Buddy, Johannes finally comes to the conclusion that Buddy's absence and silence means that he's coming home with Dad, at which time, he feels with relief, it will be too late to set out.

When Dad comes home alone in the onrush of a storm, Johannes fears that something's happened to Buddy, but hopes that he's waiting in one of their hide-outs on the farm. Unable to seek him, being housebound, Johannes begins to fear that Buddy's taken off without him. Later that night in the violent backlash from the earlier storm, the Sheriff and Buddy' mother also believe that he's run away. Later, alarmed for Buddy being exposed to such weather and afraid that he'll be apprehended and sent away to reform school, Johannes confesses their plan to his mother.

Heartsick at breaking their pact for secrecy, Johannes the next day begins to find relief and comfort in knowing that he hasn't revealed anything about their cave. And he's pleased to find the community wasting its time searching their storm-stricken area while Buddy gets farther and farther away.

Then, recalling his mother's earlier query about the whereabouts of his work shoes (which need winterizing), Johannes panics again at remembering that he's left them in the cave during their last session there when Buddy's review of the Iowa plans upset and confused him. Desperate to keep the cave a secret AND to reclaim his shoes, Johannes manages to slip away from the bustle at home and, with great trepidation, he climbs the bluff for the first time by himself.

With his guard down, but also anticipating the arrival of the ghosts now that he's coming quietly and alone, he arrives at the familiar cave, only to find that it has collapsed in a landslide caused by the night's storms.

Struck dumb at first, but daring not to go home without his shoes, Johannes for the first time ever, initiates work on his own; he begins to dig into the debris for his shoes, and in so doing, generates a fantasy about how to restore the cave before Buddy has knowledge of the disaster. Out of nowhere then, his mother (who has missed him and has sighted him high on the rocks) descends. Surprised and terrified, Johannes blurts out the secret of their cave and she, surveying the scene in horror, draws the conclusion that Buddy hasn't run away.

After getting Johannes to safety, she alerts the searchers, while he, numb from his physical efforts, basks, exhausted in his triumph at doing something special on his own. And when the searchers appear with their tragic remains, Johannes rises in sudden exaltation for, instead of finding Dad in front of him with Buddy across his arms, he SEES the ghosts he's been looking for so long, performing precisely as they did in Uncle Snorri's tale. He now can PROVE to Uncle Snorri that the ghosts are real, that they have shapes, that they even have faces.

NOTE: The novel is told from the point of view of Johannes, along with his suppositions, syntax, spelling, vocabulary, even his confusion.

There is always one moment in childhood when
the door opens and lets the future in.
(Graham Greene)

For

Wallace Stegner

CONTENTS

ORIENTATION

TIME: 1934-35   SCENE: Western rural Wisconsin

Principals

Johannes Berg (called Jonas by Ma and Uncle Snorri) (called Hansy by Dad and Buddy)

Kari Berg (Ma; daughter of Grampa Anderegg & granddaughter of Great-Granddad)

Thorwald-Jon Berg (Dad; known as Thor)

Snorri-Bjorn Berg (Dad's twin; known locally as S.B.)

Buddy Trygrud (wants to be called "Bud Trigger")

Hester Trygrud (Buddy's Maw; paramour of the Sheriff)

Borgny Gunderson (rural teacher; Berg family friend; called "Ol' Gundy" by the boys)

Sheriff Strutt (The Sheriff-Almighty to Johannes)

Rev Flogge (known as "The Preacher")

Mrs. Flogge (Mrs. Preacher's Woman to the boys)

*   *   *

Great Chief Broken Thunderhawk (for the "Wisconsin Indians")

Singing White Wolf, shamen-singer (for the Minnesota Indians)

Anderegg Community (incl The Widow Peterson, the Olsons, Hansons, Petersons, Torkelsons, Johnsons, et al)

Townfolks (incl "loony" Effie Stone)

LOCAL GLOSSARY

Poop/s, -ed, -ing	: mini-fart activity triggered by excitement, fear, worry, fun
"Terrible", "Awful"	: amazement, beyond ordinary words

PROLOGUE

The Ghost Song of Uncle Snorri

Long, long ago in Olden Times, before Norwegians came, before schoolhouses and churches and cows and the Lone Ranger disturbed his native land, Great Chief Broken Thunderhawk, most powerful of Indians, kept well the wigwams of his clan on the Wisconsin side of the Mississippi (where Great-Granddad's homestead and Anderegg Corners now sprawl over the landscape).

"Beyond the fields and nearby flood flats, through the bottoms and across on the western bank of the River, the Minnesota tribes in their typees celebrated their young, new shaman, Singing White Wolf; he of a magical voice whom they called a healer of sorrows, a slayer of shadows."

(Uff da!) Johannes fretted every time his Uncle Snorri-Bjorn began spinning the legend of the Walking Sorrows Bluff. And that happened every September in the early Thirties when Dad's twin left his ocean-riding boat for shore leave on their farm. (Uff da, for sure! What if I hear something different this time; what if he leaves out the special parts, ohhhh.). So did he worry until legend-telling came again and he'd have to wait impatiently each time Uncle Snorri stopped at the wrong places. (Like Ma says, "That's yer Uncle Snorri; loves to tease us.")

Sometimes Uncle Snorri added details for his first-time listeners and he'd string everything along to make it more "mysterious." But ma declared that "he dragged the same old stuff out every year jist to rile the community with his loony notions and the funny-peculiar names he stuck on their familiar places." Whatever changes Johannes feared never happened to alter the heart of the story. For his own special reasons then, he strained to remember it as he heard it so he could pass it on, almost word-for-word, to anybody who'd pay attention in grade-school. Most important of all, he had to make it sound real for

Buddy, ever since they began scheming over summertime plans the past winter nights.

However often he repeated himself, Uncle Snorri-Bjorn sounded as new as the first time Johannes heard him (he must fergit he's told us this before, huh?). And that made it harder to forget (if you listened with more than your ears).

"One day under a skyful of magic, Great Chief Broken Thunderhawk and Singing White Wolf paddled to their common boundary in the middle of the Mississippi and swore to forsake war, which their forefathers had kept alive since before time had a name. To prove themselves true to their promises they smoked pipes carved from the sacred quarries, slashed each other's arm in an act of Blood Brotherhood, and exchanged signals that would alert their clans to danger (how "mysterious" ahhhh; signals like everyday signs, maybe even like them mourning dove whimpers Buddy'd set off to confuse me more while he hid somewheres not easy to find).

"After making peace on the River, Great Chief Broken Thunderhawk guided his new Blood-Brother to the cave where he "meditated" (meddy-tay-ted?) and made decisions for his people. Singing White Wolf never forgot such an honor, for only a Guard of Chosen Braves knew of such a hideaway high in the tallest bluff." (A place, I'm sure, The Sheriff-Almighty Strutt could never come upon, however hard he snooped).

Because his listeners rarely interrupted or said much (too happy with their coffee, maybe?), Uncle Snorri took his own sweet time and that made Johannes more tense than ever. Yet, he loved the SOUND of Uncle Snorri's words and the way it settled around him, even if he didn't understand them all when he couldn't see them in his head (and if you can't see em how can you spell em and if you can't spell …). The way Uncle Snorri rolled language on his tongue gave it longer life: tasting "mysterious" for a long time (one of my favorite words cause it covers so many things), and dwelling on "meditation" and making "vanish" spooky. Whenever Johannes asked for meanings, the echo of the words in his own mouth chilled him with delight, and he hoped to know some day what they really said. Until then, he'd remember every syllable he could as Uncle Snorri spoke. The special words never hindered the legend:

"One day without omens (Uncle Snorri's voice as husky as if he had the croup), an enemy invaded Minnesota from the western bluffs south on the River. They fell upon Singing White Wolf, kidnapped him (like they did the Lindbergh baby that time, huh?), and demanded his tribal shores in exchange for his safety and freedom. But before the raiders could drag him downstream, Singing White Wolf with his magical voice stood tall on his captor's raft and sent forth a ghost song that shattered the bluffs of Wisconsin. The enemy stopped cold. And Great Chief Broken Thunderhawk, harkening his Blood Brother's call, launched fleets of canoes down Squaw River where it meets with the Mississippi, a battle bloodied the waters."

Uncle Snorri glowed when he dwelt on this; for whatever details colored the fighting, it always happened on water. When Buddy heard this account last fall, Johannes recalled how his face brightened with notions.

"While Great Chief Broken Thunderhawk pursued and recaptured his shaman-brother, the Guard of Chosen Braves pushed what invaders survived down the River to Eye-Away (where Buddy's Aunt Min and her houseful of daughters lived on the edge of Dee-bjuke with their four German husbands and horses).

"Such a heroic rescue cemented forever the Blood-Brotherhood. The Chief taught the Singer how to smell danger and how to lure it away; the Singer in turn chanted songs that fortified his teacher's spirit. Every season they pow-wowed; they smoked again the pipes carved from the Western Quarries (a place even Uncle Snorri-Bjorn had never been). They explored both banks of the Upper River with its un-named coulees and bluffs. Never had there been such comradeship between members of opposite tribes." ("Except in the muddy trenches of The Great War," Dad mumbled once as he shifted his quid of tobacco and listened with squinted eye).

Johannes, growing breathless, found it almost unbearable (as "mysterious" as Jesus or Buddy's Maw):

"One year at the beginning of fall, another enemy moved in from the south, this time on the eastern bank of the River, coming up from the Illanoise. And Singing White Wolf, portaging his canoe on the Wisconsin shore, came undiscovered upon a raider's camp, and overheard and decoded plans for the seizure of his Blood-Brother's bluffs. Slipping away, still unseen, Singing White Wolf paddled upstream for a day and a night, then fought a way through sloughs full of mud (and snakes?) to warn the wigwams of the Chief. (Right where the schoolhouse and the church squat now – according to Uncle Snorri – and where Blood Brothers Crick runs deepest before it disappears north of its bridge into the black Squaw River).

"While his Guard of Chosen Braves hunted game on surrounding ridges, Broken Thunderhawk, in his cave, prepared for the coming snows. Recalling the route to the sacred hideaway, Singing White Wolf crept along rocky shelves to the ledge that led to the face of the bluff. At a rustling in the air, he turned and looked into a troop of enemy scouts that popped up from moving shelters used for spying on the village far below.

"Unable to reach the cave without revealing its location, Singing White Wolf spun on his tracks and faced the oncoming force with a spine-wilting song. Once again, this enemy too froze for an unearthly moment, and off in his cave Broken Thunderhawk caught the alarm, while his Guard of Chosen Braves swooped in from the ridges to rescue the Singer once more. This time, they arrived too late and could only watch from a distance as Singing White Wolf, pierced by many flints, crumbled to earth.

"Great Chief Broken Thunderhawk, blind to the enemy before him, dashed through zinging arrows to the side of his fallen brother, and as he knelt to lift him up, he watched the light of life flicker and wane. On outstretched arms he carried the Singer along the ledge and around the bend that concealed his hideaway, while his Guard of Chosen Braves held off the raging pack.

"Safe at the entrance to his cave, the Great Chief lay his brother down and when he gazed deeper into the wounded eyes, no life quivered in the widening puddle of blood." (Each time Ma'd hear this part, she coughed and grumbled with something like "Na-men! Snorri sure is bloody for somebody cant stand meat!").

At this point, Uncle Snorri usually paused again, this time to adjust his suspenders or refill his corn-cob pipe or sip some coffee. Sometimes he strolled around the room, casting a yo-yo out, then reeling it in so stubbornly slow, every muscle in Johannes stiffened (please, Uncle Snorri, don't change nuttin now; and why you teasin us like this agin, huh?).

"Finally, with a howl of grief, Great Chief Broken Thunderhawk rose tall and moved unarmed through his Guard of Chosen Braves to curse the enemy. A sudden arrow zinged into his breast. Stiff with surprise, The Chief stopped absolutely still; then, with all the world to witness, (oh wonder of wonders, more "mysterious" than anything else in the world!), he plucked the arrow from his chest as he'd dust a feather off, and hurled it into the raiders, now screaming forward for the kill. In a flash of blue lightning, the flint exploded into a hail of razor-points ("like the quills of a flustered porkypine," Dad whispered last year when he winked at me). And in the midst of all that dying, the Chief moved backwards against the bluff, leaving his own blood in his tracks.

"When a new wave of slayers surged forth to follow the Chief to his cave, the Ghost of Singing White Wolf (ahhhh!) rose from its discarded corpse as a mist, turned the corner of the ledge and spread itself larger than a thunderhead to sobbings of a thousand mourning doves. This time, the ghost-song struck an even greater numbness on the afternoon. The world stood still. And when the Ghost of Singing White Wolf dwindled back into its pool of thickened blood, a clump of birch oozed forth to mark the sacred spot."

Weak with relief each time he found no changes in this climax, the spirit of Johannes wailed at the wonder of it all (how could such things, such things ever BE! But, will the rest remain the same now?).

"With the heartbeats and breath restored, the enemy gasped and gasped as one to find Great Chief Broken Thunderhawk, still alive, crowning the point on the Bluff, where none had seen him climb, where none could scale such vertical walls. And when the Mississippi sent in a fog along Squaw River to blot out the sight and the smell of death, the Chief dived into the sky and vanished (ahhh, "vanished," such a word, and would Uncle Snorri have other things to tell him later when Ma let him stay in Uncle Snorri's room?).

"Then everybody left on the Bluff killed each other off ("Uff da!" Ma never failed to complain then, "aint that some story to go to bed on now!)."

Uncle Snorri never failed to pause here. He'd play with his yo-yo again, encouraging some listeners' calls, their first words since he began: "Let's git it over with , S.B." "Helluva time to run outa steam, S.B.," and Ol' Hjalmer usually added "Don't give us no wooden nickels now neither!." Everybody Johannes knew called Uncle Snorri-Bjorn 'S.B.'. They welcomed him with loud laughs, slaps on the back, and sometimes nudged him (and each other), but did they really listen to his legend (like I do, huh?). Johannes didn't think so, with tears of impatience under his lids, while Uncle Snorri teased and teased the group:

"Now, from the spilled blood, good blood and bad, where warriors fell, junipers sprung up to clog and decorate the rocks and slopes, for each razor-point had ended in a scream of death. THAT is how the Howling Grief Ridges came to be named."

Johannes would remember how Ol' Gundy sniffed whenever he tried to explain such marvels at grade-school. But, while she said such Indian-sounding names meant nothing, she allowed there could have been such troubles back in Olden Times.

"After that, where else blood splashed, leaves turned red each fall; a salute to dead braves, good or bad." Johannes wondered then if he'd ever climb the ridges some year with so much blood on the oaks and the sumac. Even the idea of such a forbidden act turned ants lose in his veins and let sluggish worms crawl behind his belly button where he couldn't reach to scratch. Now listeners would wonder how much more they had to hear ("Get the lead outnow, S.B.").

"When the Minnesota people heard of their shaman's fate, they mourned long for his passing on alien soil, but when they tried to locate the cave where they'd been told the sacred bones might rest, their efforts failed and they paddled home in sorrow. Just as the Wisconsin people mourned their Chief, whom some said had been kidnapped by the sky to die alone in clouds, away from native ground. But, you must remember this (Uncle Snorri'd sometimes dig into his yellow beard with mischief chewing at his eyes), it's told that Great Chief Broken Thunderhawk perished not from wounds, but died in grief instead; grief for his Blood-Brother gone. And his spirit refused to go alone into the bosom of Manitou. Thus did his restless ghost come back to the Bluff, seeking the ghost of Singing White Wolf in the hope of going together into the Happy Lands."

At this hour, when a sigh of relief often swept over the room, Uncle Snorri would lift his pointer finger as a warning he hadn't finished, but would give anyone a chance to re-fill coffee cups or go outdoors to pee. By this time, few had the energy to resist him.

"Nobody knows the true end to our story," he'd continue with a faraway look (the kind Dad sometimes wore, and Ma too). "Some say the Ghosts never found each other and so wander the rocks to this moment (ahhh!). That's why it's known as Walking Sorrows Bluff. Where pain lingers, where the Chief, still seeking, comes out of the sky whenever clouds kiss the Point. Walking Sorrows, where storms blast the ridges when enemy ghosts remember their evil deeds and try to escape but cannot. Ahhh, Walking Sorrows Bluff, where God's Big lightning often splits rocks."

As soon as Uncle Snorri began to turn the Bluff into a poem, Ma, wherever she worked or rested, always burst upon them loud and fast: "Don't care what nobody says. That Bluff name's Anderegg Point, always been; hear that, Johannes, named fer yer Great-Granddad Johannes Anderegg and don't you fergit it!"

Then somebody usually brought up another touchy subject: "Still call it Bachelor's Drop downtown; how come?"

"Don't know better, that's what," Ma'd answer at once as Uncle Snorri, not to be side-tracked now, rambled on:

"It's believed by some that The Ghosts found each other, but they couldn't bear to leave behind the sky colors over the Point nor the sight of the Mississippi on the western horizon, and whenever the clouds kiss the Bluff, The Ghosts pow-wow in their secret cave.

"Flints from that old "treachery (trech-ree?)" are buried on the ridges and whoever comes upon one will be shielded forever from harm ("Maybe they're worth money," Buddy wonders ever time I mention arrows). But those who are lucky enough to discover the hideaway cave will have all their shadows and sorrows erased. For the Ghost of Singing White Wolf heals, and the Spirit of Broken Thunderhawk protects.

By this time every year, Ma could no longer keep still, though others looked too weary (or lazy?) to make arguments. She'd break out with: "bossshhh!" or "Nuff-a this foolishness" or "As if Johannes, as if you, Jonas, had shadows at yer age now" and she'd bustle about, shedding irritations like falling leaves while she set the table for angel food cake, or cleared space for a game of whist. Uncle Snorri always waited for her storm to fizzle before he got up to stretch again. Even when he moved around the room with the yo-yo, he teased:

"Bet you're all afraid of that hired man's ghost and that's why you don't climb the Bluff, right?" and he'd glare into various faces until somebody coughed or shifted (but who knows if that hired man really fell off at all; downtown they say he jumped or maybe someone pushed him, and he don't even count cause they found him hangin in the tree-tops dead so how can HE be livin on the Bluff then; don't belong).

"In case you fraidy-cats wanted to meet ghosts, real Indian ghosts, I mean, " Uncle Snorri'd insist, "the secret cave shouldn't be hard to locate: it's at the spot where the Mississippi shows on the horizon, this side of Minnesota. And the opening to the cave – remember? – would be marked by a clump of birch, renewed each year with skin soft as the underbelly feathers of a mourning dove. Inside the cave you'd maybe even find the bones ..."

When she heard this, Ma always aroused another commotion, reminding them of chores undone, of school in the morning (the worst of reminders), or an order to be off to bed "if you wanna stay with Uncle Snorri while he's here," and she'd push him off with a kiss: "now scoot!."

Once alone in Uncle Snorri's bed, away from Ma's concern about ghosts and blood, Johannes would work himself deep into the tick, wide-eyed restless for the sound of boots on the front stairs. He could hardly wait to hear again those details never lingered on with Ma around (mustn't let my ears get sleepy, ohhhh) and when he pretended not to know all the legend, would Uncle Snorri remember what he'd told him every time before? Each time everything unfolded like that first time, Johannes would poop with relief. When the serious moment came for Johannes to test Uncle Snorri, it went the same way, too:

"HOW could Great Chief Broken Thunderhawk climb the Bluff straight up like that, huh."

"That's the Chief's own secret; showing off his power, his own magic, I guess."

"The same like when he "vanished" then?"

"Of course he didn't VANISH, Jonas."

"You always say he did, why?"

"It sounds more spooky that way. People must have mystery or they'd be dead as door nails. Between you and me, we can stand the truth, can't we? The Chief didn't vanish at all. He just leaped through the fog into the big black bend of Squaw River. Then, with arms and both legs broken, the current carried him to a log. He hugged it and floated down to Singing White Wolf's shores to warn them there of raiders, though by that time, remember? everybody left on the Bluff had died. And Great Chief Broken Thunderhawk slept away with his wounds and became a ghost in the Singer's typee."

(Every time I tell Buddy about that leap, he wonders how many bones stuck out of the Great Chief's skin; he don't see the marvel of it at all!)

Every year Johannes asked what he'd have to do if he wanted to meet the Ghosts. He needed to see if Uncle Snorri-Bjorn remembered giving him directions before, and would they be the same ones this time, too.

"Now, if you ever found that cave, Jonas, the Ghosts of course wouldn't come out and greet you. They're shy (like most horses, huh?); they don't like noise or distraction. You must speak softly if you say anything at all."

"But how'd I know em then?"

"Well, first you must believe in them. Then, you have to sit still, empty your head, and wait. But if you believe hard enough, you'll … you'll know them."

"Don't ghosts have shapes and faces then?"

Uncle Snorri always paused before answering this most important question: "No, I don't think so … but, who can tell?"

"Oh! how'd you know em if you can't see em, huh?"

"You don't have to SEE Singing White Wolf to hear his songs, and the Great Chief would be there in silence to protect you. You'd KNOW all right. Most people never meet ghosts or have special adventures because they don't or can't believe; they're afraid of different ideas; they make too much noise inside themselves and out."

"If I could SEE the Ghosts I wouldn't be 'fraid; only hearin 'bout em scares me, cause I wouldn't know which is what if they don't have shapes or faces; I'd miss everything."

"No, you wouldn't. You'd know them if you ever met. You'd know them in your soul."

Uncle Snorri's answers remained pretty much like that, year in, year out, and the same disappointment settled on Johannes every visit. He couldn't sleep until he'd try to find out more. One last time then usually turned out the same:

"YOU ever look for ghosts, Uncle Snorri?'

"No."

"Why not?"

"Don't need to look, Jonas. It's enough to know they're all around us ... always."

"But if you could see em, how'd you think they'd look, huh? Make b'lieve you saw em ..."

"All right, but it's hard to say, Jonas. Maybe they'd have head shaved like braves, or, being chiefs, they'd probably wear their long thick hair in braids. Isn't that the way we'd expect them to look? (you mean braids, like that loony Effie Stone wears?). Golly, Jonas, you're more curious than ever before. Hey, wait a minute, why are YOU so taken with this anyway. Seems every year something like this comes up.. "

" Hafta know is all (and I'd never feel alone when Buddy aint around). Besides, I'd wanna hear ghost songs from Singing White Wolf. You say they wipe out shadows; you say he sees the future (like Ma or The Widow Peterson?)."

Uncle Snorri-Bjorn grew quiet then, and didn't remember that the last time Johannes brought this up, he'd answered in the same words:

"Jonas, you're lucky. As your Ma says, how can you have shadows at your age. Now let's go to sleep."

(Oh, but I HAVE shadows, I do, but I do!) Johannes had never mentioned that to anyone. Even Ma knew nothing about his secret shadow because he had no name for it at first, and he couldn't tell something if he couldn't find words to fit it: how a woolly blanket he couldn't see slipped out of Nowhere and wrapped itself around his spirit, pressing hard around him whenever he felt weak or afraid or sometimes shy (but never when I'm naughty, ahhhh). And it would squeeze out his air until everything turned black and the sound in his ears crawled into his nose and he just knew it would carry him off for good some day and leave no beating heart behind.

Then one night a couple of years ago during God's big freeze, a voice (like Uncle Snorri's or the Ghost of Singing White Wolf) crept into his sleep and whispered a name on his shadow, and called it The Winter-Lonely. This Something told him to fight his fears so strong and they'd run away, and never to act small, and whenever he outlasted frights and his smallness, The Winter-Lonely had no strength to take him and he'd become his own Great Chief instead, even his own Singer (whatever all that meant, ahhh). It grew easier to hold his shadow off when it had a name, but he still couldn't tell a soul of it: never to Ma or Dad, who'd worry fearfully; and least of all to let Buddy know (he'd think me loony as Ol' Gundy and that crazy Effie Stone downtown who Uncle Snorri visits when he's here). Since Buddy came into his life last fall, The Winter-Lonely stayed farther away from him (but waitin, waitin, I know fer sure).

But last year's visit, still alive in his special memory, found Johannes unable to sleep. He had to be reassured again that Uncle Snorri's legend SOUNDED real:

-You always said before when clouds kissed the Point of Walking Sorrows, it meant the Ghosts had come to their cave. So that's really where to meet em then? In the cave, huh?

-Good golly, Jonas, you still awake? He turned on his side and faced Johannes in the dark (can he hear my thoughts, like Ma can?). –One thing, Jonas boy, don't ever go looking for that cave by yourself. Agreed? Some day we'll climb up there and see what we can find (but you've promised that before and you've never had the time).

-You never been up there then?

-Of course not. Now go to sleep and I'll tell you about Norway in the morning; how I visited my Ma, your grandma, and heard again her oldest troll stories, as well as all the new ones she's collected. Sleep tight.

From the first time Johannes heard Uncle Snorri's legend at least four years ago to the first time Buddy heard it only last September,

Johannes hugged to himself one breath-catching dream: to BE in the presence of Great Chief Broken Thunderhawk and to hear a ghost song from Singing White Wolf, together in the secret sacred cave on Walking Sorrows Bluff (how can Ma insist on callin it Anderegg's Point; not a purty name at all).

He knew that Ol' Gundy and Ma and Buddy would never meet ghosts cause they couldn't b'lieve, but he'd show em; he'd b'lieve so strong he might even see IF they had shapes and faces (and think of proving THAT to Uncle Snorri-Bjorn, ahhh). Without his knowing it, Buddy helped him fight The Winter-Lonely; Buddy, without knowing it, would help him make his dream come true. He'd said it would be kinda fun to find a cave (not to wait for ghosts in but for a hidin plan, whatever under heaven that meant now), and maybe pick up flints worth money, too. How "mysterious" it all became, this breathing dream (more terrible than Jesus, more awful than Buddy's Maw).

Last fall, too, in his excitement, Johannes pooped so hard it turned into a roaring fart and Uncle Snorri'd mumbled something in a very sleepy voice: "Thus speaketh the mouth that had not tongue" (huh???) and Johannes shivered at the strange words that sounded like Bible-talk. In fact, he loved Uncle Snorri-Bjorn more with every visit. He didn't act grown-up at all, even when he had to be. Most grown-ups had so many things to be a-scared of, and they didn't like Indians nor want to do anything to make every day more excitin …

"Uff da!" Johannes drifted away on the same old worries: "the next time Uncle Snorri comes will he still sound the same? And will my everlasting dream come true, come true, huh?"

ONE

Saturday Everlasting

J ohannes listened.

A mourning dove answered itself beyond the open windows of the kitchen nook. He held his breath. The faint moan sounded closer, maybe from the lilac brush between the backhouse and the woodshed. He couldn't be sure in the rumpus Ma made at the other end of the room, where she laid out things for baking lefse.

Buddy? Finally here? But Buddy played mourning dove only when Johannes jabbered too much about Indian ghosts. Why tease him now, on this most important day? And why is he so late? He'd never been this late on any summer Saturday before (Gee whiz, we won't be able to git away at all, ohhhh).

He uncurled his bare feet from around the cushion in Great-Granddad's rocker, unfolded his arms from inside his overalls bib, and stretched forward to slow his rocking. He leaned into the window screens, ear straining. He knew Ma watched.

Only the echo of Dad's feed-truck rattling over the pass to Town came back to remind him why he had to stay home, and on this last Saturday of school-vacation, too. Dad would have taken him along without a fuss (and maybe picked up Buddy on the way?), but Ma'd said no, absolutely NO, because he still hadn't finished his summer lessons, but mostly for what he'd done to Ol' Gundy last Thursday noon. Why, Buddy didn't know about that yet (jist wait till I tell him and watch his eyes go crooked); nor had he heard about Uncle Snorri-Bjorn coming back tomorrow night (betcha that'll make him change our plans for sure).

Johannes pooped at the thought of things to happen. A weak giggle trickled out of his excitement, as a whiff from Dad's ploughed field outside the back fence wrinkled his nose with its rawness and stuck a furry finger down his throat. The dirt smelt like it had up

THERE last May. He twisted to glance up at the Point of Walking Sorrows Bluff, now pale orange in late morning sun. He had to see if it stood where it should be, to be sure it hadn't walked away. Did the Bluff approve of him and Buddy, it being in their thoughts so much?

It looked close enough to touch today, with the Howling Grief Ridges marching high above the tree-tops to his right, walling off their farm from the rest of Wisconsin. The fields facing west sloped before him to where the flood flats rolled on to Minnesota bluffs, dressed in shades of blue, not too far away.

The idea of the Miss'ippi flowing between them and his rocker sent an icicle down his backbone, just as the sight of that shoebox of a schoolhouse half a mile away, and the steeple of Mrs. Preacher's Wife's church down the road behind it, reminded him that The Winter-Lonely lurked there always, where he never wanted to be.

He turned back to Walking Sorrows to see if gathering clouds had kissed the Point. Why, from where he sat so exposed, the Ghosts of Great Chief Broken Thunderhawk and Singing White Wolf could look down through the trees and see the 'rithmetic pad turned upside down on his lap. He doubled over and pretended to work. He knew Ma watched.

Uncle Snorri's clock from Norway tick-tocked loudly on and on till it reached noon when its tin-can chime vibrated against the kettle covers in the washstand sink before clanging up through the ceiling grate to his room. If he dared sneak up there, he could maybe figure what to do till Buddy came, but he couldn't move with Ma around to read every plan that settled on his mind.

(Oh, Buddy, why you teasin me like this huh? Bein slow. How can we start down the Rivers for Eye-Away, with the sky lookin funny and Ma watchin hard? And Uncle Snorri-Bjorn comin home tomorrow, too.)

-Simply can't b'lieve it, Jonas, Ma raised her voice thinking he dozed. -Imagine, Tuesday's school again. Can you beat that! 1935's good as gone when school comes round this soon. Time for Uncle

Snorri, too. A good thing you had his postcard waitin for us last night or we'd still be wonderin when he'd show. First word since Christmas ("Be seeing you, Jonas, for supper Sunday night."), but that's yer Uncle Snorri for you. Glad we finished cleaning schoolhouse yesterday; coulda put us in a tizzy if we'd had that card beforehand. Anyway, we've had time to make his favorite things. You awake, Jonas?

-How long it'll take him to git here you s'pose? Johannes asked, eager to show Ma that he hadn't snoozed off.

-No longer than before, Jonas.

-S'pose he's got the same car then?

-Why in the world wouldn't he? Bet you'd miss that rumble seat, wouldn't you now?

-Yeah, Ma. Johannes pretended to be lost in his 'rithmetic problems.

He'd heard them say downtown that Uncle Snorri kept his sky-blue roadster-runabout in La Crosse at a girlfriend's house; then he remembered Dad telling harvesters how Uncle Snorri traded cars ever time he changes his girls. (Grown-ups always talking bout his spoonin and his sparkin, ohhh). Johannes couldn't believe that his Uncle Snorri had anything to do with girls, cause he's told him nuttin bout em, 'cept he liked visitin and listenin to that loony Effie Stone downtown (who had indoor cats and wore long braids and kept track of everybody's history which Ol' Gundy called "pure-gossip"; but who'd think-a her as anybody's sweetie, huh?). He decided not to worry bout the car or rumble seat, since things sounded good or bad only when Ma's voice made them so, and she dint sound concerned.

-If yer good, Jonas, Lord knows where he'll take you boys this year.

-Yeah, Ma (but why aint you worried bout Buddy like I am?)

He settled in such a way he seemed to be studying at the same time he could watch her fold cream and flour into a bowl of mashed potatoes, then knead some of the mixture into a ball and flatten it on the counter with the special rolling-pin that left patterns on the dough. She sprinkled drops of water on the top of the cookstove to see if it sizzled, then she took the lefse paddle and lifted the piece she'd prepared and spread it on the hot surface, where it began to bubble. Distracted for a moment, Johannes began to look forward to the sugar, cinnamon and fresh butter rolled together in some lefse (and sometimes with cranberries, if they dint cost too much; sometimes with home-made sausage.) What a memory his tongue had, tasting the smell of the baking.

-Cant b'lieve neither its over a year since Buddy came to us. 'Member that first time he saw lefse on the table? He thought I'd left some dish towels there, all folded to be put away.

Ma, humming, waited for the first piece to bake through before laying out another. -Now he cant git nuff of it like you. Between the two of you, you'll run me to the graveyard makin lefse; to say nuttin of Uncle Snorri's yen for it. Pity it don't keep good or I'd sent a sackful back with him.

Satisfied with her work (and mine?), she cleared space on the work counter for building a stack ('member last year, Buddy, ahhh …).

That summer had been so "mysterious" with those dust storms drifting dirt against everything like snow. Then, all the whispering at the Community Club about the family on County Relief soon to be settled in that rattletrap place halfway to Town. Gossip said there'd be many kids, an older girl to care for young ones, but only one of school age: a boy, a wild boy though, who Gossip called an outlaw; said he's even run away before but had to come to their country school because that's how the district boundaries lay. Johannes couldn't wait to see how such a critter looked (imagine, RUNNING AWAY from both home AND school, ahhh). Wouldn't he be fun to see, maybe git to know (what with all the other kids around him so deadly blank)? Gossip also hinted that he probably wouldn't show up at all, or stay put for long if he did. Such talk set Johannes with his hungry curiosity on edge.

But Buddy had come forth, after Ma had gone a-calling on the newcomers, hoping to get the small ones into Sunday School when it opened in the fall; and she'd invited Buddy to the Community

Club picnic held every August in their pasture, down in the weeping willows by the Crick.

THAT turned out to be the most special day he'd ever lived (till then). As he'd done with Uncle Snorri's legend, Johannes memorized every detail of this meeting, able to revive each step of it with racing blood: how he'd waded out of Blood Brothers Creek towards a tall curly boy who, clutching his overalls suspenders, strutted into his path the way Uncle Snorri imitated the gangsters he warned them about who often hid in their bluffs on runs between Chicago and Saint Paul (ahhh!) … how Buddy had stopped in front of him real close, patted him on his tow head, then stepped back to look him over before he placed a hand on each shoulder, tipped his head wideways like Ol' Odin used to do when too puzzled to bark out loud.

-Yer a purty lil mischief aint you, he finally said, -and the cleanest thing I ever seen. Who you belong to anyway?

He sounded fresh as springtime frogs.

-Wattaya mean "Lil"? Johannes piped out, scared, and so excited he pooped louder than he realized, at the same time Buddy answered with a softer poop, and without forethought on either side they butted heads. Alarmed, Johannes tried to back off fast, not knowing what he'd done. Buddy gaped at him, then winked:

-So, yer some kinda pooper, too, like me. Bet yer not a champeen though; betcha cant poop quiet without makin it a fart.

Johannes, blushing hot, slid out of Buddy's hold, baffled to find another who'd been doing what he'd done (as secretly as possible) for years. Wary in his excitement about what else this wondrous boy might say or do, Johannes backed away. Buddy moved in closer:

-Okay then, whose lil tyke are you?

Johannes drew to attention, knees trembling: - I am, I am Johannes Berg.

-Berg? A long pause with those black eyes full of reflections dancing over him. –You mean you belong to MRS Berg? Jesus, don't that take the cake!

-And aint you Buddy Trygrud? Johannes grew bolder the taller he strived to stand. –You sure don't look like Norskies.

Buddy, surprised, studied him a moment. –Guess yer right. But I aint a "Buddy" neither; I'm a Bud. You call me THAT. Bud Trigger. Like a gun.

-But Ma called you "Buddy."

-Yeah. Sure cant stop what grown-ups call us, can we. But you, you call me Bud. "Buddy," yuck; that's a baby-name.

Buddy's stare challenged him, but Johannes held fast. He'd never seen such eyes before; big as plums, digging right into him (how faded my grey ones must look, and how stringy my yellow hair compared with such tight black curls; how pale my skin against such dusky hands and face). But he couldn't escape those eyes. During the eternity they held their gaze, Johannes wondered if things looked different through different-colored eyes (Uncle Snorri-Bjorn said that many Indians had jet-black eyes; did that give them power to see in the dark?). He tried not to be the first to blink, but did.

-Sooo, yer a Berg! Now don't that ruffle the rooster. I s'pose this land belongs to …

-Yeah, and Walking Sorrows Bluff up there belongs to our farm, too. Why, that's the highest point around you know.

-Wattaya mean? Aint that Bachelors Drop? That's what they say it is downtown. Something bout a hired-man-ghost. Heard some other name too, but cant remember what.

-Oh Ma calls it Anderegg Point after her grampa; my Great-Granddad. But Uncle Snorri-Bjorn says its rightfully called Walking Sorrows, for the Indians.

-Injuns? What Injuns?

-Oh, they USED to be here. This used to be their country. Still is, Uncle Snorri …

-Uncle WHAT?

-My Uncle Snorri-Bjorn. He's away on the ocean now, works on some big boat. Goes all over the world; to Norway even.

Buddy looked him over, hushed. –You mean he's a sailor? A pause. –Never seen a real sailor before.

-Well, he used to be a lumberjack, like Dad; then they both went to The Great War, off in Yurp somewheres, and nobody else in the whole community had ever gone to France before and still come home alive. Now aint that something, huh? Afterwards Dad turned farmer, got hitched to Ma, and Uncle Snorri ...

Buddy, a head taller, looked down at him differently, but still the way 'Ol Odin did when he didn't know which bark to use.

-He'll be HERE next week, Uncle Snorri will. Comes first part-a September every year.

Johannes noticed, relieved, how Buddy's manner had changed towards him; softer, more "mysterious." –You like to see him, huh? Another pause. –If you wanna see him, you'll have to come back to our place then. Johannes rubbed away the flutter in his chest at what Ma might say and laughed back at the deep black eyes.

-And where does this Uncle Whatchamacallim get all that Indian stuff? Maybe got a squaw somewheres?

Johannes shivered at the idea. How he hated talk about Uncle Snorri-Bjorn and girls, much less having sweeties. He shook himself.

-Betcha I can poop as soft as you, Johannes said fast as with sudden boldness he reached for Buddy's hand and pulled him towards the tub of watermelons waiting for them in the weeping willow shade.

Buddy showed up at the farm a few days later, even before Uncle Snorri got back last fall. They hit it off so swell Dad said, they looked like doughboy comrades, horsing around. Uncle Snorri took to Buddy, too, same as Ma and Dad had. And from that beginning they entered into an ongoing pooping competition. Buddy remained champ, but Johannes struggled harder, even when he ended up a clucking hen, and sometimes brayed as loud as Hanson's jackass.

Every time he saw the weeping willows, he saw Buddy there. The trees grew lovelier to him all the time: fresh yellow in the springtime, then pea green before a deeper blue set in, but back to older yellow in the fall (ahhh, whatta day!).

Johannes shook off the reverie and glanced up to see if Ma had caught him dreaming, while she worked sheets of lefse into the folds of clean dish towels for storage. She hadn't. She almost always sang while she worked, sometimes in a faraway voice. She said that singing made housework go faster when you forgot to fret about what had to be done anyway. Sometimes songs like "Let the Rest of the World Go By" or "The Trail of Lonesome Pine"; she favored those from The Great War that happened long ago before his birth date back to Olden Times (whew, moren eighteen year ago they say, ahhh), those days grown-ups talked so much about when they had company and everybody hung around the table after meals, drinking coffee (did you hafta drink coffee when you got to be a grown-up, huh?). Coffee always bit his tongue, but Buddy liked it; didn't make a face after every sip neither. Ma added real cream to Buddy's cup whenever he'd done something special for her, or helped Johannes finish his chores faster. Today, between sips from her coffee cup nearby, Ma hadn't practiced those shivery hymns she sang at every funeral she'd been asked to. Instead she began that favorite of hers about a long, long trail a-winding off somewheres:

There's a long, long trail a-winding
Into the land of my dreams.
Where the nightingales are singing
And the white moon beams.
There's a long, long trail a-waiting
Until my dreams all come true …

This always brought to mind that "mysterious" short-cut over the Howling Grief Ridges down into Buddy's backyard, the last place on earth he'd ever dare to go (but I gotta try it someday jist to show me and Buddy I aint fraid-a nuttin; and think-a the surprise for all of us!).

Although Buddy lived more than two miles over the hills on Township Road, same as he did, Johannes didn't know what a mile meant. Nor had Buddy ever asked him to sneak away on that short-cut neither. Ma never took him with her when she stopped there (on business, she called it), and Dad always picked up speed, it seemed, whenever they passed by on their way to Town. Johannes could never forget how funny-peculiar Buddy's place looked, with chickens roosting on the slanted front porch, with crows playing hop-scotch on the many-colored shingles that patched the roof, and clothes to dry spread across the lower pine boughs. Many times he thought he saw The Sheriff-Almighty's car-with-the-star hidden in some shade behind old sheds, while little girls chased each other in circles through a weed-patch Ma said should be front yard grass. And he'd never seen Buddy there; not once.

Johannes heard another moan. Mourning dove again? Buddy? Or both? The Widow Peterson said mourning doves sobbed their sorrow for departed mates. At other times, they spoke for lonely ghosts. The stitch in his side burned (bethca Buddy aint heard from Aunt Min yet, and he's mad and stayin away cause we wont be able to take off for Eye-Away today or tomorrow then). A sigh, half-relief, swept over him. (If Aunt Min's card aint come, I wont hafta miss Uncle Snorri, or write that letter to Ma which I been practicing in my head ever since I knew of Buddy's plan.) Buddy'd change our plans for sure when he thought of that rumble seat and all. And by tonight or tomorrow it's maybe too late for Eye-Away anyhow. But his relief faded: what if Buddy'd made a promise to Aunt Min and would HAVE to keep it (jist cause he promised, ohhh).

Johannes shifted in the rocker until he had a glimpse of Gramma's crab apple tree beside the back fence. Sometimes, Buddy climbed into the crotch there, with branches to hide him and he'd let his legs hang down. No sign of his black hightops or everyday tennies; no sign neither of him in the swing Dad had hung from Grampa's sugar maple farther down the line. Only Solly and Sig, grazing around the tree trunks, showed restless as if waiting to be called and curried (seeking Buddy for sure cause of the way he had with horses).

Johannes wished he could see around the alcove to the backhouse and woodshed, where Buddy sometimes hid in the lilacs that filled the space between (then he'd wave a rag at me, specially if he dint want to be polite to grown-ups). No signal he could see or hear from where he sat, trapped. Only the soughing of the pines like gossip (maybe a ghost song from Singing White Wolf tryin to git through). Glancing back at Walking Sorrows, he saw the orange fade to brown while the sun slid in and out of that cloudbank drifting along the Minnesota line; heading right for them, he thought. He wisht Uncle Snorri's clock would stop, absolutely still, and with it what Ma called "Time" itself.

A cooler breeze crossed his face from the open windows and out the screendoor to the back porch. He looked up at the roll of fly paper that dropped from the ceiling and watched it turn slowly under its weight of stilled wings. Oh, he had to get out. But Ma filled the whole kitchen with her work, her songs, and her eyes. However much he needed to run against the wind and look for Buddy in some hiding place, he couldn't move. He hadn't heard Ma leave the counter when there she stood in front of him, blocking his view.

-Sky's sure lookin odd; betcha there's a storm somewhere tonight. It beats me why in the whole wide world that crazy Sheriff's gallivantin round these parts now. Whewww, she wheezed, wouldn't you know he'd run a skunk down. Almost run down Dad, too, right in our own turn-off. His dust's still hanging on the church; can trace it towards the County line. Must be onto some kind-a mess.

She shook her head again at the stink that mingled with the stirred-up dust of Township Road. Bushes swished against the sky as if pushing away the smell. Johannes stiffened. He's hurt so much from being kept at home, he refused to listen when Dad took off, much less paying attention to anybody else racing by. He hadn't even smelt the skunk (I like that bettern Ol' Gundy's store-bought stuff). What if The Sheriff-Almighty ran Buddy down like he did Ol' Odin then, splattering him all over the road and not even stopping that (goddam) car-with-the-star. Bet that's why Buddy's late, got himself run down. Johannes rattled the rocker. His belly somersaulted.

Ma lowered the sashes and turned to him: -Why look at you. A regular jumpin bean; cut-worms in yer pants now? Yer actin more a two-year-old, Jonas, than a big boy starting fifth grade. Now tell me whatsa matter (Cant, Ma, cant, ohhh).

Her voice forced him to be quiet. He wanted to get rid of her before she inspected his problems pad, but she moved too fast and licked her thumb to turn the pages faster: -You aint started yer 'rithmetic for today. I'm shamed of you.

She turned the pad rightside on his lap to the exercises he'd been trying to complete for weeks. –When yer done with these, we'll have the last of HUCK FINN tonight, right in time for the start-a school. Then you'll have them pesky book reports outa yer hair. How's that? Sure talk funny in that book now, don't they? Must be all right though; wouldn't be on the schoolhouse shelf, I s'pose.

Johannes, silenced by his fears for Buddy, couldn't look at her. With a deep sigh, she waited several moments, but he made no move.

-Well then, whyn't we go back to the spellin we started this morning? While I get Uncle Snorri's fried cakes on the way.

-Oh no, Ma, no more spelling; oh, not that again!

She puzzled over him, then tousled his sunburnt hair. Strands of it fell over his face, making him look like a puppy flirting from beneath a straw pile. She smelled of the rhubarb pies she'd set to cool in the pantry earlier, and whiffs of burnt lefse drifted off her smock to tickle his nose. She made him safe; far from his promises to Buddy, farther still from mysteries of Eye-Away. He reached for her when she tried to leave.

-You know, Jonas, you've been – we've been – real naughty this summer, leavin all the lessons I promised Miss Gunderson you'd do; to the last minute like this too. But yer spellin, that's the worst of everything.

13

Johannes cringed, bracing himself against the subject.

-What I cant for the life of me see is how you spell Ioway like you do: "E-y-e-a-w-a-y." How'd you figure that one out? Simple's Ioway is: "I-o-w-a."

-Why don't they spell it like it sounds then?

-Don't know, Jonas. That's the way it is, so that's the way you do it. You had no trouble with OHIO or even IDAHO this morning, and you even spelt part of WISCONSIN, so its not that yer slow. But you never, never get Ioway right.

She touched the arm of his chair and headed for the porch: -Betcha Buddy can spell Ioway right.

(Doncha see, Ma, "Eye-Away's" our special signal, me and Buddy's. He made it up. Means "All clear!," doncha see: "eye" for LOOK, "Away" for RUN; look-and-run when the chances come. Ah, gee Ma …)

During schooltime whenever Buddy slipped him paper with red crayon spelling "Eye-away," it meant that during recess or noon hour they'd hurry off and hide until the bell dragged them back to their desks, they all the time pretending to be playing hide-and-seek. Sometimes, they hid behind the gravestones down the road; sometimes, they climbed to Buddy's favorite spot on the roof of the girls toilet; and once they found themselves flat in the roadside ditch, covered with weeds and wild roses.

And everybody called em champeens cause nobody could ever find em. While they hid, they had their own game: thinking of how many ways to get rid of Ol' Gundy without killing her (that wouldn't be nice). Best of all, Buddy said, cause Eye-Away's where Aunt Min lived, every time they said the name, it would remind them of their plan to visit her (Doncha know this, Ma, even if I cant tell you!).

Of course she couldn't know. He'd die if she found out. She always acted like she knew everything else going on so he needed her to know this, too, but without his having to tell her. He wanted her to know without her knowing what herself; otherwise, he couldn't feel safe. But all this back-and-forth wrestling benumbed him more than being forced to spell what made no sense to him (look at all them words with "h" that nobody ever says; even in Dad's own name "Thor"). Every time Ma mentioned Ioway today, he saw only "Eye-Away" in his head. What if their secret plans dropped out by accident? That scared him. Yet he wanted someone else to know.

Uncle Snorri-Bjorn? But he'd say that he'd heard him say before: that everybody needed something secret about them to make them "interesting," whatever that meant. Maybe Dad? He wouldn't make fun of him or tattle, but even if Dad didn't tell Ma outright, she'd worm it out of him somehow. He had to be special-careful. Buddy would skin him alive if he heard these thoughts ("Why say anything? Cant you keep yer trap shut, Big Chief Thunder-Walking?").

When Ma came in from the porch with kindling, she stooped for his pencil on the floor and laid it across the 'rithmetic pad. She listened to his silence: -All right them, we'll let the spellin go fer now. See if you can finish this page of problems before Dad gits home (with Buddy, Ma ... why don't you look worried bout him too?). –You know we – you – won't have time tomorrow with Sunday School starting agin and everything else happenin at once.

She chucked him under the chin. –After what you done to yer teacher too. You hafta 'pologize to Miss Gunderson when you see her. We want school to open peaceful-like.

She went back to the stove and her baking and he took up the pencil again (already 'pologized, Ma; done it twice ... just wait till Buddy hears what I done, but cant let him know I 'pologized). He felt her eyes rummaging through his hair. Afraid that she'd see right into his head, he shook himself, hoping to shake his worries off in all directions, same as Ol' Odin did, coming out of Blood Brothers Crick.

(But Ma, cancha see the biggest thing we planned: me and Buddy s'posed to go down the Rivers today ... last chance 'fore school starts ... if I don't go along Aunt Min'll keep him there for good; said she had no kids to call her own and Buddy's Maw got one too many ... don't wanna go to Eye-Away, Ma, but gotta, gotta go, Ma, ohhh ...).

Relieved when he saw her go back to her doughnuts, his fear that The Sheriff-Almighty might run Buddy down began to fade, too. He had to believe that Buddy would be much too smart to get in the way of that car-with-the-star, and he sure knew enough to hide from the big ham inside it.

With a happy sigh, Ma settled on a stool: -When the fried cakes are done, there's only the Velkommen cake left to make. How's that fer doin on yer Uncle Snorri's short notice now?

She smiled at him as if they shared a joke, then started on of Buddy's favorite songs; the funny one about yes we have no bananas today, and the rolling pin joined with the chorus as sizzling lard sent forth hot fumes. A chunk of wood in the cookstove turned over with a hiss, then died slowly on a drawn-out breath (whispers from the Ghosts, or maybe The Winter-Lonely instead, trying to catch him before summer had a chance to leave, before Buddy got back to save him ... why aint he here yet, ohhh ...). Johannes slid deeper into the rocker and fought back; Buddy had to know he'd never tell their secrets, never break his promises to keep his trap shut around Ma.

Vacation had gone so fast, he wondered if it had happened at all. How could they get to Aunt Min's now with only two days left before school. If they couldn't go another time, they'd HAVE to leave tonight for sure (and I know yer fraid-a the dark, Buddy, even if you'd never admit it). And tomorrow ... how could he miss Uncle Snorri-Bjorn; how could he let Buddy take off by himself. (Why did everyting have to happen at once now?).

Johannes had no idea how they'd get to Eye-Away; he knew nothing about distances. They'd go, that's all. Buddy'd so decide and that took care of everything. How he dreaded that moment, though. How could he go? How could he not go? Maybe something would happen ... like getting sick, maybe. But he couldn't do that to Buddy (and Singing White Wolf would brand me a coward for sure). If they could put if off till next month instead, after Uncle Snorri left; or better still do it NEXT summer them. Tied in knots, his brain hurt so much he wanted to explode (why cant there be moren one of me, ohhh …).

Whenever Ma looked his way, he feared she'd find him all mixed-up (I WANNA tell you, Ma, but how can I squeal bout EYE-AWAY when it hadn't been part of our plan before vacation, but when we git home, me and Buddy'll tell you all bout it, let you know how Aunt Min looks, and the German husbands, and everything else). Maybe he could tell her then about looking for the cave and their ways for sneaking off, and how he waited for the Ghosts. All that plan belonged to him, and when Buddy helped him with it, he had to help Buddy with his EYE-AWAY dream (Ooh, cancha see, Ma, cancha …).

He closed his eyes and began to rock. How solid the chair remained after more than a hundred years of rocking. Ma often told him how Great-Granddad had carved it himself from a special tree in Norway, then took it apart and carried it in pieces when they left on the boat, and he'd put it together from time to time so he could rock away on deck and look over the ocean. "Still smells of sea salt," Uncle Snorri always said. (No wonder Ma likes using it when I'm not around; must carry her back to Olden Times).

As soon as he felt better, Ma's face crept in behind his lids, stiff with worry at the sight of his empty bed after no answers to her calls. Maybe he could get rid of that face after he'd written that letter (but I cant spell, ohhh …). He'd never made a letter before, except some words on a valentine for Buddy which he tore up before anybody saw it. He'd have to try (even if I cant spell, huh?). Afterwards, he'd put the letter on his pillow and Ma'd understand everything when she read how he'd only gone a-visiting like when Uncle Snorri comes to the farm. Johannes began feeling good again as soon as he'd pushed Ma's worried look away. Suddenly he realized he'd have to write to Uncle Snorri too. How could he miss him when he'd been waiting for him to come back ever since he left last year.

Johannes pumped so hard the chair turned half-around on itself, and the 'rithmetic pad slipped beside the cushion. Yet, Ma said nothing. After a while, he lifted his eyes to the horizon where the schoolhouse stood farther away through his squint, and out there beyond the ploughed field for winter wheat, someone at the schoolyard fence stood braced against the wind. Johannes stopped the rocker dead. Buddy!

Buddy must have heard The Sheriff-Almighty roaring down the road, expecting to catch Buddy at the farm, never thinking how Buddy could have run behind the roadside brush all the way to school (and if he climbed to the girls toilet roof, nobody would ever find him, 'cept Ol' Gundy, of course). Johannes smothered an excited poop. He hoped that Ma wouldn't notice Buddy if she checked the weather soon. Then a bolt struck hard: what if Mrs. Preacher's Woman had sicked The Sheriff-Almighty on him, with smiling excuses for catching Buddy and shipping him off to that "orphanage" she always bragged about (across the Miss'ippi north in "Many-apples-less").

Desperate, Johannes reached for Buddy with his eyes and tried to coax him, will him, over the field before Ma or anybody else could see him. Buddy didn't stir fast, only wobbled. Johannes rubbed his eyes and dug deeper into the distance to where the flagpole for school stood on its mound, a silver pencil against the clouds. His sight sharpened and Buddy turned into that broken half-oak at the school line fence (that crazy hollow trunk he'd tried to hide in once).

Johannes blinked at the sand beneath his lids, and wiped away the scene (whewww, wait'll I tell Buddy I took him for that rotten stump; better not say a word). In a crazy flash, he saw Buddy's Maw stumble across the furrows and "vanish."

Startled, he rubbed his eyes more, until the flagpole stood by itself again, unchanged, half a mile from Gramma's tree with red apples dangling from its branches like balls on Christmas trees. Had he really seen Buddy's Maw? It happened too fast for him to know for sure; must have been some memory running loose. But the flagpole didn't shift (jist think, only Buddy had ever shimmied up that pole all the way to the top and not slid off … I cant b'lieve youd ever fergit our last Saturday like this . .).

Johannes thought that the last day of school-vacation should be as big as the first; then you'd know if all the plans for summer had come true. If they had, as his and Buddy's almost had, you could live them over and over again during endless winter and make even better plans for the coming summer.

Uncle Snorri-Bjorn had taught him how to keep alive your special times; while in the midst of what went on, you shut your eyes, held your breath for seconds, and remembered with all your senses; and later, when you wanted to bring back that time, you shut your eyes again, held your breath, remembered what you wanted and it all happened again like that first time; sometimes even better (how "mysterious," and it worked, ahhh).

"You can live a long time on good things that happened once," Uncle Snorri said, "if you know how to store your memories."

(Whatta we goin to do now, Buddy?) Helpless, Johannes could do nothing but wait, and listen. The mourning dove must have moved. He stole a look at Ma and watched her lift a doughnut from the kettle, dust it from a bowl of powdered sugar and stack it beside others on a tray. A left-over wave of cooking spice drifted back to his nose. Uncle Snorri's clock, which clacked sometimes and sometimes clanged (like its innards cant 'member what to do), now tick-tocked naturally, then chimed twice and left a vibration in the sink. His rocker creaked; it could have been a dying cricket's omen for early snow.

✳ ✳ ✳

ITS' MAY, THE LAST day of school; picnic time. Out of the thin grove along the sunny side of the schoolhouse, a chorus of "On Wisconsin," led by Ma, reaches for heaven: the raw voices collide off-key in the scrawny tree-tops, while Old Glory, high on its pole, snaps at the shuffling clouds above and drowns the song.

Johannes hadn't been able to sing at all, too busy watching thunderheads over the Howling Grief Ridges , and when they kissed the Point of Walking Sorrows, he knew for sure the Ghosts had come to their hideaway, and that as soon as him and Buddy could be off, Great Chief Broken Thunderhawk would be guiding them along the Bluff (ready to welcome us when we came to seek his cave today, ahhh).

Johannes tried not to poop in excitement when he scanned the picnic tables gathered together on the flattest part of the schoolyard. More eager for food now than for music, mothers herded their youngest around them; older girls and boys in groups or pairs, raced for what empty places they could find on the picnic benches, and above the rattle of dishes, the murmurs of appetites (sounds like getting ready to slop the hogs, ohhh …).

When he turned back to the Bluff, Ma poked his back, the signal to sit down. Trapped between her and Miss Gunderson (Ol' Gundy, uff da!) on their plank, Johannes knew that if he squirmed too much he'd drive a lively sliver up his hinder, and wouldn't that be a rotten thing to happen on a special day like this (that day him and Buddy'd been dreamin of and plannin for all winterlong).

Across from Ol' Gundy, Buddy squeezed in on the end of the bench beside the Torkelson girls, but he gave no one his attention (he looks as struck-up as that wooden Indian at the drugstore front downtown; why, he won't even cross his eyes at me or slip a grin). On the other side of Ma, two oldtime grannies gossiped in Norwegian at the pair across from them. They sounded like squeaky mice since none of them heard or listened to each other. Johannes felt naked at this head table and worried that him and Buddy couldn't get away with every eye able to follow every bit they took.

Ma shifted inside her next-to-Sunday best, stood up, and called for attention by jingling a teaspoon against her drinking glass. Women busy with food at the sawhorse counters beneath the eaves stopped to listen; as everybody did when Ma took over: at school like this, in church, or for Community Club. Even the squeaky grannies looked her way, as if hypnotized by Preacher Flogge.

He knew she'd taken roll call with her eyes before she nodded at the old ones: -Velkommen, velkommen, her voice beamed in Norwegian. After she said something else (wisht I unnerstood Norske talk!), she spoke louder when she looked out on the others.

-Welcome, welcome, everybody else! Glad we all could make it here (whattabout Buddy's Maw, huh?). Before we fill our faces, a few words. Can you b'lieve another school year's gone! Only weeks to Decoration Day; soon after that the Fourth of July and Labor Day, then back to school again. 1935's goin fast. Uff da, how time flies.

Johannes never understood why Ma fretted about time so much. He glanced at Buddy who sat listening to Ma with serious face. He treated Ol' Gundy as if she existed no more than he, Johannes did (ohhh). Ma went on against the chirping of spring birds, her schoolmarm voice pulled at everybody's ears:

-County Agent says no more dust storms 'spected this far north. Times still not good though. Least we're all not on relief ... yet (whattabout Buddy's Maw, huh?), but no more foreclosures since last year, think-a that. Good thing Mr. Roosevelt's still with us, though some of you don't care for him. How would last winter been without his road jobs or the tree camps now? Why, they say he'll even bring us 'lectric lights some day. Imagine that!

Ma wiped her face with a paper napkin and chuckled into it: -Don't mean to blow off like some windbag politician. Now Mr. Olson of the schoolboard wants me as secretary to ask you all to thank Miss Gunderson for another year of teaching.

She nodded at 'Ol Gundy and clapped her hands, but few kids joined with their mothers when 'Ol Gundy stood up fast and sat down fast. Buddy didn't even flicker an eyelash when Johannes craned his neck to glare into that faraway face. Ma coughed into her napkin politely before going on, and Johannes closed his eyes and tried to get back to his interrupted daydream. One ear open, he rode along on her words.

-Think we should thank Borgny too for not takin that offer from the County Seat. Its not good changing teachers, you know; 'specially nowadays with so much goin on. How long you s'pose they'll let us keep our country school now, with so many one-room districts closing down? We'll hold on long's we can; hope to keep Miss Gunderson with us too (Oh, Jesus, Ma!).

One eye open, Johannes turned to Buddy for response. Nothing came (maybe he's behavin hard today cause he's 'fraid we'll start to poop and set off a commotion and waste more time 'fore we can git away). He withdrew into himself again as he heard Ma smooth out the wrinkles in her dress and cool herself (with one of them creepy undertaker fans they gave her when she sang at funerals). She cleared her throat:

-Imagine how we'd feel if we lost our dear ol' Anderegg School. She changed her voice: -Got some announcements better not fergit. First, The Widow Peterson says she'll have barn dances again this year. Central will ring emergency to let us know which Saturdays are best. And don't fergit Community Club picnic's in our pasture same's last year (when Buddy came to us, ahhh). Be here 'fore we know it with no club during summer to remind us.

Ma patted her cheeks. -Uff da! Startin early, this summery heat. Better git movin 'fore everything melts, includin us. A shame these trees we planted that Arbor Day cant grow shade a little faster. Oh, Mrs. Olson, will you please give grace. Then lead the food line with our dear grammas here.

When Ma gestured for everybody to stand, she yanked Johannes to his feet by his overalls suspenders and motioned for Buddy to come and stand in front of her. At the loud "Amen!," Buddy slipped past him without a poke. Ma directed the grannies forward, but held back the rest of their table.

-Gee, Ma, Johannes fussed, -why we always last in line, huh (wont give us time to do a thing today)?

-Shh, she warned, -good manners, that's what. There's plenty of food to go back for many times. Don't be a molly-coddle now.

-Vaer sa god! she called out to those falling into a crooked line. –"Grub's on!" like they used to call in Thorwald's lumber days. Now don't you kids fergit us mothers gonna beat you in this year's kittenball. After that, before ice cream, we'll take a pitcher of the winners. Eat now and enjoy!

Johannes looked down at the box camera Uncle Snorri-Bjorn brought her years ago (she calls it a "kodak"). She liked to take pictures of special times, when they could afford a roll of film, and once she made a snapshot of the biggest dahlia she'd ever raised, and nobody'd laughed at such foolishness.

Johannes shivered in the heat. How could they ever break away from that silly ballgame, and all this wasted time in line; why, the (dam) thing barely moved. Behind him, Ol' Gundy let out one long sigh after another, but said nothing, while Buddy, hidden by Ma's full dress, made no complaining sounds at all (don't he care if we make it to the Bluff today?).

-One more announcement, Ma's voice rang out again, -fergot to mention 4-H. County Agent agrees with me that we should start a club. You kids'll like that I know. Might even bring us prizes at County fair. So, we'll gather Monday night at our place then. After chores. You all be there.

He heard her bend to Buddy and say something about 4-H (4-H! do I hafta see these dam kids on school vacation too?). Johannes couldn't stand school for his own reasons; nobody had adventure in them; not a spark of excitement neither. Boys only thought of flushing pocket gophers from their dens. Johannes didn't think Indians would kill animals for fun, so he wouldn't do that neither. When they ran out of gopher tails for bounty, they had kittenball or peeing contests, held behind the toilets (where the girls tried to peek, but didn't tattle). Since Buddy came, he won such games; said that if you peed from some small knoll, it always looked the farthest when it hit the ground below. He could spit the farthest, too, though Johannes never tried. The losers would grumble and move away, leaving him and Buddy to play games with the girls (always a chance to skip away and hide then). But girls didn't know how to play. They squealed like baby pigs and ran circles round and round the boys who tried to run them off, That's the way it went, except the times they had to play ball to show off for the County Supervisor's unexpected visit. How could Ma understand his dread of 4-H then?

She never realized how much he hated school neither, when nobody teased him or picked fights or called him nasty names like "shit-pants" or "sissy-boy." They only looked on him as if he had two heads, each time he tried to tell about the Ghosts. Nobody ever called him "teacher's pet" neither, even when Ol' Gundy treated him like one, never scolding him the same way she did the others (but always finding something against Buddy, who'd only smile at her and wink, which turned her red). Ol' Gundy made Johannes feel smaller when she called him "poor little Jonas"; he wondered if he looked as dumb as she made him out to be. Later, outdoors, if a stray sob escaped, Buddy'd dance around him, singing "But I like you dumb, I do, I do," then he'd dodge off before tears fell, and run in circles like Ol' Odin did when he wanted to play. By school-days' end, they'd forgotten everything till the next time it happened. Ma didn't know that.

Maybe kids said things behind his back, or to their folks at home (Buddy cared not a cow-flop for what people said of him). Johannes wondered if they called him stuck-up maybe because of Great-Granddad's name on everything, or because they acted scared of Ma. Or maybe they looked richer (but only looked that way): they had the most buildings on their farm and the first telephone around and a piano and a pump organ (like in school and church), even a radio (though the batteries didn't work no more); and they had a wood-furnace with pipes to carry heat through the walls of that big house addition which Ma said Grampa Anderegg built to prove to everyone how good he'd farmed with his sons. Did anybody think him stuck-up because Dad had a feed-truck and a tractor (when it worked) and didn't have to go to town with horses? Or because he had a famous uncle, or because Ma seemed more important than Ol' Gundy at school doings, or better than Mrs. Preacher's Woman when she sang at funerals. Maybe they thought him stuck-up (behind my back) cause he KNEW about Walking Sorrows and the Ghosts. And had no fear of them.

He didn't know how to BE "stuck-up," but if he did, Ma'd (maybe) paddle his hinder purple. Now when he looked on all the Kittlesons and Johnsons and Paulsons and Knutsons and everybody else at school, he felt stranger than ever (because I have the shortest name in school ... cause Buddy'd picked me for his special pal ... cause neither of us got relatives in any of the classes ... oh, dam the 4H Club). If anybody thought him special it had to be cause he belonged to Ma (Such thoughts takin all our time today when we should be on the Bluff, ohhh ...).

The line snailed along as people inspected and sampled dishes, stood still to gossip about the food, and even talked in recipes. Johannes waited for Buddy's "Eye-Away" sign, but the signal didn't come (guess I dint 'spect it the way he loves to eat, gobbling all those things I cant stand a-tall; and today he'd have to taste a bit of everything). Ahead of him, Ma kept mumbling to Buddy, things Johannes couldn't hear (betcha its 'bout 4H Club). Behind him, Ol' Gundy, restless on her high heels, sighed deeper. He wisht he had the magic to turn her into a slug, but every time he had such naughty thoughts, Ma's face filled his head and he dried up. A blush passed over him.

The shade kept shifting. May breezes blew patches of it into different shapes and sizes. Sweat trickled from the hollow in his temple into his eye. He tried to blink away the sandy sting inside his lid. It didn't help to rub. Hoping to reach Buddy, he stepped around Ma and caught instead new light on Walking Sorrows, which made it stand taller now when blurred. Every year land changed shape, Uncle Snorri often said, but the Bluff always looked the same to him, just as Ma and Dad didn't change (unless you looked real close?). Walking Sorrows made a stubby finger out of Dad's silo far beneath it on the other side of Township Road. He dug at his eyes until the Howling Grief Ridges sharpened and he could make out Gramma's crabapple tree and Grampa's sugar maple this side the kitchen nook, and the cluster or pines near the back porch and the tops of black Norwegian spruces tall above the front yard farther back. Home never looked so grand before, so sharp. From half a mile away he could pick out bundles of blooms in the lilac brush between the backhouse and the woodshed.

People still called it the "Anderegg Place," as if Great-Granddad had never left. No one ever spoke of the "Berg Farm" but that didn't matter; it still belonged to him, so safe and everlasting. Why, even Uncle Snorri-Bjorn called it "home" those few weeks every fall.

When Johannes fretted about chores, Ma'd remind him that they all had something to show for their labor, they had a purty home; though it needed lots of fixing, it belonged to them. Not like Buddy living in that rattletrap dump the Relief People put him in (wouldn't be s'prised at all to find it leaked and had rats and bedbugs too … Buddy, you gotta come and stay with us for good, ohhh).

Even if they needed paint and patches (like the other farms on the benchlands above the flood flats), Johannes glowed with pride over Grampa Anderegg's big and many buildings in their various shades of gray and red, however faded. If some of their sheds had caved in, so had entire barns on other places; and they had the tallest silo anywhere (cracks up and down its walls don't show from here, nor do spots of missing shingles on al the roofs around). Only The Widow Peterson still had a working windmill. He wisht theirs still stood, but one summer a cyclone carried away the country store and their summer kitchen, and their windmill went along for the ride (Dad said).

Most of all, Johannes loved his house, both the old part and the later one with its many rooms and windows. Though some panes had cracked, many farmhouses had windows boarded shut. He wanted to believe his damaged windows happened when Great Chief Broken Thunderhawk or Singing White Wolf tried to visit him to let him know they waited for him on the Bluff.

Grampa Anderegg made the house look special; he had lightening rods fastened to every gable peak and beside each chimney, big red balls that captured sunbeams and looked like cow's eyes in the moon, the same kind that capped the church's steeple ("Shoulda saved his money for all the good they do," Ma'd grunt each time the church got struck by lightning, and that happened oftener than it did on Walking Sorrows Point).

Lilacs, honeysuckles, snowball bushes, and spirea filled the yards and hugged the porch that wrapped itself around three sides of the main house (Ol' Gundy called it a "ver-and-ah"). Ma planted flowers everywhere; lilies at the fancy iron gate beside the front mailbox, where rural carriers dropped the seed and mail-order catalogs they dreamed over all winter long. She put phlox and dahlias along foundations, sunflowers and hollyhocks against the barns and silo; she scattered seed along the roadside fences, which Dad kept straight and mended ("No snapped wires or rotten posts there," said townfolks passing by, "and the Berg gates open and close without falling off their hinges if you touched em"). Before you knew it, morning glories had taken over, even climbing trees to ripple on the air.

Every summer, Ma opened the horse barn gates and let Solly and Sig graze the yards and stomp down weeds (which most farms don't bother with). She let Johannes burn off dead grass in spring and fire piles of raked leaves from the elms and maples every fall. The first time Buddy helped him last year, he fell over himself (and pooped wild): "Never played with fire before," he said amazed, "and not git whupped."

Johannes loved home more since Buddy loved it now and he loved Buddy more for liking it so much (ahhh). Buddy found things in it Johannes had never thought about before. He soon saw his farm as the most special place on earth. Why, nobody else had magic flints in their hills and fields, nor ghosts like Broken Thunderhawk and Singing White Wolf. Only the Olsons had more land, but they didn't talk about it; only the Hansons had more plantings, but nobody cared. And no other farm like theirs had been split in two by Township Road, leaving house and orchard and winter fields on one side, and windbreaks hiding farm buildings and other lands on the other (a lotta places for hide-go-seek).

And jist think, too, Township Road could take em west across the County line to another road that ended at the highway that followed the Miss'ippi upstream or down; like Uncle Snorri showed em last fall in his rumble seat (how "mysterious").

Johannes had forgotten the moving line until it reached the food. He peeked around Ma again to see how shadows of rolling clouds changed the color of Walking Sorrows. Still stung by Buddy's silence, he reached around Ma's waist to poke at him. Ol' Gundy told him to stand still. Before he could do anything else, Ma thrust a plate of food at him and marched him back to their table. Buddy'd beat him to his corner (maybe we can run now, huh?), but Buddy'd gave no signal. When Ma and Ol' Gundy arrived with their plates, Johannes felt more trapped than ever as they sat down on either side of him. Ma passed paper napkins and the smell of PICNIC settled on their food. At the other end of their table, the Oldtime Grannies, already fed, snoozed on (is snoozing different in Norwegian, Ma?).

Glancing sideways at Buddy, Johannes feared that he'd forgotten everything they'd planned (we should be explorin on the Bluff, not sittin here!). But there Buddy sat, gazing on the insides of a deviled egg, too busy to raise his eyes, much less whisper "Eye-Away!." Beside him, the cross-eyed Torkelson girls giggled as they squeezed as close as they dared to him; their braids, as dried-up as dead garter snakes, wallowed in the baked beans on their plates. Buddy bent over his food (like a harvester at mealtime), and nothing else existed. At other tables, other boys did the same, well-behaved but so unnatural. Nothing mattered now but grub, and more grub, and the ballgame, and that home-made ice cream they'd been looking to all school-year long.

Johannes wondered how many of the boys liked Buddy at all, the way they let him be (scared-a the way he looks, like he cared for nobody … but me, ahhh). He'd heard whispers that Buddy belonged in reform school (what's "re-form" school, Ma, like that "orfun-edge," huh?) and only cause he'd run away that time. Those kids'd change their tune real quick if Ma ever heard em, and he wisht she would. Ma settled problems fast. But all the girls liked Buddy and kept him on the run.

Too busy trying to get Buddy's eye, Johannes couldn't eat. He stared hard at Buddy with the same devotion and impatience he had for Dad or Ma when they acted stubborn. He wanted to be sure that Buddy still liked him, for he loved Buddy as much as Uncle Snorri-Bjorn (and Ma and Dad, of course). But he didn't want Buddy to SEE how much he cared (to KNOW is differnt, to show would make me look too giggly). Sometimes he couldn't b'lieve that Buddy picked HIM for a pal; Buddy, the tallest, strongest (most "mysterious") boy in school or Town, and to think how Ma had let him come to play… and stay, so long as he wanted.

Johannes had never had a Best Friend before, because the community kids lived too far apart from him. He'd had nobody to call Special, unless you counted Ol' Odin and Uncle Snorri-Bjorn (how could you be pals with grown-ups though, even if Uncle Snorri dint act like one; how could you have dreams with half-a-collie, huh?). He'd never forget that day The Sheriff-Almighty Strutt ran Ol' Odin down as he raced along Township Road trying to find where Johannes hid from him in the blackberry scrub (and the car-with-the-star dint even stop, god-damit). Then, Buddy walked out of the willows like in a story and took the place of dog and the brother Ma said he never knew (the one Jesus called on with scarlet fever one winter night).

This noon, Buddy treated him the way he treated everybody else: he could be dead (whatever that felt like). Unable to bear it any longer, Johannes untangled the leg he'd been sitting on and stretched his tennies under the table, nearly scraping Ol' Gundy's knees.

-Behave yerself, Gramps, Buddy growled without looking up.

Johannes wilted.

-Watsa matter with you, Jonas? Ma examined him: -Fidgeting in this heat. Don't you like Mrs. Kittleson's hot dish? Awfully good you know. And you aint touched Mrs. Hanson's salad; she'll think it aint good 'nuff fer you. Look at Buddy (I have, Ma, that's all I been doin). He's eatin everything, soon be set fer more. 'Member, no ballgame, no ice cream, and no pitchers till you kids eat up (Oh, Ma, why we stuck here, me and Buddy, huh? 'cept maybe Buddy likes to eat 'stead-a lookin fer our cave).

Her voice, as always when she scolded him, unraveled the scarf he'd wrapped around his dreams. He didn't want to make Buddy mad. When Buddy called him "Gramps," he never said it in fun like Dad did (Dad said that "Johannes" sounded like Olden Times for carryin Great-Granddad's name like that). Instead, Buddy called him "Gramps" to warn that he'd lost patience with him, or considered him a pest, or a baby even, and dint wanna be bothered with him no more (maybe never, ohhh …).

Buddy with emptied plate backed off the end of his bench and strolled away to inspect what food remained. Johannes, hot and defeated, hugged his plate to his chest and pretended to eat, bent over the hot dish like a thresher.

-I don't know what's come over Jonas, Kari. Ol' Gundy complained across his back. -He's been day-dreaming all year long. I shouldn't have passed him to the next grade, you know.

He knew she stressed her words for his sake, then choked on them when her upper teeth slipped loose and settled behind her lower lip. From practice, she worked them back to where they belonged, and gabbled on:

-But, I'm sure, Kari Berg, he'll do fifth-grade work all right if you have him study some this summer. Review arithmetic and practice his spelling; that's the worst of all. And he should work on sentences, too, for that report I'll want about vacation. You know, he's got such a special memory for recalling things he likes, down to a final word; and no mind at all for other things.

Johannes burned. He wanted to poop in protest, but reared it might become a roaring fart instead (which usually happened when he got upset). Every time he tried to think of his teacher as "Miss Gunderson," she pulled a stunt like this and turned back into Ol' Gundy on the spot. He wisht he could imitate Buddy then: he wouldn't let Ol' Gundy see how much she needled him, and the more she failed to rile him, the madder she got. But Buddy never let her catch him with his schoolwork undone, and that made her madder still (but why, huh?).

Johannes stabbed at the slaw. Picnics used to be fun with all that food and fancy cakes, but today had been shattered by Buddy's funny-peculiar ways, and then Ol' Gundy butting into his summer plans. He wanted to kick her in the shins, or something worse if he dared think of it (turn her into a stinkin troll maybe ...). He waited on edge for what Ma might say before she noticed his nosiness.

-You heard what I said, didn't you, Kari? About the arithmetic? Better have him start his reading, too. He barely finished book reports this year. You can pick titles from the bookshelf when you leave.

-Good idea, Borgny, if there's somethin to interest Buddy, too,

-Yes, yes of course. Take some Mark Twain home (why does Buddy's name rattle her so much?). But you heard what I said about Johannes and his day-dreaming, didn't you?

-Course I did. Must be that restless streak in him. Runs on his Dad's side. You know how Thor's twin... Ol' Gundy adjusted her mouth.

-Guess you know what I mean, Ma went on, giving him no heed. –You know, some Norwegian men always lookin to the next sundown, ready to sail off. Always say: 'spect nuttin, nuttin's no s'prise. Snorri has such things to tell when he comes here. A reg'ler Norskie seaman who takes on ragin storms, but cant stand calm; a old-time story-spinner too, like their mother, Thor says. But talkin trolls aint good 'nuff no more; he's got Jonas heated over Indians.

Why, he's more North-Ameddican than us, I guess. A solid Norskie like that, too. Whatta shame.

-Yes, to be sure, Ol' Gundy murmured while Ma fanned away until she caught her breath again. What did Ol' Gundy know of men, Johannes puzzled, with clicking teeth and clicking high heels following her everywhere. Ma sighed:

-Aint it natural, Borgny, for a boy's imagination to be teased? Grown men feedin on that redskin stuff. Dont seem proper for civilized times.

Nobody in school ever mentioned his Indians, nor how the whole country all around them had filled with Indian deeds. The ones they told about in school lived long ago in Pilgrim Times and didn't sound real at all. Ol' Gundy said she'd never heard of peace pipe pits in Minnesota. And nobody cared, not even Ma, who cared about so many things.

-Snorri's nuttin but a kid himself; overgrown, Ma said, pausing to take a swallow of lemonade: -Never got over their time in them North Woods like Thorwald did. Musta been where he picked up all that Indian stuff. Thanks God, Thor's got his shoes on the ground. Likes to poke fun in front of others sometimes though, 'bout wantin to be off on some ocean-goin boat (now wouldn't that be somethin, Ma!).

A tray of food passed over him. Johannes heard Ma thank Mrs. Johnson before she dipped something from a bowl onto his plate. He couldn't eat a thing. Looking for Buddy, he finally saw him moving towards the boys backhouse, with no sign for him to follow (what if he goes off alone today, ohhh ...). Helpless, Johannes sank deeper into himself, all ears (how long would Ol' Gundy and Ma fergit that he still sat trapped between em?).

-Do you think it's a good idea, Kari, for Johannes to be with Buddy ... so much? Why, they're "inseparable (in-sepper-bull?)" in the schoolyard and have little time for anybody else.

-Aint nuttin wrong with Buddy, Borgny, Ma said in a whisper louder than talk. –If anyone should know, it's me. Dont see why yer worried.

Johannes knew Ma'd stand by Buddy, but he didn't like the way her voice carried on the breeze. No sight of Buddy yet (like he'd "vanished"), but he couldn't believe Buddy'd start their plan without him. The sharpness in Ol' Gundy's voice kept him small and still:

-Honestly, Kari Berg, he practically lived with you all winter long. Just because you promised the Relief People you'd keep an eye on him, I don't think they meant you should adopt him.

-Dint do nuttin extra, Borgny. He adopted us. What's wrong, anyhow?

-Can't you see? The boy's almost two years older, and much bigger grown. Pardon my mentioning it, but that can't but be "contaminating."

(Oh, what's contam-bin-eight, Ma ... and why do you grown-ups talk a-lot when we're right in front-a you, like now; besides, I aint that much smaller neither.)

Ma turned sharply: -Well, he had to be somewheres out-a the weather. And he lives the farthest away. Had to keep him; dint want no kid gettin lost in a white-out, or freezin to death on them slippery hills. Then ... (Ma's voice sounds rosy) then he became a habit. A good habit.

Johannes thought he heard Ol' Gundy's insides churn.

-Maybe he's wild to look at sometimes, Ma went on, but you cant blame the kid now. Kept my promise to keep my eye on him, and I find him reg'lar unnerneath.

Johannes beamed at Ma's praise of Buddy and hoped that she wouldn't catch him listening. He tried to think of nothing but the hot dish in front of him, and all those vegetables his belly didn't want. And why did Ol' Gundy hate his Special Friend so hard (ohhh ...).

She wouldn't rest: -But Kari, he can't help being touched by what he comes from. That woman with those unwashed bas . . brats, that shack with chickens in the house, AND ... Ol' Gundy gasped, -that sister of hers down in Dubuque ("Dee-bjuke" ahhh). They say SHE keeps a house, a HOUSE, if you know what I mean.

-Know what you mean, Borgny, but Buddy cant be blamed fer that, no moren for his Paw bein shut away with TB. Thanks God for that District Sanitorium!

Ol' Gundy acted like Ol' Odin with a bean-filled sock, not letting go: -Besides, Kari, he swears ... cusses.

Ma paused for a moment. -Never heard him cuss myself. Had plenty chances. But Johannes knows better anyway.

He warmed at the faith she showed in him and squirmed against the slivers on the bench. (Oh, Ma, poopin's so much safer than cussin when yer glad or mad; you can always say you couldn't help it, unless you made a fart too big for church or school ... and I'm workin all the time to be champeen.) He dared not poop now.

Too warm to settle against Ma's softness, he leaned away from Ol' Gundy as far as he could. Boys always joked about how she'd look bare (nuttin but a bundle-a sticks, I bet, with no meat on em neither), and that always made Johannes wonder how other grown-ups would look undressed, 'specially Dad or Ma or Uncle Snorri-Bjorn (would they look funny-ha-ha nekkid?). When he heard Ma tell Dad sometimes how "finicky" or "downright persnickety" Ol' Gundy could become, he thought it had something to do with being bare or skinny. He loved the way Ma smelt in the heat, reminding him of his heifer's breath when he inhaled it: green grass sweet and cozy, while Ol' Gundy wore a store-bought scent that stung his eyes and Dad said stunk like something pickled. He listened to them eat, but hoped to hear more things he'd never know about until Buddy got back (what if he dont come back, ohhh ...).

Before long, Ol' Gundy started on another track: -Something else to interest you. I've smelled smoke on Buddy, too. YES!

-Screamin catfits, Borgny, Ma put down her fork, -where'd the sam hill a kid git tobacco now? He couldn't buy a penny-postcard. Thor dont smoke, only has his snoose sometimes.

Johannes wondered then if Ma knew Buddy's Maw smoked cigarettes, or so he'd heard downtown. He caught the flutter of Ol' Gundy's purple hankie when she rubbed her mouth back into place and edged in to whisper overhead:

-That's nothing, Kari. Listen to this. I've caught him ... caught him pestering the girls.

Ma looked around for Buddy, then hooted so loud, the kids across their table jumped, all ears, and several mothers turned their way.

-Getting into their bloomers, I mean. Ol' Gundy gasped, - even caught him on the roof of the girls toilet peering through the cupola slats (But, Ma, Buddy dont care for no girls, ever).

-Don't you see, Kari, his voice is changing, and ...

-Better be, Ma snapped, - if he's normal; better be a-grow-in. What proof you got on this here bloomer stuff now?

-Well ... the girls told me ... hinted to me ... and when she glanced across to the Torkelsons, they wiggled off the bench and fled in a rush of giggles.

-So there! Jist what you'd expect. Ma went back to her food.

Her silence fell over the table (a window shade pulled down against the sun), but before emptiness could fill the space across from him, Molly Johnson and a baby brother plunked down fast and simply stared at him; only the freckles on their chins and cheekbones breathed (like my two heads, huh?). Molly's braids had come apart and hung loose as stiff as twine (Molly? Molly-coddle?). Johannes twisted around for a chance to squeeze away; maybe he could slip under the table and crawl around Ol' Gundy's purple shoes.

Then he saw Buddy (ahhh ...). Weak-kneed with relief, Johannes watched him come into the shade of the eaves and sample more food before loading another plate. He took his time at it, too, giving them the chance to finish their gossip about him before his return would spoil it; that's what Johannes decided (wisht I dint give a dam what people said, but when he's too polite with grown-ups, maybe that's on purpose, huh).

Ma, rested, came back to life: -Not worryin at all, Borgny. Always said Buddy's good for Jonas. Might teach him to look out for himself. Jonas cant do a thing on his own. Always holdin back, always waitin. That aint good in a kid. He's got nobody nearby to play with neither; not good bein round grown-ups all the time. Why you s'pose I send lunch with him to school when it's easier to run home at noon; want him to mingle with the others, let him watch how Buddy does it (Buddy cant stand them kids neither, Ma, but he can smile and fool em, I cant do that like I cant spell).

Ol' Gundy sat so still, Johannes dreaded what she might work up next, but Ma went on:

-Jonas listens to Buddy, too. Buddy minds better than Jonas and favors doin chores. Thor thinks the world of him.

He's bright. Wants to learn everything, the names of what's in the grain bins, how to run the rusty cutters and mowers and planters in the machine sheds. He dont even mind the chickens which Jonas hates; thinks they stink too much.

-To be honest, Kari, smart kids give me the creeps. You don't know what's going on inside; always planning things, I fear.

-Thanks God, that aint a problem for Jonas. Oh, he can be a little mischief, but he's usually too bashful for his own good. Buddy makes him lively. Even laughs off his Indian daydreams. One boy alone is only half a boy. I say; takes two to make a REAL one.

Ma paused, fanned herself, and sounded faraway: -Wish Jonas could be more ... ordinary though.

(Ma, what's this "or-dee-nair-ee" now? Why you grown-ups always talk about us like this?).

-Don't know what you, mean. About "ordinary" ...

-Well, boys gotta be 'fraid of something or they'd be impossible. Jonas aint 'fraid of all the things he's s'posed to fear; instead he's scared-a what should be helping him, like Sunday School, the Sheriff, even school sometimes.

-Pardon my butting in, But I think if you made Jonas work like other boys his age, he'd have no time for gathering wool.

-Maybe yer right. Ma lingered over the words like she did when she sat alone with her thoughts out loud: -but he's not so big and strong yet; cant 'ford him gettin sick in times like this. Maybe even losing him, too. Ma sighed into her napkin. –But we'll find 'nuff for him to do this summer, you'll see.

(Ma, why you always say I'm small and weak; I'm not; I'm almost big, as strong, as ... besides, you never LET me do nuttin on my own).

-Did you try Mrs Olson's chow-chow, Borgny? Ma spoke in a sudden change of voice, then smiled at Buddy as he slipped into his place. He smiled back at her and twinkled, but refused to notice Johannes, who tried to get his attention. Buddy turned to the new things on his plate instead.

Ma pulled Johannes back from his crouched position and peered at him from the side of her face as she ladled out another scoop of that hot dish his stomach couldn't stand. The stillness over the schoolyard hung lower while serious eating went on. Birds chirped and fluttered in grand confusion. Breezes played tag in the tree-tops. And Old Glory snapped away at the thunderheads on high (as hopeless as Ol' Odin runnin after crows).

Fighting back a touch of The Winter-Lonely, Johannes again stretched a leg under the table. He reached Buddy's knee and tapped. No response. He dared not kick, however good the idea made him feel. Now what about those new chores Ma talked about (bet Buddy wont mind them at all since his Maw's on Relief and has no work for him and he don't have to help me unless he wants to). What else could there be to do after learning to milk some older cows and caring for his heifer and the everyday chores around the house and gardens? But ... Ma's 4-H business threatened him. What did Buddy think of that? Wouldn't it turn their winter plans upside down and inside out? He tapped Buddy's knee again. Buddy, unreachable, studied a blob of lime jello he tried to balance on his knife. His eyes danced with green reflections and saw nothing else, much less Johannes (oh, where are the signs we use when stuck with grown-ups, huh?).

Johannes rubbed at his eyes and the move sent his elbow into Ol' Gundy's ribs and knocked the fork out of her hand.

He had to see if Walking Sorrows still stood there and if it looked the same at home. Nothing seemed real today. He pinched his left side to be sure he hadn't just snoozed off. Then back to the Bluff and its clouds.

-Honestly, Johannes, don't know what to do with you. Why cant you behave like all the other kids? See how they settled down, busy eatin' like you should be. Oh, thank you, Buddy for getting Miss Gunderson another fork. Now, Jonas, whatcha lookin at:

He couldn't hold back another minute.

-Gee, Ma, look! Aint Walking Sorrows jist terrible underneath that sky, and the Howling Grief Ridges, too. Why, they're jist too terrible in all them shades of orange and blue!

Lost in his awe of the midday light, Johannes forgot for a moment where he sat. -I'm sure that Ghosts of Great Chief Broken Thunderhawk and Singing White Wolf are up there now, cause the clouds keep kissin the Point. Then, louder, for Buddy's benefit, -and the Ghosts are waitin ... waitin ... in their cave.

-Heavens, what's come over you? Got sunstroke, son?

Ma pressed her palm across his brow. -Now what's so special about Anderegg's Point today? Only a pile-a rocks to make you fall; a pile-a rocks with rattlers too.

-See what I mean, Ol' Gundy nodded, pleased, - always trying to tell us about caves and ghosts up there.

-You know, Borgny, every visit Uncle Snorri brings up this same ol' stuff, so ... c'mon, Jonas, git back in yer shoes fast, doncha think. You aint finished yer salad; its dryin up on you.

Johannes closed his eyes while he diddled with his food and tried to imagine either of them on the Bluff. He never believed that Dad or Uncle Snorri-Bjorn had never been up there, but he'd not expect Ma to go nor Ol' Gundy in her high heels. Apart from walling their farm off from the rest of Wisconsin, the Bluff meant nothing to her, Ma'd say to those who asked why she hadn't climbed it; did she fear the ghost of that hired man, the one that kept everyone away, and she'd answer loud and sharp: "Fiddlesticks!" Because it stood there tall and always silent, nobody paid it heed ('cept loony Effie Stone), and people wondered why it could be special when they saw it every day; even when lightning struck it every summer, too.

Johannes turned to see what made Ma quiet. She gazed at Buddy, fixed, like they shared a secret he shouldn't know. He tried for their attention by smiling wide (as wide as Dagwood ever did), but Buddy stared beyond him (thinks I've blurted out our plan, I'm sure; that's why he's actin like this). He leaned forward as far as he could without touching Ol' Gundy's purple dress (like I always tole you, I'd never tell a soul ... not even if . . when . . we found the cave; cross my heart and cross it more, ohhh ...).

Buddy stiffened and stabbed him with his sudden voice: "Eye-Away!" he gulped.

Amidst a racket of turned-over dishes, Buddy slid backwards off the bench, scrambled to his feet, and dashed around the far corner of the schoolhouse for the windbreak between the toilets and the line fence.

-Psst! came hisses from tables nearby. -Hey, Buddy, look! Here come yer maw!

All faces turned from the picnic to the empty place in front of Ol' Gundy.

-Bet she's tightern a coot, too, a wee voice shrilled. -Sure looks kinda tight now, donchee, shrieked another.

Buddy's MAW! Johannes spun around so fast, his elbow rattled along Ol' Gundy's ribs again, his face smashed into Ma's arm. Sure enough! Under the smarting sun, Buddy's Maw climbed out of a dip in Township Road where it rolled up past the schoolhouse gate. Icicles trembled in his chest. What if she goes right on by, he worried, each time she stopped to look behind her. But she headed their way, stepping high through the sand between the ruts (musta walked a hunnert miles and in this dusty heat too).

-C'mon, Borgny, Ma commanded as she reached across his forehead for Ol' Gundy. –Gotta welcome Hester Trygrud; no one else'll bother.

Johannes heard Ol' Gundy's shaky "harrumph!" when Ma lifted him by his suspenders and planted him feet-first on the ground. –Now run and git a clean plate for Buddy's Ma – Mother; let her have yer seat. Better bring two, Jonas. You never know … put the other one in Buddy's place. You boys can roost somewheres else.

-Be s'prised if Sheriff Strut aint far behind, Ma whispered as she dragged Ol' Gundy off.

In this "mysterious" arrival of Buddy's Maw, Johannes even forgot the Bluff. With Ma's watchfulness side-tracked for now, he rushed free to join Buddy before she knew he'd gone. As always, her manner had silenced the gathering and it allowed him time, too. He moved backward into the shelter of the eaves, where he stood beside un-cut cakes, not wanting to miss a minute of such a special time (why, Buddy's Maw had never been to school before, not even to Community Club).

Ma waited at the gate, while Ol' Gundy fluttered behind her, taking tiny steps to catch up. Her thinness made her lean against the breeze (tryin to push it away, huh). Did that fat nose on her flat face keep her from blowin over; he remembered overhearing Mrs. Preacher's Woman at some church supper say that Ol' Gundy covered herself with such white powder to make her nose look smaller (aint grown-ups funny-peculiar though). He'd heard Ma tell Dad many times that Ol' Gundy should dress her age, too (whatever that meant, cause all those purple clothes she wore looked odd, not friendly to little kids at all). And when she spoke in fancy words, Johannes closed his mind. Such blabber! He'd grown so used to her ways, he'd completely forget she limped, and when reminded, he blushed inside, like now, for his unkind thought. Uncle Snorri-Bjorn called her his "favorite movie star," whatever that meant too, but then, he also called Ma his "little woman" and Ma as big as his heifer LaVon (Dad would joke; why cant grown-ups ever say that they really mean, huh). Impossible to imagine Ma as skinny as Ol' Gundy, or hauling lard like Preacher Flogge. He favored Ma being big, not sow-fat like Mrs. Kittleson, but soft to lean against and solid too. How purty she looked when she didn't know he watched her, and she never changed her face with painted looks as Ol' Gundy did, and like Buddy's Maw now coming through the gate.

Johannes gaped at the white-white hair and the pink-pink cheeks, a white and pink he'd never seen before. Last year Uncle Snorri told Ma, after they'd seen Buddy's Maw downtown, he "found her somewhat old to be Jean Harlow," that she tried too hard to hide her age, she looked ten times worse instead (what's Jean-Harlow, Ma?).

When Hester Trygrud took the hand Ma offered, a tiny devil wind skimmed across the sand and swallowed her in dust. The pattern of birds on her dress took off in spiral flight that lifted her skirt from her knees, bunched it around her breasts for an instant, revealing black things that made her underneath as spooky as midnight shadows (not at all like what the Sears Roebuck catlog showed in the backhouse). The top half of her looked too heavy for the broomstick legs that kept her balanced.

Joshing laughter broke out in the schoolyard, and Johannes thought of the times downtown he'd heard Dad and the men at whist talk of Hester Trygrud being such a sport. Sport? He couldn't for all the tea in China SEE how she could play kittenball on the Mothers Team with tits as big as Wilda-no-Tail's. Ma didn't have tits, she said, but the top of her she called her bosom (boo-zoom?) and sometimes Dad mentioned boobies. The men in Town also said that Buddy's Maw smoked like a chimney and drank like a fish, while other things he listened to made his ignorance itch.

Mouth still agape, Johannes couldn't lower his eye. He waited for Buddy's Maw to finger her dress down over her hips, then shake out her hair, which made him think of dusty milkweed pods exploding every fall. She pressed the redness on her lips, then took Ma's hand again. It all had happened in seconds (Whewww!).

In her usual way, Ma's voice (clear as the dinner bell at home and making everything sound ordinary as everyday) led them amongst the tables where she had every mother greet Buddy's Maw. Johannes strained for a closer look (Buddy's Maw sure dont look real; how "mysterious," stranger than Jesus or Uncle Snorri).

He drew in his breath at the idea of Buddy running to hide from his maw; how could anybody be 'shamed of their maw? And Buddy 'specially, who feared nobody (and scared-a almost nuttin but blood and the dark and high places).

-Eye-Away! Whatsa matter. Gone stone deef?

The muffled whoop reached his ear after a clod of dirt bounced off his neck. Johannes whirled around to meet Buddy's signal from the girls toilet. While he wavered between him and Ma, he sighted The Sheriff-Almighty careening out of the hills down Township Road, the car-with-the-star bouncing out of every dip, looking mean and wild and moving in on him (and Buddy, ohhh …).

All eyes followed, all voices cheered each appearance that brought the Sheriff closer. The star-on-the-car faded into The Winter-Lonely and Johannes took off. With arrows zinging in his ears, he fled fleeter than a fawn, through high weeds past Buddy into the schoolyard fence.

His legs hadn't stopped running when Buddy caught up to him and untangled him from the barbed wire.

-Christa-mighty, Gramps. Got dynamite in yer pants? You know when I cry "Eye-Away!" I mean look-and-run, not goin nuts.

Once through the fence, they left everything undone behind and raced each other through the planted field for home. Dad's silo beckoned and Johannes choked with wonder at such forbidden freedom. He pinched himself as cloudbanks overhead formed dazzling snowdrifts just for him and spread themselves back and forth against the sun and soaked the Bluff in waves of shifting color and when the cloud shadows swooped upon them, him and Buddy rushed away from darting sunbeams that caught them, he thought, stabbed them, and sometimes plunged them headlong to the ground, then raised them up and stabbed them more while they stumbled ahead of their feet between furrows of sprouting oats.

Johannes gasped at the terrible presence that stood so soon before them. How young the sky this noon and huge, and Walking Sorrows taller than he'd ever seen it, with the Howling Grief Ridges hiding behind it.

At the backyard gate, Solly and Sig, their ears perked, stretched their long necks to greet them, their muffled whinnies riding the winds of spring.

Johannes wiped his tears. He knew that Ghosts looked down (and maybe smiled, huh?).

*   *   *

-SNOOZIN GOOD, AINT YOU, Ma said when she picked up the problems pad from the floor. -Tired from haulin all that water this mornin? Wont Buddy be tongue-tied when he sees what you done; for his tub too.

Johannes opened his eyes wide to wipe away how Ma would look, standing by his empty bed with that letter he didn't know how to write.

-Musta wore you out yesterday with that polishin and all. Shame Buddy couldn't be there to help (Quit sayin Buddy's name like that like nuttin's wrong when bein late like this aint natural now, and Buddy dont like bein at that schoolhouse less he had to).

Yesterday Johannes stuck a note in the kitchen door, telling Buddy he'd be helping Ma clean schoolhouse as they did each month of the school year and yesterday Dad wanted him to help her with special things if he didn't get in the way. And Tuesday school again, uff da!

Ma moved closer to the screens. She scanned the sky and watched Solly and Sig standing stock still at the back fence, their necks stretched long, sniffing the weather.

-Sure glad you got that water in. Too bad we cant afford to fix the porch pump; hoped we'd had it done 'fore Uncle Snorri came this year. He'll think we gone back to Olden Times for sure, or ready for the Poor Farm.

-We still poor, Ma?

-Course we are. Same's everybody else, Jonas. But we're so lucky we aint on relief ... yet. Now dont make that a stew. We live best we can. No shame bein poor. Besides, its how you hope that matters.

-Yeah, Ma.

She rolled the window shades to the top to let in more light: -Dont like how the northwest looks. And the horses actin strange. Even heard some geese goin south, I thought; too early for that, aint it (musta been Buddy, ohhh)?

Whenever Ma looked anxious, Johannes paid attention. He jolted forward so fast, the rocker moved with him again. He hadn't heard wild geese; he'd forgotten to listen just as he'd missed The Sheriff-Almighty racing by.

-Now settle down, sweetheart. You know why yer stayin in. And you aint finished a single lesson all summerlong, and here we are.

-Aint fair, Ma. Buddy dint git vacation lessons.

-Buddy always done his work on time; not like you, leavin it all to the last minit.

(Sure, Ma. Buddy wont let Mrs Preacher's Woman git a hand on him, if he dont study, and ship him to that place in Many-apples-less; he dont let Ol' Gundy trick him into misbehaving neither and that makes her maddern a badger when she cant make him mad at her ... wisht I could be like that.)

Ma left the windows and pushed his hair off of his face again: -My, aint we lookin like a troll (dont call me that!). Have to clip yer hair tonight fer sure before yer bath. Maybe Buddy's, too ... (he must be all right the way she keeps mentioning him and worries bout the weather instead).

The touch of her hand soothed him while she looked deep into his face (cant you SEE, Ma, I gotta get out and find Buddy 'fore lightning comes; cant you see THAT, when yer so good at seein everything else!). He dropped his eyes. His sigh turned partly-sob. She looked away, then closed the problems pad and stuck it under her arm.

-Know what? We'll throw this out for now. Buddy can help you later. He's good at 'rithmetic. Why, you can do multiplications in yer tubs tonight. How's that sound?

-Fine, Ma. He had to say something or she'd think he didn't feel good and she'd send him up to bed.

-A good chance now to work on sentences. You know Miss Gunderson always wants vacation stories soon as school begins.

Defeated again, he couldn't sort out any of the things spinning foolish in his head. He looked on in helpless silence while Ma sharpened his pencil with a paring knife and laid an open writing tablet in his lap. He stared down at the lined pages glaring at him. How could he make that letter to Ma (AND the extra one for Uncle Snorri, uff da!), much less WRITE about his summertime with Buddy for all the school to know.

The clock clanked twice with the pain of winter truck chains.

-Good, Ma said. –Only two a-clock. Aint we been busy now; all that's left to do is Uncle Snorri's Velkommen cake to fix.

Humming with satisfaction, she went back to the counter where she poured dough into three round tins, leveled each with a gentle shake, checked the wood in the cookstove, then placed the pans on racks inside the oven. She wiped her hands on her smock and smiled at him.

-Now while that's goin on, back to my sewin. And you can git yer story started.

He leaned as far out from his chair as he could to watch her move through the open sliding doors into the sitting room. There Gramma's sewing machine sat in the bay, surrounded by hanging geraniums.

-You know what? She stopped in the middle of the room and talked back at him, -I'm makin a shirt for Buddy same as yers. If yer both good and do what I say, I'll embroider yer names on the pockets afterwards. Wont that be something You two'll be the fanciest pair in school.

(Maybe I can sneak off when she settles down, her back to me).

45

When he said nothing, she turned, thrust her head towards him and whispered loud as if a roomful of others listened: -And dont try sneakin off, or jumpin around so the cake falls. What'd we tell Uncle Snorri if you spoiled his favorite cake?

While she dug through her sewing basket, he heard her mumble to herself something about early fall and winter, and more about geese going south. Why hadn't he heard that if she had? It had to be Buddy then, with another sign (but why today); jist think, he could imitate anything so good it even fooled Ma (and maybe Uncle Snorri-Bjorn or Dad). Johannes listened hard.

Only the whirring of the machine then filled the downstairs, melded with Ma's song about a long long way to Tipper-something. Not loud, but with a stubborn up-and-down drone that sounded like the hurt inside him felt which he couldn't touch. She pumped the pedal fast or slow according to which parts of cloth she worked on, and those shifts in speed wiped out her higher notes. She said her voice sang alto (whatever that meant).

(Oh, Buddy, whatcha doin to me anyhow? We shoulda been to Eye-Away and BACK a month ago!)

How could Buddy wait like this till the last minute and maybe get found out. And only two free days left to go (and be back for school, too, ohhh …).

Johannes had no picture in his head of Ioway, except that nobody said it the way they wanted you to spell it. According to Buddy, Ioway lay south of the sunset on the Minnesota side of the Miss'ippi, a blotch of pink in his geography book, but colored red on the wall map at school. He could trace there the boundary crooks in the River, but distance meant nothing on paper. Did color? Wisconsin, the shade of Ol' Gundy's purple dresses, and Minnesota green as horse tank moss. Yet the scenery hadn't changed colors last year when they rode in Uncle Snorri's rumble seat along one bank of the River to the other (how "mysterious" …).

Uncle Snorri told him once that you could BE in any place you wanted, even if your body couldn't go there (like saying "Eye-Away" amounted to BEING there almost?); but like with the Ghosts, you had to think big and not give up (Oh, wouldn't it be better to BE in Ioway without having to GO there, huh?).

This puzzlement brought back Ma's troubled face, the one she wore that morning he barely remembered when she came to his bed to tell him that Jesus had called Grampa Anderegg home to heaven in his sleep. Could heaven be much father away then Eye-Away if you went straight up in the air then as far as you went down the Miss'ippi? He never asked questions 'bout heaven cause everybody got funny-peculiar looks on em and said nobody's been there to tell; same way with hell, nobody'd seen it, when I'd ask what state hell's in. But, Buddy HAD been to Eye-Away (so there!).

He chewed the pencil's eraser and flipped through the empty tablet. Vacation hadn't started with the school picnic. Vacation only began the minute they raced home to change their clothes. He pooped at the remembrance, every detail too alive to ever fade away.

He glanced up at the ceiling register and dreamed that Buddy had gotten to his room without him knowing how, and waited for him to be free of Ma (whenever that time comes).

*   *   *

ONCE ACROSS THE FIELD that day and up the backstairs to his room, Johannes flops on his bed so winded he wonders if he'll ever catch his breath. Buddy hits the floor, panting:

-I'm croakin fast, he gasps. They can't even munch on the chunks of angel food they'd filched on their way through the pantry. In the momentary quietness that descends, Johannes is satisfied now to rest on his back and only daydream about their plans instead of chasing them since they'd come this far without being found out and stopped. He waits for Buddy to decide what to do, and when, and how.

His room had windows in three walls: a long pair in the gable looking west over Gramma's crabapple tree and Grampa's sugar maple all the way to the schoolhouse. In the slopes of the ceiling, double dormers faced each other, the southern set of sashes gave onto the pines along the driveway to the back porch; the northern pair looked out from the desk Dad had built for him out of egg cartons, and from there, Johannes could stare as long as he wanted through the tree-tops up at the Bluff. When breezes rustled the branches, Walking Sorrows blinked at him, inviting him to come forward and try to find the cave. Except from the rocker in the kitchen alcove, the Bluff couldn't be seen from any part of the house. He loved his room for having such a secret, as much as he fancied its "mysterious" color which Ma called "Norwegian Blue," same paint she'd used on Uncle Snorri's room upstairs in the main house.

Ma often told Johannes (she thinks I dont hang on to nuttin) that his room had first been the loft in the cabin Great-Granddad Anderegg put up long long ago, when him and the Gundersons had the only homes for miles around ("if you made-a hole through the outside kitchen wall, youd see the old-time logs now hidden behind boards."). She loved to tell how later, after Grampa Anderegg and his sons made money on the farm, they joined the new house to the cabin cause they needed much more space. From this big addition, which faced east and looked up to the first bend in Township Road, nothing could be seen of Walking Sorrows Bluff or its ridges. The black Norwegian spruces cut off views.

Johannes searched the stains in his ceiling for new designs that could be signs of Ghosts. He never pointed out anything like that to Buddy, though, and because he never talked of ghosts, that convinced Johannes that Buddy really feared them (not like me, but I wont let him know I know his weakness).

Pinpricks of brightness tried to penetrate the pulled-down window shades and turned the room into an invitation for a nap. All at once, Buddy rolled over, sat up and yelled: -Cripes! Musta gonnasleep. Aint that the shitfits. How the sam hill did that happen now. He shook himself and stared around him, still surprised. A pair of squirrels quivering on the outside window sills dived into the trees. –How long you think we snoozed? Hey, Gramps, you sleepin, too? But … shhhh.

Buddy crept on his knees to the grate in the floor and peered through it. He'd see nothing but the cookstove top, Johannes knew, but he watched the way Buddy listened until he backed away, scratching his head. He went to the west windows, peeked around the shades, before moving into the dormers.

Unconcerned, Johannes brought up his present worry: –Why you dint talk to me at school, huh? How'd I make you mad?

–Couldn't risk it, Hansy. Couldn't git you talkin or we'd never git off and you even spillin our plans maybe. But, shhh.

Johannes didn't move. Even with Ma gone, the house contained her spirit; that's what made home welcome and so safe, but it unsettled him to find Buddy nervous. Ma couldn't have walked home in the time they'd been gone from school. He tried to switch Buddy's attention:

–You SURE, Buddy – Bud – you never been up there, by yerself, I mean; cross yer heart and hope to …

–Whatta you think. Why'd I go up there alone (betcha that means he's scared-a them high places, like I thought)?

Relieved, Johannes leaped from his pillow across the bed and landed at Buddy's feet. The whole floor shook.

–Shhh! She'll hear you all the way to the picnic! C'mon Gramps, shake a leg. If she gits back fore we git off, then what?

Stung, Johannes climbed out of his best overalls and kicked them across the room. He shuffled out of the tennies he wore for school or for going to town, not bothering to unlace them. He fumbled through his chore clothes muddled in a bundle underneath his bed. Buddy, already changed, had hung his discards on empty wall hooks, and tugged on the black high-tops he wore for walking the short-cut. He tip-toed to the gable and looked out again. –Swear I heard a car. Cant see nuttin from there though.

-Course not. If a car's for us, they drive down to the back porch; never use the front. Cant see any car from up here; only lights at night.

Johannes squeezed into his stiff barnshoes which pinched until he stomped each foot into place.

-Holy criminy, yer so dam noisy. Yer a reg'ler little fart blossom.

-Aint neither!

-Yer worsen Ol' Gundy tryin to catch fly-balls. Now tie them shoes real good.

Johannes poked at him, but Buddy raised a finger and whispered: -Somethin funny's goin on here. Thought I heard the phone crank too.

-Maybe Dad's in from the fields; for a bite to eat, I bet.

-You know, Hansy, we gotta move real slow and listen. Still cant figure how I konked out like that, dam it. And you too, another dam!

-Guess you musta et too much. Maybe yer part pig, huh?

-Shhhh.

-We better sneak out by the front through the bushes and spruces, then we can git back to the route I got laid out.

Near the bed, Buddy opened the door to the main upstairs. Finger to lips, he tip-toed into the hall. Johannes, turned Indian scout on the track of a bear, stalked him down the long stretch towards the open stairwell at the end, next to Uncle Snorri's room. Ma never wanted him or Buddy running all over the house, so any chance to ramble through its different parts became an exploration.

Johannes lagged behind Buddy when he passed where a hired girl had slept, and the rooms which hired men took over from dead uncles during Grampa's time. He stopped short at one closed door (would the ghost of the bachelor who fell off the Bluff be there; he dint deserve bein ON the Bluff), then passed the spare rooms for company across from the open stairway to the attic (wisht Ma would let us play up there other than on rainy days). When Buddy, scowling, turned to urge him on, Johannes skipped down the strip of carpet to Uncle Snorri's door which Ma usually kept locked.

But not today. Both door and windows stood wide open. He dashed inside to the sea chest with a mermaid painted on its hump-backed lid, a chest large enough to crawl into, and it covered half the front window when Uncle Snorri opened it. Several times Johannes tried to open it, but Ma kept it locked too.

He turned to find Buddy at the foot of the feather bed, studying what Ol' Gundy called a "sampler" in its frame over the headboard. He remembered the time Uncle Snorri asked Ma to embroider the words stamped on it, which Ma said she didn't understand, but because the letters looked so fancy, she wanted to fill them in with colored threads. HE could read the words, but wondered in the whole wide world what any of it meant: THEN BE HIS FATE AS HE FASHIONS IT. Anyway, it sure looked purty hangin over the wooden bed (did Buddy know what it said?).

-Gramps, got no time for snoopin now. Buddy yanked him back into the hall.

-Why aint things locked up like they s'posed to be, huh?

-Its cleanin time, 'member. Yer Ma tole us last night she's airin out the house all week and we can begin beatin carpets in the morning. Ought-a be fun, havin something to pound on (whatta way to start vacation!).

Johannes fretted when Buddy, moving ahead again, motioned for him to stay where he stood at the top of the stairs. He listened, then both grinned. They'd been so lucky up till now. Satisfied that no dangers really lurked, Buddy beckoned him to the central landing. Each tread had its own squeak or groan. They pressed themselves against the descending rail or the opposite wall and tried to step as lightly as they could away from each protesting sound. From open windows downstairs, whiffs of lilac rose on honeysuckle breezes. Johannes had to sneeze but one hard look from Buddy and he swallowed fast, and proceeded one foot ahead of the other like he did when walking barefoot-ed around broken glass.

He let Buddy reach the front door first, where the narrow windows on either side of it looked into the shadows of the porch ("ver-and-ah") to their goal beyond. Ma kept this door locked, too; not from fear of the gangsters Uncle Snorri warned about (whoever heard of such a funny-ha-ha thing for here) but to keep Johannes from getting away to the many hiding places he knew about in the hedges and across the road in the sheds and barns. The few times he'd managed to get away on his own, and only for fun, Ma caught him before he got anywheres.

Buddy stretched for the key high on its nail behind the window curtain, where it hung unseen, but out of reach for Johannes. Buddy fumbled around, then went to the other window frame; nothing there either. Somebody hadn't put the key back there it belonged and the door wouldn't budge an inch without it. The boys turned to each other, stumped.

At the end of the central hall downstairs, two sets of double sliding doors, both opened wide, looked through the sitting room into the kitchen, where the cookstove stared right back at them. Dangerous territory, jist in case. But for the open doors, they could have sneaked into the sitting room to wait. Johannes favored that area most of all with it davenport and fat chairs to romp on, the long-legged table for the radio and its batteries, the pump organ Ma played many nights, and Gramma's sewing machine in the window bay. Lots of room where he could sprawl over the rag rugs with the funnies (underneath all them hangin plants everwhere that dropped blossoms on his head). Nothing tickled him more than the Katzenjammer Kids, and he liked Popeye's Olive Oyl cause she looked so much like The Widow Peterson. Buddy grunted, no knowing what to do, Johannes thought; with everything so open they couldn't pass unnoticed if someone lingered in those rooms.

Maybe they could escape through the bedroom beside the bottom of the stairs. That most "mysterious" room of all, where Dad and Ma slept in Grampa's tall polished bed. That's where he sometimes heard them talking, even laughing, in the middle of the night when he'd steal down to the pantry for sugar cookies (grown-ups sure act queer, makin such funny-peculiar noises). He stepped into the room, then backed flat against the inside wall when he saw that the door to the sitting room at the far end stood open, too. He held his breath.

Sunlight seeped through lace curtains and cast more patterns on the bedspread, which, Ma said, his Gramma Berg had crocheted for her long ago and sent to her by Uncle-Snorri Bjorn. Something else made that bed extra-special, too:

"That's where Johannes first saw the light-a day," she'd tell company, "right where the stork dropped you; 'member that, Jonas, you who 'member everything so good!"

He wisht he could remember something that terrible, that extra-awful, but he know storks only from the funnies and in books, and it made him dizzy to think of being carried around like that, hanging from a big long bill, the way he toted butter slung from knotted dish towels to Ma's oldest friends. One time he'd asked Uncle Snorri about this and he said that some things should be "mysterious," some things shouldn't have answers. But Johannes couldn't see how the stork got by such heavy furniture, with doors and windows shut tight too. The Widow Peterson said that doctors, not storks, brought babies in hospitals. He'd never seen a doctor, certainly not a hospital (what do they look like, huh?), though the County Nurse who pricked them against smallpox smelt like medicine (and that's when I saw how Buddy hated blood when the pin used on him made him bleed). The only time he asked Buddy about the stork, Buddy's mouth flapped open and he snorted like a boar, which sent Johannes into hiding from that question ever after. Worst of it, Buddy not only called him Big Chief Pooper Stork, but the dumbest kid in the whole purple world.

-Why you hidin now, Gramps? First you cant git outa the picnic quick a-nuff; now yer diddlin all over the place.

When Buddy discovered him, he tugged him back into the hall: -Sure you dint hear nuttin? No car? No phone? Numbed by their adventure, Johannes shook his head. Buddy slapped his own and beckoned Johannes to follow.

Rooms had purposes, Ma said, which meant that they had no reason for gallivanting through most of them. But they couldn't help that today, Johannes thought, as he trailed Buddy to the double doors opposite Ma's room. They had no choice but to slip through the north half of the house to the back stoop, then make it around the foundation of the summer kitchen outdoors before anybody caught them. That's if their luck still held. Johannes pooped (ohhh …).

Buddy slid one of the panels into the wall and they found themselves on the threshold of the one place Johannes gladly stayed away from, the front room (which Ol' Gundy called The "par-ler"). It smelt forbidden-spooky. Draperies (soaked in blood looks like) darkened much of each long window. Gramma's Christmas cactus (that never bloomed till Easter) and Boston ferns (all of em old as all-git-out) nodded at each other from their corner stands. The dried-blood carpet matched the curtains and the cover on Grampa's Norwegian Bible. That book, too heavy to lift, rested with its goose-pimply drawings, on a chilly marble table-top beside the album of the dead, where he could never find the likeness of that brother he'd never seen, nor the bachelor uncles. Other furniture lined the walls, solid as the upright piano (Ma dint care to play cause she had enough of that in church and school). Above the horsehair settee (Ma called it that), flanked by companion armchairs, Gramma and Gramp Anderegg in oval picture frames of their own, gazed stoney-eyed through bulging glass, at the wall where a charcoal sketch of how Great-Granddad might have looked in Olden Times hung by itself.

Ma'd tried to explain the room to him, but he couldn't keep things straight, except for two events: Ma and Dad had been hitched there cause Dad wouldn't go to church, and in the wedding picture on the piano, he stood stiffer than the scarecrow in the melon patch. Later Johannes had been baptized there with Ol' Gundy and Uncle Snorri-

Bjorn standing up for him (whatever that meant, but Ma said she'd explain it in due time … when he'd unnerstand).

Now Ma opened the front room only for something she considered special (like when the Mrs Preacher's Woman and her man stayed for Sunday noontime meals?). Worst of all for Johannes, the front room held a memory (maybe it's still only a dream) he had a Grampa Anderegg in a fancy box which rested on sawhorses in the middle of the floor, and when he tried to touch the sleeping face, Ma pulled him away and said something about "the dead." That word gave him goose-bumps.

While Buddy took in everything around him for a hushed moment, Johannes crept back to the album. As soon as he touched it, the Bible next to it opened on itself to a picture of God's Big Lightning splitting rocks in two (one of them pitchers Ma said he'd git wrong ideas from; made, Uncle Snorri said, by some man in France long, long ago).

-Jeez, Gramps, yer into everything. Yer the snoopiest lil thunderbugger I even seen. WE gotta shake a leg.

Buddy shoved open the panels to the adjoining dining room. Ma used this mostly for company, too, unless she had the kitchen messed-up during canning times; and ever since that cyclone blew the summer kitchen off, she used the room for harvest crews. Every season Johannes heard ladies whisper about how "uppity (??)" it looked to feed working men in such a fancy place while they fed theirs in kitchens and on benches. Once again Buddy stopped, silent as he looked around.

Johannes liked this forbidden room; it smelt more friendly; over the long oval central table, two hanging kerosene lamps with crystals (jist like icicles, ahhh) cast tiny rainbows across the room to Gramma's corner cabinets filled with cut-glass that also raised blue and red reflections on itself, and made lady visitors cluck and coo. Ma never let him handle the gold-edged bowls and platters.

Scowling, Buddy pulled at him again. They moved fast along the table with its many chairs pushed in, then both jumped back from the telephone on the wall beside the swinging pantry door. The phone gave Johannes chills, 'specially when Central rang six long times for EMERGENCY (how exciting, ahhh), and that meant fires, floods, or accidents for Anderegg Corners, but seldom anything good other than The Widow Peterson's barn dance announcements. Set too high on the wall for him to reach, Dad explained once that Ma didn't want him to rubber on the party line and learn to gossip that way.

They pressed around the sideboard and continued along the wainscotting to the swinging door that led to the backstairs and the outdoor stoop. –Whewwww, whatta relief! they exclaimed as one. They sighed from released tension and snickered at the sound of their shoes which has begun to squish from such tight treading. But when they tried the outside door, it didn't budge either.

–What's goin on here, Johannes cried, then whispered, –this door's never locked; dont think its got a key.

For an hour it seemed they stood in silence for a moment, both knowing that the only way out left for them ran through the kitchen from the pantry, past the windowed alcove to the back porch. But once outdoors, anybody watching could see them all the way to the schoolhouse. It seemed another hour before breath came back naturally. They had no choice but to risk their sacred plans.

They started forward, one foot at a time, as they'd done last winter when testing new ice on Blood Brothers Crick. The swinging door from the pantry into the kitchen whimpered like a pup sometimes, Johannes remembered, so he barely touched it and backed away. To their surprise, it opened inward without a sound, but the sudden brightness of the kitchen almost blinded them. Startled, then in a spurt, they flat-footed it across the waxed linoleum for the back door.

And there sat Ma in Great Granddad's rocker in the nook, sorting dirty clothes. They all turned to stone.

Ma spoke first: –Whatta you two think yer up to? Her eyes swept over them from their workshoes to theirs caps. –Runnin away like that and spoilin the ballgame too.

Nailed to their spot, Johannes looked down at his feet and let a poop that burst into a baffled fart. He shuffled fast and smiled at her with all of his teeth.

-Dont be cute now, Jonas. Cant stand nuttin cute. You can dry up and blow away is what.

He sagged against the alcove wall beside Buddy who'd turned drugstore Indian again.

-Dint 'spect to fine ME here now, didcha? But aint the both-a you a pair! What's up yer sleeves?

Buddy braced himself to keep his high-tops from sliding on the slippery floors. Johannes dared not look at him: -But Ma, how'd you ...

-Dont worry, boys. Dint sprout wings if that's what's got you scared. She busied herself with the sorting baskets while they still held their breath. –When I looked and dint find you, Miss Gunderson saw you at our backyard gate. So Sheriff Strutt drove me home is all. Wanted me to call the County Seat for him, but that's not yer business. MY business is whatcha up to now, on such a sticky day, and in them heavy barnshoes too.

No response. The Uncle Snorri-clock ticked louder in the frozen moment.

-Look at me boys! Got notions now?

They both looked up at once, still avoiding each other.

-Dont know what's in yer heads, but sure dont need you runnin off to the end of nowheres, gettin into troubles. She paused. –You want walk home dead sometime? Then what'd we do? And Buddy's Maw – Mother – too?

-What makes you think ... we aint ... Buddy nudged him.

-Johannes! Watch yer grammer, and you, too, Buddy. You hear me? Never let me catch you on them rocks, she nodded up at Walking Sorrows, -with all them walls to fall off, and timber rattlers waitin. Dont want you near the Squaw neither; that's down the river to yer graves fer sure.

She squinted at them: -You want Jesus callin you 'fore yer time now?

(What's Jesus got to do with it, huh? Ah, Ma, Jesus dont care 'bout no bluff or river; he's too purty and in them funny nightgowns too; why he couldn't even find us . . maybe …).

The clock chimed and set off a flurry of flies.

-Know whatcha do? Work on that tree house Uncle Snorri started fer you last fall, so long's you don't slide down that corncrib roof again and rip off yer … pants. Or, you can go down the crick and splash where the cows cross, long's you keep an eye fer copperheads. You wont need yer heavy shoes then. Do yer feet good runnin bare like that.

Ma pushed aside her work, got up, snatched her kitchen smock from a hook, and bustled off to the counter. There she dragged out coffee beans and grinder.

-Company comin, Ma?

-Miss Gunderson's walkin som-a the ladies over after they clean up. Gonna give em early lilacs. Mr. Olson'll carry em home.

Ma poured fresh beans into the funnel and began to grind away. Encircled in coffee fumes, she sputtered on: -Imagine you two, runnin off from the ballgame like that; even leavin yer ice cream. Dont know what to make-a such thing. Planned to give you the rest-a the day off, but if yer gonna stand there like a pair-a constipated trolls, you might as well fill my washtubs for tomorrow. She dumped the fresh grounds into the coffee pot and set aside an egg for adding later. –Be so good to wash outdoors again, but there's no water in the rain barrels from April. Uff da! County Agent hopes we wont be dry this summer too.

That turned Buddy loose. Nodding at Johannes, he opened the screendoor and shoved Johannes out ahead of him. They staggered across the porch, but kept their faces turned away as each slid down against a pillar to the planks and sat there back to back. Vibrations tinkled in the dinner bell beside the steps. Grasshoppers whirred with the sputtering of Dad's tractor off on the far forty beyond the crick. Johannes slapped at his fingers of sweat that crawled down the insides of his legs.

-See what I mean, Buddy growled, -like I tole you, you too dam slow!

Johannes watched fat robins on the grass, pulling up fat worms and stretching them until they snapped. He had to change the subject fast; he didn't want Buddy mad today:

-Think the spade's still under the porch, huh?

-Yeah, felt fer it last night … but see whatcha done few slow-pokin around; yer nuttin but a limpin loony.

-Think we'll really see the Miss'ippi up there? Johannes tried hard to fight off the blame. He turned to find Buddy unlacing his shoes: -Now whatcha doin?

-You heard what she said, Gramps. She'll sure as hell know something's up if we keep our shoes on.

-But we cant climb no rocks barefoot-ed.

-Course not, cutesy, but cancha see?

-See what, huh?

-We gotta go barefoot-ed 'round here, that's what. Gotta be special-careful.

Buddy begged attention as he put his face against Johannes: -I know, we'll hide the shoes in the corncrib and nobody'd think they're there till we can sneak off. Then we'll put em on along the way. That's swell, yeah! Keep em right there under the tree house where we s'posed to be workin anyways. Sound good?

Johannes saw the light. He nodded so eagerly in agreement he pulled both shoelaces into knots and sat there, unable to untangle them, furious enough to cry.

-Oh, Buddy, Ma called, coming to the screen, -yer Maw – yer Mother – said you can stay over next couple of days when she's off to see yer Pa. I tole her you could stay all summer if you wanted, and that's if her and yer sister aint got chores for you; or … if you don't behave.

Buddy's face cracked with a smile so wide, Johannes saw the space between his front teeth quiver. –C'mon, Hansy, he laughed, leaping barefoot from the porch.

Taken off-guard, Johannes still struggled with his shoes and could only watch Buddy drag out the sawhorses and planks from the woodshed, set them up between Gramma's apple tree and Grampa's sugar maple, turn up the washtubs stacked against the porch foundation, grab two pails from the outside cellar steps, and dash across township Road to the pumphouse between the barns. Johannes heard Ma behind him take the copper boiler from the porch wall and drag it to the kitchen stove where it would set a-top the reservoir, waiting to be filled. Then Ma came out to help him with his shoes:

-Now aint he a good boy though. She watched Buddy disappear.

-Oh, Ma, we dint mean to spoil the ballgame, honest. But couldn't help it, Ma, cause … cause The Sheriff Almighty … I feared he'd take Buddy off (him or that Mrs Preacher's Woman!).

-Jonas, baby, you and the Sheriff! Now why in all the world would he take Buddy anywheres?

-Dint he go after him before?

-NOT Sheriff Strutt. But if a kid runs away, who's to look fer him and bring him home? That's what a sheriff's paid for. Such notions you got. Anyway, we dint feel like playin ball today; too hot and all that food we put away. No good for the system.

When she finished undoing his laces, Ma pulled him to his feet, but he ducked her hand when she swatted at the seat of his overalls, and sent him flying off the porch.

-Dont fergit yer pail, Jonas!

Blushing, he ran back to her: -No, one's nuff. Help Buddy all you can, but dont strain yerself, carryin two at once. You bring yer water for the boiler.

He knew Ma watched him till he "vanished" through the gates.

By the time he got to the pump, Buddy had one pail full; while he hunkered to wait for the second one to fill, Johannes fussed about how long they'd have this hated chore to do. The porch pump broke down last Thanksgiving, right after Jesus called Ol' Hjalmer home, and nobody else in Anderegg Corners knew about house wells or pumps (which had to be primed with boiling water every winter anyway). "Couldn't 'ford a town plumber," Ma always scolded each time Dad wanted to bring one home. So they learned to carry water across Township Road and it became such a part of daily chores, they forgot about minding it, except Johannes. "Besides," Ma'd say whenever it came up, "much better drinkin water than the porch pump offered anyway. It's from the same spring that waters the cows and feeds the horses' tank. Cold, clear, clean."

Johannes found it easier and more fun to fill Ma's tubs last winter from the drifts around the house. They stacked the tubs so high with snow, the melt spilled all over the kitchen floor (and how we giggled cleanin up the mess).

When Buddy set off on a balancing act, water splashing from each side of him, Johannes hurried to fill half a pail, then take off after him. He tried not to trip over himself as he usually did if he hurried.

-That's more like it, boys. Ma beamed, coming to meet them. –Shouldn't take many more for rinsing and the boiler. –You go off then, do what you want till supper.

After emptying the pail she took from Johannes, Ma joined Buddy, who'd set up the wringer between the tubs. As she brushed the washboard and re-arranged it, she gave orders while she worked:

-One thing more. When I call you kids, want answers quick; dont wanna be holdin no cold meals. First ring-a the bell's a warnin, git yerselves together; second ring means twenny minits to yer plate. No third ring. But if I hafta use that auction-megaphone of Grampa's, you jist go hungry's all. That aint no fun now, is it?

A nosey bluejay swooped around before landing on a plunger and squawked at them.

-You boys'll look after each other, wont you, Ma added before Buddy trotted off again.

Johannes could tell whenever Ma had Meaning in her face, cause her eyes drilled right into you for what seemed forever, daring you to blink. After the way she'd exchanged looks with Buddy, he knew she wouldn't pester them if they done their chores and dint come late to table. He'd depend on Buddy playin his "pertecter" (that's what Uncle Snorri-Bjorn called him last fall). But the way Ma'd warned, that dinner bell might be a problem, and if she had to use that megaphone, uff da! He must never forget that she meant business then.

He started after Buddy, but she held him back:

-'member, Jonas, you wont be selfish will you now? She looked deep into him. -If Buddy's gonna be around a lot this summer, too, you treat him like a brother (the one I never seen, huh?) and he can stay long's he wants. If yer real good, Dad might try to git batteries for the radio. Then you can hear The Lone Ranger agin.

He looked back at her with blank eyes (cant bear to tell her I cant stand The Lone Ranger and that Tonto talkin silly). Dint she know that everything he had belonged to Buddy anyway, cause soon they'd be Blood Brothers (once Buddy got over bein scared-a blood). And maybe this summer, he'd even find out if the Ghosts had shapes (or ... braids?).

-'fraid its too late for us to go, Johannes complained when he got back to the pump. He leaned, resigned, against the cooler where a bowl of purple jello floated on the water and he pushed at the container filled with butter balls.

-There's still time fer us, Hansy; days already longer. But we gotta keep busy till the company gits here. That'll be our chance. Cant be moren half past two right now. He paused. -Maybe we'll hafta miss meals sometimes if we git busy and dont hear the bell or that other thing.

Johannes watched Buddy fill his first pail: -Think we'll see the Miss'ippi today?

-You and that goddam river ...

Every time a cussword prickled the air, Johannes flinched at the exciting (but naughty?) sound of it.

-Its the only way to tell if ... Uncle Snorri says it's the only way to ...

-Jeez, Gramps, you sure lucky yer maw dont whup you. Wonder why though, if you rile her much as you rile me ... sometimes.

Sparkling with mischief, Buddy's eyes hugged Johannes: -anyway you rile me good, Big Chief Fartin Thunder. And he pushed his weight against the pump.

They'd just finished with the water when frantic blackbirds alerted them. Before they ducked into the backhouse, Johannes caught sight of Ol' Gundy leading the ladies past the path to the back porch, where Solly and Sig grazed (but they wont hurt you cause they like to sniff at everybody). By the time the babble reached the front gate, Johannes had managed to throw himself into the shrubs around the "ver-and-ah." He lay close to the ground, ears reaching out.

-Who'da thought she had the nerve to show up in the first place, someone huffed.

-And then to haul off with the Sheriff like that; right in our very eyes. Ol' Gundy snorted into her hankie. –Why ... why he hasn't got the morals of a tom-cat (what's more-alla, Ma?)!

-Sure does take the cake now, dont it, with her man a-dyin slow like that.

Their hissing sounds mingled with the rustling leaves and birds. Sprays of spirea nodded in bewilderment. But for Ol' Gundy's voice, Johannes couldn't tell one complainer from another; they all whined and scolded alike. Most grown-ups all sounded the same to him, like most of them looked a-like too, unless he'd noticed something special in them to remember ... something hard to do.

-Oh, Borgny, Ma called through the front door screen (she has that key now?), -bring the ladies in this way; much cooler in the dining room. Best lilacs on the north side, too. But first we gotta have some coffee.

Disappointed that he couldn't hear more about Buddy's Maw, Johannes backed away when he could, and saw Buddy, beyond the porch, start off ahead of him. Their shoes, tied by their laces, hung from each shoulder; he dragged the spade behind him.

-Do we gotta take the spade now, Johannes fretted when he caught up.

-Can never tell, Hansy. Might hafta clear the cave of junk … that's if we ever find one. Anyway, we'll have it up there jist in case; yer paw wont miss this rusty thing. And dont you fergit yer shoes next time neither.

Buddy tossed the brown pair at Johannes, while he put his black ones on, and riding a current of brewing coffee, they "vanished" into black Norwegian spruces..

* * *

JOHANNES SAT UP WITH a jolt. Ah, that day. His blood raced now as fast as it had then, making it more impossible to share such times with anyone (even Buddy dont know how specially-unforgettable this vacation's been to me). The letter to Ma wouldn't take shape, much less the story Ol' Gundy wanted.

The hum of the sewing machine joined the buzzing of bugs in summer fields, and Ma's singing mixed up with it all:

Work, for the night is coming,
Work, thru the morning hours;
Work, while the dew is sparkling,
Work 'mid springing flow'rs;
Work, when the day grow brighter,
Work in the glowing sun,
Work, for the night is coming
When man's work is done.

(but that's all we do, Ma, is work, almost all-a time) but this song at least didn't bend him in two like the final ones she practiced for every funeral in the world.

Ma couldn't see him without leaving her chair and looking into the alcove. Maybe he could get away to his room. Once up there, he'd try to crawl out of the north dormer into the elms. Then off on his own to the tree house where Buddy might be hiding, or on to the horse barn where he's maybe currying Solly and Sig, or greasing their harnesses, which he likes to do. Then, wondrous thought, what if he, Johannes, went alone to the Bluff jist to prove he could git there on his own (now wouldn't that pinch Buddy's titties when he heard!). He sighed a sob. He hardly dared think this way, much less trying to reach Walking Sorrows by himself.

He'd no sooner placed a foot on the floor to deaden the creak in the rocker than Ma tip-toed in to check the cake, then slipped out without a glance his way. Yet he knew that she'd seen what she needed to know.

He'd never been lucky with sneaky things, always being unmasked and right away too. Buddy never got caught in anything he shouldn't be doing. Even Ol' Gundy couldn't bring him down. But Johannes at least could DREAM of going to the Bluff alone, following the trail Buddy laid out in words and making a map of it in his head as he memorized the possible twists and turns and climbs, and the best way to take off from the house, and even how to get back differently:

The quickest way to the face of the Bluff had to be head-on, but how could they ever climb such cliffs, and besides, Walking Sorrows overshadowed Anderegg Corners like a wall so nobody could try anything without the whole community knowing; even if everybody stayed away from the place for fear of that hired man's mad ghost (the nerve of calling Broken Thunderhawk's sacred bluff "Bachelor's Drop," ohhh ...). After the snow had melted and before the end of school, Buddy had made his route so clear to Johannes that Johannes said (with the map in my head) that he'd be able to find his way to the top with eyes closed tight (ahhh ...), even locate the cave alone ... if he had to. These plans kept them worked-up long before they could actually take off on that last day of school (when nobody'd notice, huh?).

Once they got behind the black Norwegian spruces, they'd skirt the vegetable garden and orchard which lay behind the house in protected coves at the bottom of the ridge slopes. From there, a gentle rise to the high field that marked the end of cropland. Above that, rocky benches began, step-like through sumac underbrush and blackberry bramble, till they reached the ledge that you could see from every angle below, as it ran below the crests of the Howling Grief Ridges to the base of Walking Sorrows Point, where it rose like a fortress, thick and wide and high (Uncle Snorri called it a "castle keep" whatever that meant now); flat on top with no sign of a growing thing up there. Elsewhere, junipers sprung out of the cracks and crevaces of the rocky walls … (how "mysterious").

Buddy also had a plan for getting them back in a roundabout way without being seen. They'd retrace the way they'd climbed, but instead of coming out of the spruces beyond the front porch (in case people milled about the yard), they'd run across Township Road farther above the mailbox at the front gate, and disappear into the windbreak that separated the farm buildings from the house. Ah, yes, and when they came to the corncrib beneath their tree house, they'd leave their sandy shoes there, and nobody would ever know from which direction they'd arrived. Johannes wished that he could have made such plans, but unlike Buddy, he remembered details (Buddy dont remember good, 'specially when it comes to the Ghosts), which he couldn't tell a soul (not even Uncle Snorri-Bjorn, unless, when he takes me to the Bluff some time, I run ahead and lead the way instead).

Once again he tried to stop the rockers with his foot, and once again Ma stepped in to check the cake; then, as before, left without a word, though he knew she noticed how busy he must have looked. The speed of the machine slowed, then hurried, then stopped, before repeating itself over and over. He gave up trying to get to his room and lay back against the chair while zinging arrows flew past his ears and disappeared. He watched ground sparrows outside the windows scuttle along the fences (they look smaller than the dust balls in the attic).

*　*　*

IT'S PICNIC DAY AGAIN. Time at last to test their trail (will Buddy bring them to their goal, ahhh …). Johannes catches up with Buddy as soon as he gets into his shoes, then outruns him through gates and fences. Those first minutes he races against his own excitement, a galloping calf clicking its hooves at the thunderheads of May, at the clouds now kissing the Point of Walking Sorrows. He can't remain inside himself at such an invitation from the Ghosts, into whose grounds him and Buddy trespass (we're Indian scouts now; will the Ghosts charge us, chase us off, as they maybe done to that hired man?).

After such an explosion of energy, Johannes fades at the edge of the high field. He stumbles along, trying not to trample corn shoots, and turns an ankle every time dirt pours into his shoes and drags him back. When Buddy eagerly reaches for his arm to slow him down, Johannes shakes free and forces himself ahead again, if only but a few feet. This land belonged to him just as the Bluff belonged to Broken Thunderhawk.

When they got to the first of the benches, after stomping their way through head-tall brush, Buddy regained the lead and kept it by hoisting himself onto the rocks with the aid of the spade handle, then pulling Johannes up after him. High on the wider shelf without scrub, they threw themselves into the grass as thick as a rug and found their surprised faces buried in violets. They pooped, then giggled, and tore off their shirts and slapped at the muddy sweat that freckled their arms.

Johannes wavered between awe and dread. He looked over his left shoulder to the ledge. Below them a million feet straight down, the windows to his north dormer stared up at him whenever breezes ruffled the tree-tops. He drew in his breath and clutched at the flowers under his nose. Ol' Gundy said that violets made Wisconsin famous for their juicy stems and head that nodded half-awake (and such a noble color too). He waited for Buddy to mention the Ghosts (and if he dont, I'll know fer sure he's too scared to talk-a them).

Breaking their silence first, Buddy sounded funny-peculiar (not funny-ha-ha as he should feel now): "Yer Maw sure hates rattlers, donchee? Aint you scared?

Johannes shook his head. He remembered the squishy softness of the snake he'd stepped on near the Crick, but he'd always wanted a snake for a pet, not to run from them, if he could ever make Ma understand that not everybody hated snakes like grown-ups did. Every time he saw a purple snake plant, he searched hard around it, but never found one there.

-I aint 'fraid though, Buddy insisted, looking at Johannes in a way that begged him to be scared as well: -Betcha we wont see any this far up. Only a good snake is a dead one.

-Why you wanna kill snakes anyway? Doncha know a dead one calls back others to it?

-Who sez?

-The Widow Peterson sez so. But I aint scared-a snakes!

-You look puny. Whatcha 'fraid-a then? GHOSTS, maybe? He laughed too hard and sudden.

-Ghosts? Course not, Buddy – Bud! Aint that why we're up here, huh? Doncha 'member nuttin? I'm only 'fraid-a missin em. And here we are right where they should be almost.

-Yer loony as that Effie Stone. "Hansy, Hansy, with ghosts in his pantsy!"

Johannes turned away. Buddy moved in closer: -You really b'lieve there's ghosts? Up here? Up on the top? Maybe the hired man that jumped off the bluff that time left a ghost behind ...

-Whatta you mean, JUMPED?

-You know they say downtown he dint FALL off a-tall. Some say he jumped; went nuts over some wimmens (sounds like Dad now); others think he got himself PUSHED. Aint that why they call this

Bachelor's Drop? Now if he got pushed and left a ghost behind, wouldn't it be riled to find us up here now? Aint that what they call trespassin, too?

-Yer full-a purple turds is what! That's only grown-up talk; got nuttin to do with Walking Sorrows. Besides, that hired man's ghost wont be here; it's home's in them tree-tops. I'm waitin for REAL ghosts, for Great Chief ... (but what if my Ghosts wont wanta stick 'round us Norskies, huh?).

Johannes tried to cut his doubts, but they flipped back at him: if the name of Walking Sorrows changed, maybe his Ghosts wouldn't know where to go, 'specially with names like "Anderegg Point" or "Bachelor's Drop," and what would such names mean in Indian? And Buddy b'lievin talk of the hired man bein pushed (did the real Ghosts push him off for bein where he dint belong ... like me and Buddy now?).

-Whatsa matter, Hansy, scared-a something?

-Dry up and blow away.

-Betcha yer Uncle S.B. made up YER ghosts, like everything else. Now if this Thunder- bugger lived at all, whyn't nobody else talk 'bout him but you and yer Uncle S.B.; Ol' Gundy dont say nuttin and she's always blabberin 'bout somethin.

Johannes wanted Buddy to shut up, but dared not tell him.

-Guess it dont hurt none, if you dont git to b'lievin stuff like that (now you sound like Ma!).

-What's "b'lievin"? I jist know, is all. And Uncle ...

-Never stretches things, I s'pose. HOWJA know? You only see yer uncle coupla weeks a year. Okay, Hansy, less pertend. Whatta think you'd do IF we ... IF we run into some ghosts up there, what then?

Johannes couldn't say anything at first (why, he's finally mentioned ghosts!), until Buddy prodded him again:

-I think ... I think I'd ... I'd die.

-Yes – indeedy, like I thought. Yer jist a 'fraidy-cat.

-Oh, I wouldn't die of bein 'fraid!

-No? Then from what?

-Dunno. Nuttin. Nuttin, I guess.

-C'mon, Hansy, whatcha'd die of it you aint scared-a any ghosts we run .. might run into?

Johannes paused to let an icicle run down his throat and right on through his insides this time:

-I guess I'd die ... I'd die . . of wonderment! He glanced up at the fleecy sky. –Jist die of wonderment is what, cause it'd be so TERRIBLE!

Buddy sprang to his feet and yanked Johannes out of the violets. –Nuff fool talk! Yer more loony than I thought. Sound like some piss-cutter ... you.

-Can't we wait awhile, Bud? Now that we're already here? (BEING here is the most important thing of all and you gotta be quiet and sit still if you wanna hear a ghost song.)

-We aint even started yet to look for caves.

-So what. It's there. Right at the spot where you can see the Miss'ippi, I'm sure.

-"I'm sure." How you so "sure" now?

-"Doncha 'member nuttin I tole you a-tall?" Johannes repeated a familiar refrain.

Buddy scratched at an ant running around his neck: -Maybe Ol' Gundy's right 'bout you; always gatherin wool.

-But Buddy ...

-Dont fergit, I'm not a Buddy, I'm a Bud!

-I tole you what the first signs are a hunnert times.

-I know. All winterlong. Dont make em true.

-When Great Chief Broken Thunderhawk leaped off the Bluff and Singing White Wolf's Spirit kept the enemy from the cave, it all happened where the Miss'ippi showed, and that's where the cave'll be. So there!

-Bull balls, Hansy! Buddy cocked his head like Ol' Odin did when he tried to understand. A smile quivered on his chin: -Me Tonto! You nutsy!

All a-fire, Johannes prattled on: -And Uncle Snorri says ...

-Yer Uncle's a sailor, Hansy, not a Injun scout.

-says that a clump of white burch will …

-yeah. You already told me … a hunnert times.

-But, you never let me finish.

-Oh, I know the rest-a it, Big Chief Walking Thunder. C'mon, we're wastin time.

-Yer 'fraid-a ghosts, is all, Johannes mumbled under his breath.

Buddy pulled at him and nodded to the barren Point of the Bluff. There it loomed massive ahead of them, almost orange in the sunbaked stains of afternoon. Above them, a hawk spun spirals on the sky.

-Sure dont see what yer Maw finds wrong up there. Buddy's croak softened to a hush, as he pushed ahead: -But aint it wild though?

The wildness only excited Johannes more as he trudged on behind. Wolves no longer howled and kept people awake all night like in Olden Times, people said, but bears might still find sleep in caves, and timber rattlers favored shade. He couldn't worry about all that. Uncle Snorri said that Indians treated wild things like relatives; they even talked with animals (bats included, huh?), like he did with Solly and Sig, like he'd done with Ol' Odin before. But what would he say now to a bear or a left-over wolf? Maybe he should-a practiced on the woodchuck under the silo, or that badger in the pasture.

Moving on, he looked up and watched Walking Sorrows come to meet them. He pinched his side to be sure he hadn't left his body. His breath tightened when he stopped to study the Point. Energies frozen by the marvel of the moment, he wanted to rest again, and ponder: how had his magic gotten Broken Thunderhawk to the top? Why had he jumped off the Point when he could-a hid in one of the ridges that fanned out from the Bluff? These questions muddled him (what if Uncle Snorri's clues are wrong? What is he's a liar, too, ohhh …). He broke into a sweat, this time cold.

-Fer Chrissakes, Gramps, git the lead out. Buddy called from the next shelf where he'd hoisted himself again. -Yer so loony today.

Gotta sunstroke or something? Gimme yer hand. We gotta make tracks.

For an hour they explored. Cliffs rising from the ledge yielded empty promises: they dug into crevices stuffed with fallen stones and brush; they inspected mounds caved in on themselves; everything crumbly and prickly with stiffened moss like that mold on the cheese Ma hung in the cellar for weeks. From the evidence around them, there musta been dead warriors everywhere: all these crazy junipers, black against the sandstone, clinging to the rock by invisible toes. If you got kilt by a arrow's flint (like those zinging past me some times?), would you turn juniper, too, stickin outa the Bluff instead of bein held down by graveyard dirt?

At each clump of birch near the outer ledge, Johannes whirled around for a sight of the Miss'ippi; each time, nothing showed but purple Minnesota distance. How could anybody, much less noble Ghosts, get through such mess? And to call it better than The Happy Hunting Grounds? He dared not lose hope.

Whenever Buddy thought he'd found a clue and backed away shaking his head, Johannes reminded him that a secret cave HAD to be hard to find, or it wouldn't be secret (or "sacred" neither) if any ole someone could come right up to it and jist walk in. The more the net of doubts tightened around him, the faster Johannes walked to keep up behind Buddy. He had to prove that the cave would soon appear as it looked inside his head, and that would prove that Uncle Snorri hadn't lied like windbags in church insisted.

After pushing through a last bramble of blackberries which sprung from a heap of shale and concealed them from the backyard at home, Buddy followed the shelf around a bend in the base of the Point, and they found themselves beneath an overhang, in a jumble of boulders. This unexpected shelter seemed to Johannes to be several times the size of his back porch, but the ledge plunged out of sight at its far end and he stared, stunned, beside him down another million feet into the tops of oaks, elms, maples with no sign of a farm or field; only woods to the end of nowhere. And not a line to show a river.

Buddy held back from the edge. His baffled face on the vast space to the west tickled Johannes (yep, I know fer sure now, he's scared-a high places too, but I wont let him know). Behind Buddy, saplings screened off the back wall of rock and cushioned the scattered stones. They aroused not a sound of bug or bird. They looked into each other's blank astonishment, too defeated to say a thing.

Johannes, desperate, pointed at a single clump of birch leaning out into the air away from the rim of the ledge (the spot where Singing White Wolf died!): -Look, Buddy, look! We found the place!

His outburst brought Buddy back to life with a loud poop: -Crimminy, Gramps! Dont most birches grow like that. We been seein em like that all afternoon.

-This one's special, see. Full-grown and tender at the same time; pure white too, not rusty like the others.

-Yer rilin me! Worsen Ol' Gundy. And you think yer a champeen pooper too.

Buddy let out a blast, then jumped high and tried to touch the ceiling of the overhang. When he failed in a third effort, he sat down hard and rested his chin on the grip of the spade. He shut Johannes out of his thoughts.

Defeated some more, Johannes crept to the rim of this porch and studied the distance. Maybe if he searched strong enough, he'd drag the Miss'ippi out-a that purple haze.

The horizon remained unchanged. He crept back to the bend where the world they'd left behind lay like a tiny dream far below. He pinched his side again. He closed one eye, held up a thumb and blotted out the schoolhouse, then erased the church with a slight move to the right. Imagine getting rid of such places by moving a finger! To his left, the blackberry bramble shut off any sight of his farm buildings, as if home had never been at all. That idea chilled him more than being on these forbidden heights; yet, there he sat for real, unable to find the River. Too discouraged to be afraid, or maybe too afraid to be discouraged, he rested his eyes. What's left to do, he puzzled, when everything depended on the sighting of the

Miss'ippi. No zinging flints whistled past his ears with answers or ideas (Uncle Snorri's stories cant be jist lies or jokes; they always SOUND so true).

The echo of a rattler sizzled in his head, then passed. Behind the scrub, the wall holding up the overhang began to smell as earth-heavy as the graveyard after a burial. Why, The Winter-Lonely could slip right out of the rocks and crush him like a bug for sure if he didn't stay tip-top sharp. But what to do? Nowhere left to move ahead to (and how can we turn back with nuttin to show for our wintertime plans, ohhh …).

Johannes edged away from the clump of birch to see what Buddy had in mind. But no sign of him. How could THAT happen (had he "vanished" like Broken Thunderhawk)? Before he could cry out in terror, a muffled noise seeped out of the growth against the back wall, and before Johannes could locate the sound, Buddy's face darted out of the boughs that drooped over the center boulder:

-Holy jumpin shitfits, Hansy! Guess what I found! Right here in the wall …

Johannes, weak with relief, cringed at the delicious words:
-a'nother hole, I s'pose.

-Honest, Gramps, b'lieve it or not, I found us a cave.

-And howcha find it, huh? Smelt it maybe …

-Sure did!

-Stop pullin my leg, Buddy … Bud. Yet, he pooped so hard at the promise of it all, it turned into a rattling fart.

-And you stop trying to be champeen now, Buddy scolded as he motioned for Johannes to crawl onto the boulder. –While you sat moonin over dead Injuns, this here wet breeze came outta the brush and … and … well, see fer yerself then.

When Johannes got near enough, Buddy pulled him across the boulder, twisted him around, and shoved him feet-first into the hole that opened behind the brush. Resisting all the way, Johannes grabbed at the air overhead, but couldn't keep from sliding through darkness onto a clutter of pebbles.

-See it? Look! Whatta you think, Hansy? Buddy almost sobbed in excitement, as he fell in on top of Johannes. -So, here it is! And here we are!

Johannes saw nothing at first in this new world of reeking earth. He'd expected the discovery of their cave to be such an awful event that music would sing from the sky. And maybe even the Ghosts (with shapes ... and braids?) to make them welcome. No music, no Ghosts now, only a cyclone-cellar dampness to pucker his nose. He'd never seen Buddy this lively before, dancing around like a prize-fighter, punching the air, and tapping the walls with the point of the spade.

-Now aint this the cat's pajamas! Anyways it will be, soon's I clear away the junk and smooth out the walls and find fresh sand for the floor.

Wavering, Johannes looked around from his knees. It took time for his sight to sharpen, and when it did, the first thing he saw turned out not to be a rotting clothes-line sagging across one corner, but a tangle of cobwebs furry with silt strung between him and the dull light. A bat flexed in the upper shadows. Nothing scared him more than anything he knew (unless trolls existed too). Bats drank your blood, The Widow Peterson said, and he needed all the blood he had if he hoped to catch up to Buddy somehow. His heart jumped and he backed away, not wanting to touch a thing, nor have any of this rawness close in on him. Spiders wiggled under his skin.

-Whatta think, Hansy? Buddy bent over him, too overcome to notice how Johannes held back. -Got nuttin to say? First we'll git rid-a the brush, then we can roll that boulder off out front. Be easier to git in here to work ...

Johannes, eyes still on the bat, mumbled at last: -How'd you know this is the RIGHT cave, huh?

-RIGHT cave? Whatta you mean? It's a CAVE, Gramps. Aint that what we're lookin fer? Aint that what we planned? RIGHT cave!

-But we planned to hunt for the Great Chief's secret cave.

-Oh, shit, Gramps, what's the differns? A cave's a cave. Some small, some big. Besides, how we know fer sure HE … he ever had one. How we know fer sure yer Ol' Thunder-snorter ever lived. At all. Buddy shook his head and turned his back.

Rage struck Johannes with such force for an instant, he shuddered at the ugliness of what he felt, and got into himself again by inching backwards along the wall to the half-blocked hole.

-Jeez, now whattsa matter, Hansy? Buddy turned to watch him leave. He wore the same puzzled look Ol' Odin showed each time Johannes bawled him out. –Jist think, we found ourselves a cave fer summer. Aint that swell? Aint it now?

Still shaken by that flash of hatred, Johannes, on the verge of sobs, threw himself on the ledge outside, and stared into the west. (He's heard my story inside and out and still cant say the names straight once … "Thunder-snorter," humpff!).

He bit hard into the sand on his lips. Ma always warned that if he cried about things, he's destroy what he wanted most. And who could mean more to him than Buddy (and Ma and Dad, of course), even if he hated him a few minutes ago for not letting him cry over his disappointment. How could Buddy have been fooling him all along with such an open face while he listened and planned, even found a way to get us here. He forced back tears; neither dared he cry should the Ghost of Broken Thunderhawk see him, and wouldn't show himself to a crybaby, and Buddy'd think for sure he acted like a third-grader (or a baby troll).

Johannes wiped his face and worked his way to the rim of the ledge, where he let his legs drop over. He never cried like many kids, about everything. Because of his age, his size, and his shyness, Ma insisted that he should be afraid of high places, of storms and ghosts and snakes, and the dark, and even trolls. When he said that none of these things bothered him (I can prove it too), Ma'd look worried and got right back insisting on what she wanted him to fear and treat him like he did. One thing: he couldn't be sure about trolls though:

Did trolls climb bluffs in North Ameddica? Uncle Snorri said they stayed in Norway's mountains; The Widow Peterson said they lived under bridges anywhere, waiting to pounce on naughty kids and eat them. And when Ma said the same things, anything Ma said always sounded true. But he couldn't really believe in trolls (or anything) that made people laugh as hard as Uncle Snorri laughed.

Just to be sure that trolls didn't live there, Johannes dared himself to peek under the bridge over Blood Brothers Crick every chance he got (other kids never went near the bridge unless they had to, then they ran over it too fast to be scared). When he found nothing there, he wished Dad would stop and let him look under the crick bridges on the way to Town, but he'd never want Dad to see he had any interest in TROLLS. For Ma's sake he'd pretend to be afraid sometimes, even cry a little. But in front of Buddy on the Bluff he could never cry.

He raised his chin in case Buddy caught his weakness, then drew back his legs so he wouldn't be scolded for acting careless (jist cause Buddy's scare-a high places, I'm s'posed to be the same). He rotated his head around the vastness of the sky, where more hawks circled; he explored the horizon some more, but it looked farther away as colors changed. Whatever the differences in Uncle Snorri's legend every year, one thing never changed: the secret cave of Great Chief Broken Thunderhawk looked out to where the Miss'ippi, in a streak of light reflected from the sun, underlined the bottoms of the Minnesota bluffs. Nothing like that showed today.

Behind him, Buddy hacked away with the spade, then carried armfuls of branches to toss over the ledge; careful not to stumble over Johannes, who lay back on his elbows as if in a trance, yet much aware of what went on around him. Several times, he peered over his shoulder and saw the private smile on Buddy's face that always teased him, cause it meant satisfactions he didn't know about (why, he acts like I'm not here a-tall and dont even give a tinkers dam). Finally, Johannes swung around on his hinder to make his presence felt.

He didn't recognize the spot they'd reached such a short time ago. With the growth torn away from the back wall, and everything pulled away from the largest boulder, and the hole in full view, the area looked more than ever like a porch without pillars. He never imagined they'd have to MAKE a cave though; he expected it to be there (according to Uncle Snorri's signs) waiting for them to walk into. When Buddy, grunting in his labors, nodded at Johannes with a mischievous glance, Johannes leaped to his feet. Suddenly forgiven and just as quickly energized, he wanted to help.

He didn't know what to do, nor where or how to begin. He'd never dug at anything before, except with a hoe in the garden. He watched how Buddy grasped the spade handle and hoped to remember to hold it that way, and where to place his foot, and how much muscle he needed to strain, when the moment came for him to grab the spade. He moved back to the blackberry bramble that concealed them from the farm. He pulled off his shirt and let it fall into an apron around his waist. He waited, all but panting, ready to spring. When Buddy paused to wipe off sweat, Johannes lunged for the spade, and missed. Shaming himself as much as he'd jolted Buddy, he swung about-face and attacked the bramble.

He broke off twigs, stripped dead leaves, and wrestled with boughs that sprung back at him, whipping his arms and face. Furious, he bent back stalks, and stood on them until they snapped. One handful fought back with thorns, and with roots loosened, flung, him backwards against the ground with shredded stems in his hands. Fumes burned nose and throat. He sneezed.

-Whatta hell you doin? Buddy yelled out of the blue -Why you tear this up now?

Johannes blinked back.

-Dincha see, Gramps, this brush hid us from yer maw. Now if she ever looks up here, she can see us come and go like a coupla bare-assed crows. See fer yerself, Big Chief Thunder Walking.

Johannes turned and looked down that million feet, shocked:

The shadow of Dad's silo threw a thick thumb across the cowbarn loft. This side of the kitchen wing, Ma's smock billowed back and forth along the clothes lines as she wiped them clean for hanging out tomorrow's wash, everything sharp and clear.

-Looks like Ma's hooked up to a pulley, dont it, slidin back and forth like that. Johannes didn't know what else to do but make it funny-ha-ha.

Buddy didn't laugh. He hunkered and wiped his face, then looked away.

Johannes realized that Mr Olson had carried off the ladies, but he suddenly wondered about the time when he saw Dad's tractor sputtering homeward along the pasture lane with a parade of cows in tow. He even made out Wilda-No-Tail lingering far behind (waitin to be searched fer later). He forgot the time.

At first after Ol' Odin left them, the cows didn't know what to do without a dog to round them up; now with him and Buddy not on hand, Dad had to do Ol' Odin's work. How good Ol' Odin worked the herd, just like he kept barn cats and chickens from crossing the road to bother the house or mess the yard. Few cars passed through Anderegg Corners, so every one he heard acoming, Ol' Odin thought it meant company for them and he'd race to meet it with a barking welcome. How he missed his half-a-collie ... the way he'd trail after him on the way to school, slinking along the brush that hid the fences from the road ...

-See what I mean? Buddy interrupted sharply. He stood up, stretched, and squatted fast again. -From now on when we're up here you gonna have to stand guard; listen for the dinner bell or that megahorn she calls through.

-But I gotta help!

-But somebody's gotta watch and listen and that's not gonna be me. So that's 'bout the size of it.

It sounded final. They glared at each other for several heartbeats, each locked in himself, until Johannes gave way. Nothing scared him more on earth than making Buddy madder, or not saying a word with is face gone far away and alone, too (like Ma and Dad sometimes). He couldn't bear that kind of silence.

-Now if youda left that bramble stand ... Buddy softened, -I know that. If you watch good, I'll leave that pile in the corner of the cave for last and we'll clear it out together.

How's that sound? We'll even pretend it covers the bones of ... the bones of whatchamacallim you always gabbin 'bout. Okay?

Johannes caught the twinkle in Buddy's voice and dived for the spade again. He kicked it out of Buddy's hand, grabbed it, and dashed for the hole in the wall. They tumbled together against the boulder half-blocking their way.

Buddy stiffened: -Didcha hear the bell now?

-Dint hear nuttin.

-See what I mean. You shoulda been ...

-She always rings it twice or more.

-All the same, shoulda been listenin.

Scolded and worried, Johannes waited for Buddy to finish digging around the main boulder, and when he ordered him to help, they threw themselves against it and pushed. Each time the boulder moved a bit, Buddy packed small stones into the space pried free.

-Never fergit, Hansy, this is secret. Like we always said. Buddy caught his breath: -Cant tell nobody 'bout this, not even yer maw; sure's hell, NOT yer maw. Gotta be careful talking in front-a wimmens or they'll spoil yer plans (why Buddy sounds like Dad some more).

They stepped back from the entry to the cave and with what strength remained, they threw themselves against the obstacle again, forcing it to see-saw.

-'Member, this gotta be kept secret, Buddy panted, -dont s'pose yer Ol' Chief Bugger-thunder'd let anybody find his cave by telling. Same's with our cave then.

OUR CAVE! Johannes coughed. That living icicle melted down his back so fast he forgot to listen for anything. He pinched Buddy's leg before he pinched himself, and when Buddy snarled back at him, he knew, relieved, that they hadn't dreamt all this. Our cave! Johannes shoved himself against the boulder with such force he squeezed his balls and the sudden pain made him push all the more.

When the stone broke free, they rolled it in a crooked path to the rim where it teetered several times, then fell. Up through the splintering treetops below, their names rose out of the distance.

-Johannes! Buddy!

-Jeeze! Yer maw! I DID hear somethin back there.

Buddy tossed the spade into the cave and started off like a deer, then turned back to drag Johannes along the ledge. Once away from the shelves, Johannes found the rest of the way downhill much shorter and quicker than the climb.

They froze again when Ma's voice sharpened in the megaphone: -What'd I say 'bout my calls? If yer not at table in ten minits, no carmel puddin tonight.

They made it together across Township Road on the route as planned, sneaked to the barnyard fence behind the windbreak, then shifted their panic to a studied stride as they rounded the corner below the cow barn. And there stood Ma in the pumphouse door, at rest from scouring milk cans. She squinted towards Blood Brothers Crick.

They froze as solid as they had on the kitchen linoleum.

-Sure am 'shamed-a you, Jonas. Hidin when I ring, no answer when I call. And you, too, Buddy. Didcha fergit tonight?

Too winded now to risk an answer, Johannes shut his eyes and dropped his head. He hadn't forgotten.

-You s'posed to begin milkin Wilda-No-Tail, 'member? And now Dad's gone ahead and started chores alone.

-Lemme try milkin, Mrs Berg. I wanna learn so bad.

-Why Buddy! No, it's all right this time. From now on when I ring or call, better answer fast, boys. Hate to hafta use that horn; whole community can hear me.

Not yet released, they stood close together and listened to her rinse cream can covers. Everything would be fine, Johannes wanted to believe, if he could tell her not to fear for them, that nothing could happen to them on the Bluff if they behaved themselves. If he could tell her that much, they wouldn't have to hide and lie (uff da! hate telling lies; cant 'member later that I told).

-What on earth's wrong now? Too much fiddling in the crick? Off to the house. Food's in the warmer and if you dont clean it up, I wont begin TOM SAWYER tonight.

When Johannes opened his eyes on their sandy feet, he gasped. They'd forgotten to hide their shoes.

*　*　*

"WHEWWW! CLOSE CALL!" BUDDY'D warned (and on the first day of vacation too). Reliving that moment brought ticklish chills. Johannes sat up and blinked, then shook imaginary sand from his feet. Dad had been so taken that night when he heard how Buddy wanted to milk that Ma forgot to pester them about their shoes (at least she made it look that way), and that night before their bedtime reading, she praised Buddy's offer instead of scolding them some more for being late.

Ever since he started staying over, day after day, Buddy turned their chores into games (or tried to), which made them go faster and gave them extra time when they finally got away. Buddy wanted to help Dad with everything, with work Dad wouldn't let Johannes try yet: like pushing hay from the lofts for the cows and horses … or running the tractor (when it worked) till Ma put a stop to that, saying it made Johannes jealous. Buddy didn't mind tiresome things like pumping water, or raking and stacking hay and grain, or cranking the grindstone for Dad's sickle blades (while I struggled not to spill the water I had to pour into the trough). After Dad showed Buddy how to curry Solly and Sig, and when to braid their manes and tails, the horses grew so close to him they tried to clip-clop after him wherever he went, or whinnied at the sight of him (like Ol' Odin used to whimper after me at every turn).

With each new thing he learned, Buddy asked a million questions which Johannes cared not a bean about, and Dad always had a zillion answers; more ways about how to do this or that than he could shake a shingle at. Dad made Buddy his pal (like he tries to treat me) not like a kid at all. And if Buddy didn't care for Dad so much, he'd never let him call him "Buddy" like he let Ma. And Johannes knew how Buddy liked to be called "Gramps' Big Brother," or his "Protector." He sure had saved them on their first day out (guess he wants to be a milkin champeen too).

With fears fading of Buddy being in The Sheriff-Almighty's hands, Johannes decided that Dad had run into him somewhere, though Buddy always took the short-cut to the farm in daylight. Dad would never stop at the Trygrud shack except to drop or pick up Ma there. He bet they'd run into each other downtown on the street or in a store, and Dad would carry him back like he'd done before (talkin blue streaks all the way). He slowed the rocker and settled back, calmed by his own assurance that the way things might be would be true (hope they git here fast so I can give him Uncle Snorri's news and we wont wanta leave for Eye-Away then and I wont have to write them – goddam – letters neither.) Johannes hugged himself.

-How you comin, Ma asked from the sitting room door.

-Miss Gunderson says with yer kind-a memory writin 'bout summer ought to be the easiest schoolwork of all. When you finish a page, I'll look it over. Then we'll try one of them cinnamon rolls you helped me make this morning. And we'll fergit bad spellin for now. How's that?

-Oh, Ma, gotta move. My hiney's sore from so much sittin.

She said nothing as Solly and Sig clumped past the screens and looked in at home, surprised, ears stiff. The wind glided over their coats; they shook their manes and backed away.

-Guess I better take Solly and Sig to their stalls case a storm hits fast.

-Sit still, Jonas. Their gates are open; they know what to do when they hafta.

-What if lightnin strikes nearby like when it burnt off Wilda's tail, or when it hit the tree that time by Gramma Johnson's brooder coop and knocked her flat (and she dint come to for days, ahhh).

-Dont need yer tricks now. If you cant settle down, maybe should loosen up that hinder with some birch ... Better yet, git Sheriff Strutt give you a lesson when he flies back this way. All I hafta do fer him to stop is wave a towel.

Johannes hid his smile. He knew by the change in Ma's voice (with some funny-ha-ha in it?), she didn't really mean such threats, but he pretended to take them serious so she wouldn't look like a dunce if Dad heard about it and teased her for being such a windbag (but never blowin hard 'nuff to matter).

Johannes took up pencil and bent over the tablet. The red lines on the paper turned into angleworms the way they wiggled around after a rain. He couldn't write a word about summer, but he'd try to get Ma's letter out of his head on to paper. He nibbled the pencil's eraser: "Dear Ma," he put down at the top of the sheet and lay back to see if the rest of the words came by themselves. The sewing machine hummed along with Ma doing "Abide With Me" again. Pine shadows wavered across the window glass; breezes shifted into winds from a new direction.

His eyelids drooped and he saw Dad rushing home with Buddy on the runningboard, something Dad never let Johannes ride. The feed-truck "vanished" into the shade over the road and came out the other end of it as Uncle Snorri's sky-blue runabout instead (ahhh). It slowed down for a lady who had her thumb stuck out ("called hitchhiking," Buddy said once; best way to git around when you had no car or cash). Peering through cheesecloth fuzziness, Johannes saw Uncle Snorri leap from the driver's window, skate up to the lady, take her hand and bring it to his mouth (yick!): "Why Aunt Min, let me haul you off to Buddy!," and he dumped her into the rumble seat so fast, Johannes couldn't see her face, and the car sped into the distance.

AUNT MIN!

His heart skipped. He shook his eyes open and pinched his leg, but the picture wouldn't wipe out (must be a sign or warning from Singing White Wolf; Uncle Snorri said that as part of his shaman's job, he had to make dreams and "visions" happen). No wonder Buddy's not here, not if Aunt Min had come. Betcha fer sure that's what's happened; 'stead-a sendin that card they'd waited for so long, she wanted s'prise him, like me and Buddy planned to s'prise her. Convinced that Singing White Wolf had alerted him, Johannes went into turmoil:

He knew that if Aunt Min had come, she meant only to take Buddy back. He had to stop her. He had to save Buddy from Aunt Min this time, not from The Sheriff-Almighty (but how, ohhh ... how could he git away from Ma). Wouldn't it be the biggest s'prise of all if he sneaked through the short-cut and dropped right down into Buddy's backyard. The idea of such an escape released a poop that turned into a blasting fart the very moment the sewing machine stopped.

-Johannes! Know what I said 'bout actin cute! Think yer some lil girl now? Even they aint cute no more if they're actin cutesy.

-Cant help it, Ma (dont girls poop, huh?).

-See, Solly and Sig are headin fer their stalls. Gotta know where yer at if there's a storm a-comin. Please dont bounce around. The cake'll fall; should be most done by now.

-Yeah, Ma.

-Besides, need you here to try yer shirts on, too. Makin yers the same's Buddy's, cause yer growin fast (dont wanna grow fast, Ma ... not yet, not yet, and hafta drink coffee, and . .). -Soon's I find matchin buttons, we'll see if the shirts fit right and make what changes then.

Nearly frantic, Johannes had to find a way out of the house. If he did, he wouldn't dare take the short-cut now and get lost in the woods, but if he didn't hurry up Township Road, he'd meet Dad coming home. But, jist think if he made it, he'd SEE Aunt Min (and wouldn't hafta go to Eye-Away), and he'd see more of Buddy's Maw (still as "mysterious" as Jesus or The Ghosts), and get to talk to BOTH of them (ahhh ... but uff da, what would I ever say, huh?).

A flight of flints zinged past his ears in such a crooked way it hurt. He blinked (ahhh ...).

-Gotta go to the toilet, Ma. He almost shouted.

-Why, use the slop-jar in the cellar, Jonas.

-Gotta do number-two. Real bad.

-All right then. But dont squat long. Be sure to latch the door inside; dont want papers blowin all over creation and back.

-Yeah, Ma.

When he got to the back porch steps, she called through the sitting room screens: -Now dont be studying that catalog so much you doze and fall into the pit agin. Want Uncle Snorri to hear-a that?

-No, Ma ... yeah (but its funny-ha-ha lookin in the book at all them funny-peculiar things ladies wear unnerneath).

He leaped into the wind, but didn't signal at the woodshed where Buddy hid sometimes (he wont be there now if Aunt Min's at his house). The sewing machine looked straight out after him. Ma saw him the minute he went through the backhouse door and the minute he'd come out. He had to act special-careful.

In case Ma looked in on him, which she often did, Johannes dropped his overalls and settled over the smallest of the three holes in the wide bench. A breeze trickled up and whistled at his hinder. He giggled, then shivered some; he'd made it this far (and all that ways to go, how now?). He peered through the quarter moon carved in the door. Ma filled the whole window. If she'd go into another room for a second, he could dash around the lilacs into Township Road, and she wouldn't know.

Before he heard it passing along the brush behind him, he smelled the skunk on The Sheriff-Almighty's car, then it honked twice for greeting as it headed back for Town. In the excitement over Aunt Min's visit, he'd forgotten all about her distrust of the Sheriff.

He'd never dwelt on the times Buddy'd explained to him why Aunt Min would never come to see him here; not after he wrote her about the Sheriff hanging around his Maw. Then Buddy showed what Aunt Min wrote back; said she had no truck with the law (whatever that meant), and if Buddy wanted to see her he'd have to come down like he'd done before and she'd "protect him this time for sure" (and keep him for good too), and with them German husbands and horses too. No wonder Buddy wanted to go down the rivers to Eye-Away. Johannes had forgotten all of that, and it hurt being so dumb. Of course Aunt Min couldn't be in Wisconsin; not with The Sheriff-Almighty on the loose.

Disappointed, yet relieved, that The Law wouldn't find Buddy with Aunt Min, Johannes re-assured himself that Dad HAD picked him up or why wouldn't Ma look worried otherwise (unless that's why she kept eyes on the weather). If Dad DIDN'T have him, maybe he'd gone down to the horses to hide in their mangers as they'd both done many times. Johannes perked up at the sudden idea of running off to Solly and Sig. But he knew Ma watched, even if she didn't look at him.

Why the Aunt Min dream, he puzzled. He couldn't get rid of her. Buddy never talked about other relatives, not even his regular family; not a word about his sister out of school who cared for the youngest (Mrs Preacher's Woman said she should have a husband somewheres); nothing about his Pa being sick and stuck away. Only Aunt Min seemed to matter to him. How lonesome it must be not having family stories to churn around inside you like those Ma had on hand at the drop of a word. A wave of affection for Buddy in such a plight swept over him, and Aunt Min figured larger in his thoughts (and what did she look like huh?).

Johannes had no living aunt, no grandparents that he remembered ('cept for Grampa Anderegg's face in the box that spooky time). Dad's paw and sisters died in Norway long ago in Olden Times, but Gramma Berg still lived there, too old and poor to travel but still collecting and spinning troll tales (Uncle Snorri tells us every fall).

Just think, Ma'd remind him, Gramma Berg taught Dad and Snorri and her neighbors how to read. Then Dad'd say how someday when they had extra money (whoever heard-a such a funny-ha-ha thing), they'd call on her like Uncle Snorri does each time his boat hits Norway. Ma never had sisters; only four brothers, all of them now dead of war or "in-flu-ensa," but she didn't let you forget that one brother played Norwegian fiddle, another had been an auctioneer, and two knew how to raise crops good. Ol' Gundy said that Ma kept a "family tree" inside her head (whatever that meant if he dared to ask):

Many times he heard how Great-Granddad Anderegg brought Grampa and Gramma, newly-hitched, with him when he left the Old Country … how Gramma Anderegg carried a shoot of a crabapple tree from her fjord, just as Grampa later planted a sugar maple from Canada beside it there at the backyard fence (Uncle Snorri-Bjorn always says apples from Norway and syrup from North-Ameddica made the best mix ever) … and all world heard about how Great-Granddad homesteaded their farm and how Grampa added all the land and, full of dollars later, built the big house and everything else to show how good he managed. Then Ma loved to tell how after The Great War, she took over the farm for Grampa when sickness took the farmer sons … and then, how Dad became one of the hired men to help her hold things together (Uncle Snorri teased Dad sometimes by callin him "the hired hand," ahhh …). And Ma always wiped away a tear when she told the rest of their history: How some years after The Great War, Grampa and Gramma left Ma with the hired men and crossed the ocean again; this time to stand at the graves of their soldier sons who'd perished in the fields of France … how after that pain, they went back to Norway to visit the orchards of their native fjord, where Gramma died, and Grampa buried her there beside the church they'd married in, and he came home to Wisconsin to die himself, of grief … four years after the stork dropped Johannes in Ma's bed, she'd remind him (and it all sounds too "mysterious," ahhh).

Hard to believe that everybody didn't have such exciting things to tell about their people. He'd watch Buddy's eyes grow wide whenever he listened to Ma. But … Buddy had his own Aunt Min. Johannes felt cheated sometimes without an aunt like that, until he realized that NOBODY else in all the world had an Uncle Snorri in their life (so there!).

When Johannes peered through the backhouse moon again, he caught Ma coming onto the porch. She took down one of the copper bath tubs that hung on the outer wall (like the Viking war shields in Uncle Snorri's tattoo). He hoped she'd take it to the kitchen and be gone long enough for him to run. But, she leaned the tub against the pillar outside the kitchen door instead, and gazed off at the weather some more with that faraway face that baffled, sometimes scared, him too.

What did she look for? What did she see? Did grown-ups have their own Winter-Lonely? Uncle Snorri-Bjorn had boats; Dad had fields and animals; Buddy had Aunt Min; and he had The Ghosts of Walking Sorrows. What did Ma have when she looked that way and sang about long, long trails a-winding into somewheres. Would she see him now if he crept away, close to the ground. But he knew she watched.

Too late anyway. Before he could fasten his overalls, she went back to her sewing. He let his pants drop and decided to wait until she called (there might still be a chance to flee). After testing different positions, he found that if he hunkered mid-bench and leaned against the back wall, Ma's face appeared like a flower bud in the middle of the moon. He gave up further thoughts of short-cut, Bluff, or even Township Road. He'd be satisfied to make it to Solly and Sig, for nothing ('cept snugglin on Ma's bosom) wiped away confusion more than burying his face against the velvet nose of a horse.

But Aunt Min wouldn't leave him alone; even when he knew now why she couldn't be here; still hung around (would Singing White Wolf bother with Aunt Min, or make Buddy git him all mixed-up pretending to be mournin doves or geese goin south before their time, huh?). Johannes wondered again why Aunt Min got dragged into his plans when she had nothing to do with Walking Sorrows Bluff. What a birthday present that had been that night last June when Buddy brought her into their summer dreams.

*   *   *

THE JUNE NIGHT IS sticky. Johannes wakes up wet. Afraid of swallowing his precious Blackjack gum, he sticks it to the bedpost and gets up to pee. Stray moonbeams point him to the stair rail where the slop jar sits, the fancy one with violets painted on the cover and bluebirds flying around inside (Gramma favored it, Ma said, but she never smiles when she hears me and Buddy call it our holy thunder-mug).

Every night he'd been waking up like this, as bad as in winter when he thought of some problem he had to work out on the school blackboard the next morning, and he didn't know how to do it. This night he didn't worry about school, or Jesus, or grown-ups, but fretted instead over the ways Ma kept them off Walking Sorrows without even mentioning the Bluff. That made it harder than ever to complete their cave.

-Aint 'fraid-a Injun Joe, are you? Buddy teased from his pillow.

Johannes almost missed the pot. –Shhh, why you wakin up? You usually snore like somethin dead.

-Dont hafta make noise bein awake now. You still mad?

-Whatcha mean?

-Why you run out like you did tonight, makin yer Maw feel bad and on yer birthday too. And after she baked that big fat cake fer you ...

-Well, she shouldnt-a said what she did, Johannes muttered, moving out of the puddle of moonlight. –Askin if Broken Thunderhawk belonged the same tribe as Injun Joe. And you no better yerself, laughin so hard and runnin round me yellin "Me,

Tonto, me Tonto!" (I hate Tonto. I hate Tom Sawyer. I hate you too when you act like that ... ohhh, but I dont though).

Buddy raised himself on his elbows and stretched, willing to listen: -think you got more spunk that Mrs Preacher's Woman, always riled 'bout somethin? But you still rile me good ... sometimes.

-You know Broken Thunderhawk wouldn't talk dumb like Tonto; wouldn't act mean like Injun Joe. Why you side with Ma then? You know my warriors are the bravest braves on earth (so there!).

-Hansy, you aint ever seen a live Injun, 'cept that pair we saw in Town once, drunk as, drunk as ... (as yer Maw maybe?) as horny skunks (what's "hor-nee," Ma?).

Johannes, ever eager for anything about Buddy's Maw, smarted at what he'd almost blurted out. He shifted gears fast:

-YER the one's scared-a Injun Joe, he challenged as he climbed back into the sheets.

-The way you take to that silly story Ma reads. A cave with girls runnin 'round inside? How you figger that?

Johannes feared that Buddy might get ideas from Ma's reading nightly. He didn't trust the way Buddy paid attention, all politeness, with a dreamy look, and how he laughed at the right time whenever Ma looked up from the book, expecting to find them tickled. Whatever would he do if Buddy decided to imitate Huck or Tom, but wouldn't let him help to fix up their cave (no, the cave belongs to me!). The Lone Ranger, Tom and Huck, and trolls ... all of it foolishness when their own hills had the best stories of all. Nobody'd listen (though Uncle Snorri seemed to think they did) or ever pass them on, but Dad. At least he didn't butt in and agree with Ma when she scolded him about his Ghosts. Buddy should know better, laughing at the purpose of their (his?) plans.

Johannes glanced at the shadow beside him: -If yer not a-scared, why you not sleepin, huh?

-Thinkin 'bout the cave.

-In the TOM SAWYER book?

-That's only kid-stuff, Hansy; WE mean business.

-You mean . . our … cave then?

-Sure aint any others. But we jist gotta hurry up with it, that's all.

-Yeah, yeah, or we wont have a place to sit and wait for the Ghosts to come.

-Cripes sake, Gramps, you still dont unnerstand a thing.

Buddy turned his face to the south dormer where moonlight flooded the floor and cast shadows of the pines against the walls around him.

-Doncha see, Hansy, when we finish the cave I'll … WE'll have a good place to hide in; even live in if we hafta.

-We dont needta HIDE from Broken …

-BUT, we might need a place to hide sometime. Maybe from the Sheriff, maybe even from yer Maw. 'Fore we take off for Aunt Min's, that is.

(AUNT MIN?) Johannes sat up straight and lost his voice. He'd never heard of such a thing (you mean WE'RE going down the rivers to EYE-AWAY, ohhh …).

-Think-a it, Hansy. While the Sheriff's ridin the roads, maybe draggin the crick and Squaw River fer us, we'll be safe here in our cave for a day or two, waitin to start behind em; yep, BEHIND em. How's that sound now?

The world spun too fast for Johannes to discover it.

-Unnerstand? Buddy mumbled, slipping into sleep.

Of course he didn't understand. Johannes, too confused to think, couldn't even poop (AUNT MIN! Must be another game). All winter they'd planned to search for the cave with Singing White Wolf's bones, and for the magic flints on the ground around it. And while Buddy hunted arrows, he'd sit ready to receive The Ghosts. Wouldn't that be too wondrous, too terrible for earthly words! Even if they couldn't see or touch The Ghosts, they'd be in their presence like Uncle Snorri-Bjorn explained it every fall. He'd have secrets nobody else could know, and he'd believe so hard, he'd prove that The Ghosts had shapes, maybe faces (and wouldn't THAT fill Uncle Snorri's pipe, huh?). And when Buddy got over being scared of being cut, they'd become true Blood Brothers, too.

(Now Aunt Min's mixin up our dreams, ohhh …). Buddy had to be fooling about going to Eye-Away. Only the other day he showed Johannes a picture postcard from her: she said she'd be away until he got another card to say she's home again (back to Dee-bjuke on the River, ahhh …).

Sprawling across most of the bed, and restless as Ol' Odin chasing rabbits in his dreams, Buddy cared no more for their summer plans than Ma. Wider awake than before, Johannes pushed against the metal tubes of the bedstead and stared out at the moon, hanging in the boughs. A mosquito whined in his ear; a whip-poor-will crooned in the fog that began to creep in from the marsh. But where is Eye-Away? And where's his Aunt Min gone (only rich folk went places away from home)? Buddy had to be teasing again! Maybe sleeping in the moonlight makes him loony; maybe in the morning he won't remember this, and they could cook up other ways to get away from Ma.

After their first time on the Bluff, days on end marched off to Nowhere. Sometimes a week or more "vanished" before they got back to work there. Ma, true to her promises to Ol' Gundy, had chores for them the minute they looked idle: berries to find and pick, vegetables and rows of flowers to hoe, kindling to split every day for the cookstove, and eggs to fetch from all the crazy places hens dropped them; all of that before milking time each night (Dad dint let me milk Wilda-No-Tail in the mornin), after pumping water for the house and cows. But the worst never-ending job of all: them (goddam) cucumbers to take care of for that 4-H Club Ma made him join, so it wouldn't look funny-peculiar if her own boy took no part in something she'd started for the other kids. All this work ended only to begin again and again, forever.

He wisht he could boot that County Agent in the balls for bringin up 4H to Ma; and kick Ol' Gundy's hinder purpler that her high heels. Buddy never fussed over chores. That kept Johannes from complaining for fear he'd look unable to keep up (sure dont wanna be any kind-a champeen, though).

Ma never brought up picnic day again. She had quieter ways of keeping them in hand. These tested all their schemes and tricks. She changed her mind about attending daytime meetings of the Ladies Aid at church, or her County Homemakers at school; she invited all those ladies to meet at the farm instead. She no longer went to Town to trade like before but kept that for Wednesday nights and Saturday afternoons, when Johannes (and Buddy) went along; there she'd catch up on gossip and have Johannes carry vegetables and fruit to Mrs Preacher's Woman (ever time Buddy ducks away from me this side of parsonage, leavin me alone with them stuck-up lil Town-girls). At home they never knew where or when Ma'd show up out of nowhere; that kept their plans on alert: a couple weeks back, she almost bumped into em on their way down from the high field, where, she said, she'd gone for bluebells; and day before yesterday, they smacked right into her as they crept, ever so carefully, 'round to the corncrib and they s'prised each other so hard, Buddy dropped their workshoes in the bed of lilies there before she even noticed them. Never knew where Ma'd be next.

When she sent them off to play, she never interfered, but how could they get to the Bluff and back with such little time to spare. They knew what the sound of the bell meant, and, worst of all, her call by megaphone. "Twice, though, they failed deliberately to answer, so she wouldn't think it odd when they came in late and couldn't help it. Dad said nothing about how they played, so long as they did their chores and brought him morning and afternoon water and coffee when he worked the farther fields. Dad said he trusted Buddy to hold the reins (whatever that meant).

Real freedom came only when Ma sang at funerals and Dad helped with the box. Those times, Ol' Gundy always offered to look after Johannes (and Buddy, whose name she'd never speak) until the folks returned. Easy to take off from Ol' Gundy then; she'd be too upset to tattle on them. But Jesus had been lazy that summer, not calling on the old ones he chose to take to Heaven every heat wave. So there hadn't been many funerals (maybe next month, huh?).

If it rained for stretches, they played at many things: they made "houses" out of crates and cardboard boxes for the barn cats and their many kittens ... or, if Dad couldn't see them, they scaled the loft rafters of the barns and jumped into fresh hay piled halfway up the walls (ahhh, leapin like Broken Thunderhawk from Walking Sorrows Bluff!) ... once, to hide from each other, they buried themselves in granary bins, but had to be careful how to breathe, and how not to crush the winter watermelons stored there for New Year's Day dessert ... once in awhile, Ma let them dig in the things from Olden Times now packed all over the attic. But they had the most fun of all when they tried to find out what some of Uncle Snorri's "souvenirs" meant; strange objects from all over the worlds he visited (how "mysterious," ahhh ...), but which Ma tried to keep under lock and key. But the most important thing, they remembered never to look restless, even when she read to them each night.

Tonight though on his birthday he had to run off when Ma dragged in Injun Joe like that. It made him as mad as the many times she reminded him that Jesus watched and knew everything he did. He dint wanna be looked after all-a time. Not by nobody, not even by Buddy (who did it in a secret way, I know). While he dint like the idea of Aunt Min mixin up their summer, he had to admire – tongue-tied – how Buddy had a plan for everything. Maybe he could be like that after he heard ghostsongs from Singing White Wolf, and maybe even learn to poop as smooth as Buddy could. But their cave ... if they dint git goin full blast on it soon, there'd be no more vacation left. And he hoped with all his heart that daylight made Buddy fergit Aunt Min.

Buddy snored in a sing-song way and took up more of the bed. Johannes beamed down at him, splotched with shadows, and forgave him for making him confused. He batted at the pesky mosquito still favoring his ear, and sighed, wider awake than before with misery and relief equally together. Maybe Aunt Min's card would never come (ahhh …). If Buddy didn't go to his house every few weeks to look for mail, Ma stopped there on their way to Town to see if Hester Trygrud had things for him to do. Later, Johannes heard her tell Dad she never liked to stop when she saw the Sheriff's car in the backyard brush. When Buddy did go home, he tried to get back the same day or early the next morning in time for Johannes not to worry. One time, though, he didn't return for two whole nights, and Johannes burned with fever, convinced that The Sheriff –Almighty had run him down or shot him dead in the head for cussin at home, or somethin. Ever time Buddy came back with nuttin to show, Johannes wisht harder than ever that Aunt Min would "vanish" like Broken Thunderhawk, 'specially after Buddy showed him an ole letter once that said she'd like to have him with her for good, cause she dint want him growin up around TB.

Now the idea of Eye-Away (OF GOIN THERE! ohhh …) coated him with a dread as green, he thought, as the scum that covered part of the crick. And each time, he wanted to know where and why Aunt Min stayed away so long, Buddy's mouth fell open like it did the time he asked him about the stork. (And yet, I wanna see the Miss'ippi, ahhh …).

The cave worried Johannes the most. Once beneath the overhang again, they had not time to fool around. Buddy pitched in at once, leveling the floor, squaring the inside walls, while Johannes, ordered as usual to stand guard and be alert, had only to watch his farmyard far below, with heat waves and his sadness around him. It dint seem right even when he said he unnerstood the reasons.

Baffled, he got up to pee again; he'd never outlive the teasing if he wet the bed. After last night's lemonade and fuss (and now Aunt Min) he felt wet all over. Buddy slept on, sounding like those ZZZs looked in the funnies. He backed away from the "holy thunder mug" and went to the south dormer to look out towards the barns in case fires had started there from heated hay. He crossed to the other dormer and with wonder gazed up at Walking Sorrows Point. It looked haunted under the moon; he couldn't believe they'd ever been up there, nor could he believe that Buddy wouldn't let him help:

Could Ma really be the reasons, huh? Up on the rocks in daylight, it sounded natural to stand guard, but alone at night, oldtime suspicions gnawed: he couldnt work cause he dint know how to learn, or never did things right after bein showed, and ever time he tried somethin on his own, everything went haywire. How could the cave be his then if he couldn't help fix it up, and how could it belong to Buddy either when he dint b'lieve that Broken Thunderhawk had even lived.

He turned back to the sleeper. The Widow Peterson told him once that the moon looking on you while you slept made you wake up loony (is that what happened to Effie Stone, huh?). He moved to make a shadow that hid part of Buddy's face. In doing so that touch of violence flared again for an instant, but before its ugliness scared him cold, a wave of tenderness overwhelmed him (how could anybody in all the world hate Buddy!).

(Wonder if he KNOWS I know how scared-a ghosts he has to be or why act gangster-tough each time I mention em, huh?) Johannes looked back to a wedding last fall when some grown-ups got hitched by candles inside the church and he'd wanted Buddy to hide with him in the graveyard and dare other kids to find em, but Buddy – and the other kids – said NO! They dint wanna miss the weddin cake and all that (think-a given up some maybe-ghosts for cake; hadta mean bein scared or they wouldn't-a covered up that way). Dad said lots of brave people stayed fearful all their lives of things they couldn't see or touch. (But Buddy – Bud – I'll never let nobody know yer scared-a anything).

Suddenly he wanted to hug. He didn't dare. Instead, he reached over to brush the fuzz sprouting in the pit of an outflung arm. Johannes wondered why he didn't grow hair like that, and whenever they compared themselves down here, Buddy looked different every time, in shape and color too, and Johannes remained forever the same (a dried-up tobacco worm). Dad didn't seem bothered though when he asked about such things; he said you could go through lots of changes in the years ahead.

(Yet, how'd you become Blood Brothers when yer almost brothers anyway, or when one of em's still 'fraid-a blood? Let him have the cave then and I hope it takes forever and wears him down to nuttin, and even if I dont wanna go to Eye-Away, jist wait'll I show you I aint no baby neither. CANT let you go down there by yerself and never come back here agin, ohhh …).

The silver discs on Grampa's maple rustled beyond the western screens. Under moonlight, dew on the fields turned into carpet of lightning bugs that rippled their way towards the house, aiming to roll over the windowsills to damped his bedroom floor. A screech-owl from the cowbarn told the whippoor-will to shut up. The bird sounds tickled him. He remembered how taken he'd been with the owl Uncle Snorri wore home once; clamped to his shoulder it turned its white head all the way around (what magic, ahhh …). Given to him, Uncle Snorri said, by an Indian brother. But Dad had butted in and laughed and said: "You mean yer Indian brother-in-law," and Ma hadn't joked at all (Grown-ups talkin all the time and sayin nuttin, ohhh …).

Johannes turned back to the bed and studied the snarled curls beside him, more than ever the way Ol' Odin looked and even sounded (dreamin bout Eye-Away already, huh?). He blotted out more moonlight, then carefully lifted the sheet with a glowing curiosity to peek beneath, and just as carefully pulled it back into place. He lifted his head and looked straight into the grinning eyes of Buddy, so suddenly awake.

Johannes stiffened. Buddy winked. And that turned out to be the night when Aunt Min joined their summer plans.

*　*　*

HE DIDN'T HEAR MA'S call until he opened his eyes and saw her (through the backhouse door) standing at the woodbox on the porch: -Johannes, cant you hear me? You all right? Wantcha to bring some kindling when you come.

Giving up any chance of escaping, he ran out, fastening the bib of his overalls on the way to the shed. When he reached the porch and dumped his armful of chips into the box there, Ma held the kitchen door open: -Gracious grief, Jonas , thought youd fallen in agin.

He sniffed the air (and freedom) as Solly and Sig had done: -Oh, Ma, lemme ... lemme stay outside awhile. A lil while, huh (I love storms, and wind)?

She hustled him indoors and swatted at the flies that tried to follow. He stood at the windows while Ma fussed with the cushions in the rocker. He said nothing more when she breezed by: -If you dont wanna write on yer story, you can churn butter for me. How's that? Take yer pick (Buddy made good butter when she let him try, but I only turn out curds).

Ma raised her voice from the pantry door: -You know Buddy cant be here all the time. Doncha see, his Ma – his mother – has things for him to do same's I have for you (but Ma, his Maw's on relief and dont have chores a-tall). Here I give you time for schoolwork and you dont 'preciate it. Besides, he's gotta have some time home, or she'll think we kidnapped him (like happened to that Lindbergh baby, huh?).

-How can she be home if she's gallivantin with The Sheriff-Almighty (all over hell and back; let him do her chores). Uff da! Johannes caught himself too late and saw his words stuck in a balloon over his head like in the funnies.

-Johannes Berg! Ma came into the middle of the room, -you lil gossip. Now where you hear such things? Buddy say somethin?

-Oh, no Ma, no. He never talks bout home. But everybody else does. At school ... downtown ...

-Sure got big ears fer yer age. Its all none-a yer business is what. So let things be. Hear me? She looked him over for a long minute: -Let's git back to yer sentences.

When Ma finished setting out the cream for making butter, Johannes climbed back into Great-Granddad's rocker and curled himself into the smallest ball he could. Before settling down to churn, Ma brought him the cinnamon roll she'd promised earlier and put it on the sill in front of him. He heard the milk gurgle as it slopped from the pitcher into a glass, but he had no appetite after the day's fuss and worry (oh, Buddy, why do I hurt so much?). Ma checked the sky again, then picked up his tablet and pencil from the floor (oh, Ma, wont this day never end, why ... why its everlastin!).

She examined the open pages: -"What Happened to ME on Vacation." After reading the title, she paused: -But there . . where's yer story? Why, Jonas you aint even started it.

She turned the page over and read aloud from the top: "Dear Ma." She stopped again, looked at him puzzled: -Jonas, she finally said: -how sweet. Yer gone pertend yer story's a letter jist for me? Must say that's sure different.

-Hope Ol' Gundy likes it then (but how can I 'member what I say when I hafta lie like this!).

-Dont make funna yer teacher, Jonas dear. Callin her names like that. If her ways are sometimes odd, she's got the right intentions. And she's so good to look after you when I hafta sing. The way Ma frowned on him sprayed him with shame. –Miss Gunderson's got problems you know nutting of. We must help her all we can. No good still stuck in her family like that, and at her age too. Ma mumbled the last words to herself.

(Ol' Gundy must be thirty-two at least. Oldern anyone he knew 'cept Ma and Dad and Uncle Snorri-Bjorn, but they dint count, bein yer folks: folks arent too old or young, jist yer folks, which is different from BEING old like other people).

-Dont be mean to Miss Gunderson then, will you, Jonas. When yer grown she wont seem so queer. You'll 'preciate her like you'll 'preciate yer Ma and Dad when we're no longer here. Unnerstand?

Ma waited for his uncertain nod before handing back his tablet: -With a memory like you got, should be easy fillin up the pages. And none-a that Indian stuff neither, she warned him as she moved away from the nook. –Why, yer a lil Norwegian boy growin up in North-

Ameddica and should be thinkin on other things. On Mr Lincoln maybe, or Tom Sawyer. Or even that Paul Bunyan to be sure.

-Oh, Ma, he almost wailed, -cant think-a what to write (hope Dad gits here soon so I wont hafta try).

She headed back to his chair: -What? With all the things that's happened the past months? Look back, Jonas. Might start with the Sunday School picnic last spring; first time we had it in that park downtown where we saw deer, even a bear and wolf, and all-a you rode there in Hanson's cattle-truck (like a bunch-a steers, too; but Buddy dint go, not bein part of Sunday School, even if he wouldnt mind The Widow Peterson for Bible Class).

Ma ran her fingers over the back of the rocker as she dug up more things to remember: -then we had the Fourth of July in our pasture with all them boughten fireworks Dad's lumbar cronies brought on their way to The Dakotas; 'member how they teased you and Dad 'bout goin with em to the wheat fields (Buddy begged to go alone …). You b'lieved em and ran and hid so you wouldnt hafta leave, 'member that (yeah, Ma, buried myself in the mangers and Solly and Sig dint even whinny to give me away).

He hoped she'd leave him soon, but she rambled on: -but course you cant fergit to tell 'bout raising yer own cucumbers for the 4-H Club you wanted no part of, BUT when you and Buddy sold enuff fer new school overalls, you changed yer tune then, dint you (dont mention cukes, Ma, never hated anything so much; took all that time away from Walking Sorrows). –How's that fer a start now?

She tousled his hair and went off to the pantry. He watched her drag out the porcelain churn, empty jugs of cream into it, then wash down its paddle, before she settled on a high stool with a crock between her legs. She sat across the room from him and began one of the Norwegian country songs she sang while doing lively housework, her movements with the tune. He liked such music when he didn't have to listen to the words he didn't know. The longer she sang, the more time he had to dream (she thinks I'm workin on my story).

Johannes counted as important only those days him and Buddy got away to the cave, and the memory of them remained forever real, while whole weeks between such times sank into lazy gloom. How could Ma 'spect him to write about what he'd forgotten, how could he let Ol' Gundy parade his secret summer in front-a everybody else in school (ohhh …).

Between songs, Ma flared with another idea: -You know, Jonas, tell whatcha did when you went to town Wednesday nights and Saturdays. Up and down the streets, you and Buddy, takin in everything. Tell what you saw. Who you met. How you spent that extra nickel Dad sometimes had to spare.

-Yeah Ma.

He bent double over the tablet, working the pencil fast, how much harder 'tis , pretending to be busy. He wouldn't let kids at school know a thing 'bout him and Buddy; about how big and proud he felt in Town when they walked the sidewalks on either side-a Dad and everybody greeted em and spoke-a them as "the Berg boys in from behind the hills." Them Town kids dint even know Buddy's real name, nor anything of Walking Sorrows' Ghosts. And later, when Johannes suspected that people might be laughing at them, he dreamed of what such stuck-up people'd do if they saw him coming down Main Street with Great Chief Broken Thunderhawk on one arm and Singing White Wolf on the other (with Buddy catchin up behind … maybe?).

Ma rotated with the churning, but now and then she paused to remind him of something else to put on paper (she's livin the whole summer like it only happened this mornin and I can only bring back what I cant fergit … maybe four, maybe five times in all, includin last Thursday too. Now Ma'll be 'membering all over the place till the clock stops):

-Tell 'bout yer baby chicks too, and how they died; dont let on they perished cause you dint plug up the hole in the brooder house where some weasel managed to squeeze through … And dont fergit the day you picked blueberries in the marsh, then tripped over the pail when you tried to beat Buddy home, and you squashed berries all over yerself and stayed BLUE fer days; even goin to churchlike that and Buddy callin you a bluejay (and much differnt names, Ma, when we got alone) ... Oh, yes, you cant fergit how you stepped on that snake in the pasture and it dint even bite you (too s'prised like me to bite, I guess).

All the while she remembered things, between her songs, he made himself busier with the pencil, chewing on the eraser now and then, to make it look like he copied everything she said. He had to be special-careful though; she's almost made him spill the beans about the letter he'd begun for her, then thinking it the opening of his story ... whewww, another close call, Buddy. Without knowing anything about it, she could make you give away any secret you had, 'specially if you had to lie about it.

Ma's singing slowed as the whirling in the churn grew muffled. Uncle Snorri's clock struck four. Where'd they be tomorrow at this time, Johannes tried to wonder. Would they be off to Eye-Away, or would he still be sitting here like this, waiting for the sky-blue runabout to dash up to the back porch. And what surprises would he have this year for them, along with his Indian legends, you could never tell (Oh, Uncle Snorri-Bjorn, what if I hafta miss you, ohhh ...).

If he lived a million years he'd never forget last fall when Uncle Snorri took him and Buddy to their first-time movies in La Crosse. Tongue-tied, he watched something silly with Shirley Temple (who looked jist like she did in the bottom of his cereal bowl), but he dint really like it cause it jumped around so much and everybody talked funny-peculiar. Afterwards, they showed pictures for next week's movies, all about soldiers fighting Indians, and he wisht they could have seen that show instead (but why did everybody wanta kill off Indians like that, huh?).

As happened when school started a few days later: Buddy divided the kids into soldiers and Indians, himself playing Sergeant Someone, and he named Johannes Big Chief Swinging Wolf Fingers, a renegade who everybody had to hunt down and kill.

"Know its only games," Ma'd told Ol' Gundy when she heard of it, "but is it nice pertendin to kill anybody now?"

Nobody else said a thing.

Then, memory of memories, before heading home in the rumbleseat, Uncle Snorri drove them across the Miss'ippi and along the Minnesota Bluffs. And Johannes swore he SAW his two chiefs smoking peace pipes in the middle of the River, but Buddy, busy counting wild geese landing on the sloughs, only farted back at him. He'd never told about that in school either.

Johannes gazed out at the clouds about to bury the Minnesota bluffs. He wished a storm would hurry and break hard enough to keep them out of Eye-Away, and he wouldn't need to think of writing letters till tomorrow, or maybe never, once Buddy hears of Uncle Snorri's visit.

What would he have up his sleeves this year (besides new tattoos)? Maybe he'd take them north of the County Seat where Indians lived and had pow-wows with drums and dancing and lots of feathers. That place, Uncle Snorri told him once, had a mission (mish-un?), where they tried to make Indians into white men, and that truly puzzled him (how can such things be, huh?). Must be powerful magic. If he could only ask Singing White Wolf which ghostsong would work such a thing, would it work the other way around, too (turning me into a hee-thun?). Maybe that county's where The Ghosts would really be (not here with us Norskies who stole their bluffs and coulees; but with their own kin, ohhh ... and dancin with feathers, ahhh).

-How we doing? Ma brought him back.

-Oh, gee, Ma, still dont know what to write. We did nuttin but work all-a time.

-Whatcha mean you did "nuttin but work all-a time." You poor lil thing (she calls me that in Norwegian, I know). Course you dint work all-a time. Think-a the times Dad let you out-a chores. Whatsa matter with you anyhow? Musta had some fav'rit work like Buddy. Sure looked like you had fun sometimes; know Buddy did. Yer shameful, Johannes Berg, makin yer folks out to be slave drivers and you actin like ... like Mr Lincoln's slaves. Now you know that aint true.

She turned her back on him, hurt. Johannes hurt then, too, when he saw what his words had done (course I dint/don't feel like no slave; how could I when I dont know what bein a slave is like). Though nothing counted like the Bluff, he guessed they had had other fun, if you thought about it:

He never minded carrying coffee and water to Dad. On the way home, him and Buddy could take their time and watch the bull play in the pasture with the cows, or they'd try to catch one of the steers, and when they failed each time, Buddy (all excited) always asked: "Howcha like yer balls cut off like that? Heard Maw say the Sheriff eats em; pig nuts, too; maybe that's what makes him mean (how "mysterious" ... oww). And they liked to prod the purple boar in the pig-pen and get him so wound-up he'd drop his zig-zag ding-dong on the ground and step on it when he whirled around each time they jabbed at him (that must hurt, too ... owww).

Ma stood up, re-arranged her smock, and inspected the inside of the churn before sitting down again. Back at work, still silent, she made Johannes burn to see how sad he'd made her. He didn't know what to do when she behaved this way. He wanted her back cheerful, like when she played ante-I-over the granary roof (lettin me and Buddy be her partners by turn). When Ma shut him out with silence, that scared him worse than any scolding words or threats (of The Sheriff-Almighty or bats).

(Sure we had fun sometimes, Ma, but not the kind to thinkabout till now). Neither did he mind looking for Wilda-No-Tail whenever she strayed from the herd and got lost in the pasture somehow (whatta way for his heifer's ma to act). Dad found a cowbell for her, but she learned to walk in such a way that clapper barely sounded (she jist likes stayin off behind). After they'd find her in her usual spot, looking drunk in the middle of Blood Brothers Crick, they took time to jump into the water, too, keeping away from the dark places in the bends too deep to wade. Before coaxing her back to the cow lane, they sometimes hung willow wreaths or morning glories around her neck, and she'd moo after them.

To be honest (dont let Ma know), he didn't mind hunting stray eggs dropped outdoors by nutty hens because he might find a snake in such a nest and he could capture it and hide it in his room (though snakes dashed off so fast, and Buddy hated em). Helping to bind barley, oats, or even buckwheat didn't bother him too much, for between their season he had the chance to help with building haystacks, which is mind turned into wigwams, just as last fall him and Buddy turned corn shucks into typees (and all-a time Buddy askin what's the excitement to make me poop so much).

-You day-dreamin, Jonas? Fergetting yer sentences?

Relieved to have her voice come back, he almost shouted:

-No, Ma! He hesitated before admitting again: -cant write good when nutting really special happened I can tell somebody.

-Whatcha mean, nuttin "really special"? Dont wanta hear such words again. Johannes Berg, we could – you could – write a book. Where'd you spend vacation anyway, outa yer head in bed?

Ma stood up and checked the contents of the churn: -Cant begin to mention all the other things that come to mind. Why not tell 'bout The Widow Peterson's barn dances where Buddy learned to hoppwaltz and you wouldnt even try to square dance (yeah, Buddy actin like a champeen too, foolin with them cross-eyed Torkelson girls and lookin like he wanted to, uff da!) … And there's yer tree-house you'll have to show Uncle Snorri (we dint do a single thing on that, Ma, but at least you dint find our workshoes in the corncrib underneath, ahhh …).

-Course you wont fergit about our threshin; how it felt to ride the grain wagon, while Buddy tossed sheaves to the machine and later dumped sacks into their proper bins, and how the both-a you ate with the menfolk afterwards. Regular farmers, you. Still you say nuttin happened to you. Jonas, yer too smart to act so dumb.

-Yeah, Ma.

At the mention of threshers, Johannes perked. Of all the things she'd been reminding him about, this he couldn't fergit. When Buddy begged Dad to let him work with the men, Dad had Johannes ride the flat-bed wagon back and forth between the threshing rig and the granary, and because he looked so small to be noticed much amongst the sacks of grain, he took in the gossip rolling around him; lots of new stuff, too, on Buddy's Maw (which made her even more "mysterious"). He couldn't write that though, when he dint know what it meant and couldnt spell the new words even if he unnerstood em.

The men talked about Hester Tryrud's melons (is there a 4-H Club for grown-ups, too?), and what she could do with them, then something about their size and The Sheriff-Almighty Strutt, and while size didn't matter much, Dad had said in passing, it make lots of differences sometimes; sometimes mighty handy. Then, when Dad spied Johannes up front between the sacks, he motioned to the men and they turned their talk to weather (ohhh …).

During coffee breaks he didn't want to inspect the steam engine with Buddy, but hid behind a tree trunk and heard more things he couldn't believe: how The Sheriff-Almighty had run Ol' Odin down while chasing after Buddy's Maw, and Johannes puzzled over why Buddy's Maw had to be CHASED in the first place, unless they meant such times as when he had to chase Wilda-No-Tail out of new corn before the loony cow ate herself dead (imagine anybody CHASING Ma!).

"Oh, Strutt's all right in his way," Dad had said, "if he shook them wimmens off his tail; chasin pussy like that all over hell and back, gettin hung up like a hound in heat" … (Oh, Ma, where's hell at anyway; nobody tells me nuttin.) Bewildered, Johannes soaked up everything he heard: why would The Sheriff-Almighty chase cats and hit Ol' Odin instead (and not even stop that dam car-with-the-star)? If that big ham didn't know the difference between dogs and cats, that made him more dangerous than ever. And why did men always mix girls up with Uncle Snorri: "Yep, Thor," someone had said, "Strutt's like yer twin, S.B." and Dad had answered: "No, Snorri LIKES his wimmens; Strutt's only fer the hunt." Johannes wished he understood what Dad said to make the threshers slap their forehead or their knees. They sounded worse than the ladies when they chirped over everything, and didn't say what they meant, but hid behind other words he never knew (jist like grown-ups). At least the menfolk didn't hug or stick up their noses. They only cussed and laughed loud (how did grown-ups ever unnerstand a thing, huh?).

After the threshers ate their noontime meal, Johannes climbed back on the wagon with a cupcake in his fist. When the men noticed him again, they got busier with their work and said nothing more about Buddy's Maw, nor anything else he wanted to hear.

What would Ma say now if she knew what he really couldn't forget about the threshing. He shook his hair out of his eyes and watched her lift the fat lump of butter from the churn. She forced it into a wooden mold that shaped it into smaller balls with designs on them. Later, she'd wrap each one in a piece of waxed paper and he'd bring them all to the spring-house cooler. In the coming days, he'd carry some of these to Ma's oldest friends ("Bein neighborly," Ma said when he wondered why).

(Wisht I could tell you, Ma, how hard I tried to find The Ghosts all summer long, but never had time to sit still long a-nuff to let em come to me like Uncle Snorri taught; never by myself neither, with Buddy makin noise; dint know how to look anyway, with no pitchers of em). Did the man who drew the feedstore calendar know how that chief looked? And the one who made the Indian on the bakin powder can? Did all the chiefs wear ropey braids (like Effie Stone) and have feathers in their hair?).

-'member somethin else, Jonas. Ma sounded her regular self again. –You gotta tell how you got lost that time. You know, that time you took a short-cut after carryin butter to Gramma Hanson.

She looked steady at him, waiting for him to look back: -Dint know what to do when it got dark and no sign-a you. No Buddy here to help us look. Then Hanson's barkin dog showed us where you lay in the moonlight; snoozing in the graveyard 'gainst the Anderegg stones. You all tuckered out, with two coons sniffin at yer toes. You mean to say you dont 'member THAT?

-Never been lost, Ma. How many times I tole you I stopped there on purpose. Forgot time and went to sleep, I s'pose (had to practice sitting still to see if ordinary ghosts came by).

-You dint think-a haunted things? She came across the room and bent over him, a big question on her face.

-You know I aint scared-a ghosts, Ma (like many grown-ups are). The graveyard's peaceful, but Buddy wont go near the place at night (dont worry, Buddy, I wont let nobody know that yer 'fraid-a anything).

-Course he wont go with you. She scanned his face. -Buddy respects the dead, is all. Dont YOU think them old ones earned their sleep? Look at Great-Granddad Anderegg: over a hundred years on this earth, and Grampa beside him, almost as old, and yer farmer-uncles restin too. You wanna romp on their graves then? For shame.

-Dint do nuttin shameful.

-Maybe so. Dint you feel a tiny bit a-scared? Aint lil boys like you s'posed to be 'fraid-a ghosts? The dark? Even trolls?

-No such a thing as trolls (or are there? Uncle Snorri's never said YES or NO about em).

-Can't be sure now, can we, sweetheart. But we gotta to b'lieve in some fearful things.

-Why's everybody so fearful of the graveyard and The Ghosts of Walking Sorrows. And everything else that's differnt, huh?

-Lord's mercy, child, such questions.

Ma returned to her high stool and leaned against the counter. She fanned herself with the skirt of her smock: -Who's fearful of what? Well, first-a all, aint no ghosts up there; whatever people say. Only rattlers in pairs and deadly places to slip off. And then, aint no reason unner the sun fer goin to the graveyard after dark. Ever.

Johannes couldn't hold his tongue: -Only wanted to practice bein still 'fore I run into Great Chief ...

Ma dropped her smock and clenched her hands: -Jonas, Jonas, here we go agin! Big Chief whatsoever. Doncha know by this time that's only yer Uncle Snorri's story. Like all them funny names he puts on ever place around us. He's got stories wilder than Dad's; you gotta take salt with everything yer Uncle says. No harm done if you dont b'lieve such foolishness.

Ma shook her head and went back to wrapping butter balls. Her voice, saddened, slowed and that gave Johannes courage:

-But Walking Sorrows ...

-Named fer Great-Granddad doncha dare fergit it: Anderegg Point. Nuttin weepy or spooky 'bout that!

-Downtown they still call it Bachelor Drop.

-They dont know what theyre sayin.

-Names all over the map are Indian, Ma.

-Maybe so. Cant you see what's differnt though? Them names are the Ameddican way of sayin what the Indians said in their own talk long ago.

-Many still are true for now: Miss'ippi ... Wisconsin ... Minnesota. Why dont we hear 'bout OUR Indians 'stead-a Pocohontas, Squanto, and them others; they dont sound fer real a-tall.

-I know, I know. Why you worry on such things now?

Sensing her confusion, Johannes pressed on: -S'pose I meet The Ghosts, would they talk Ameddican, if they talked; or Norwegian maybe?

-Course not! They'd talk Indian. Uff da! Ma caught herself.

Johannes tried to keep her befuddled: -What would our names mean in Indian talk? And why do Indian names sound queer when turned into Ameddican, and they sound so purty too?

Ma came back to his chair. Her voice saddened him more when it sounded suddenly tired: -Better dump such notions, Jonas; clear yer head. Else people'll think yer nuts. Better stick with the trolls.

-You said yerself they maybe aint real neither. Besides, they're nasty. Said so yerself, Ma.

-Least we know what they're s'posed to be. Dont know what to expect from yer Indian chiefs and their ghosts and all that creepy stuff. Yer head'll be mixed all together if you hold to things like that. Now let's git back to our – yer – sentences. Or wanna fill and clean the lamps instead?

She touched his shoulder on the way to the porch for the kerosene can. Johannes grabbed his pencil fast.

-When that's done, everything's ready fer supper, she said on her way back to the shelf above the sink where lamps waited to be filled and their chimneys polished: -And after that only Uncle Snorri's cake to frost.

-Ma, Johannes called out after her: -Why you hate Indians, huh?

-Johannes, baby! She stopped in her tracks and turned a wounded face: -Dont hate nobody, Jonas; you sure know that by this time. Where'd you git such notions now?

He hoped he wouldn't bring back her silence. –I mean … everybody else sure seems to hate em …

-Don't know no better; plain dumb, is what. Gotta let all God's creatures live like they do. You know that from Sunday School. But YER Indians, Jonas … yer Indians aint fer sure; they're Uncle Snorri Indians. He dont even put names on his tribes.

-They AINT jist stories, Ma!

-I know, I know. He does git carried away when he's … when he's . . carried away. Uncle Snorri's lot like Dad. Likes to talk tall, then gits … carried away. Least Dad's tales are true. You gotta find the differnce 'tween what Is and what Aint. And that's 'bout the size of it. (But THAT'S what's true for me, Ma, what you say AINT!).

Johannes watched her fill the lamps, screw the cap back on the oil can, and hold each globe up to the window light to see if she'd left smudges when she washed them earlier (wisht I could help you, Ma, but you know I leave finger marks; not like Buddy, ohhh …).

She used her church voice when she spoke again: -You been good all summer; not a word-a Indian stuff. Now today you bring it up agin, like you never stopped. Been sayin to myself: "My Jonas is a-growin-up; like Buddy, leavin kiddie things behind," and now, now you disappoint me. So much, she added, on her way to the porch with the kerosene can.

His spirit drooped (grown up? feel no differnt than before, Ma). When Jonas asked her not long ago if Santa and the Easter Bunny belonged with "kiddie things," she looked so upside-down he never mentioned that again. And the holidays as always came and went. Now he'd made her look inside-out again; it hurt. He could read Ma's many changing voices: what she liked or couldn't stand, what she thought of someone or something, what she needed, and he always seemed to realize when she wanted to sit by herself in Great-Granddad's rocker, too. Best of all, she never whined. How it hurt to "disappoint" her.

(Oh, I dont wanna grow up and be like grown-ups, Ma. They scared-a everything. They aint no fun neither, 'cept Uncle Snorri-Bjorn and Dad, and you sometimes. But grown-ups never give me answers 'bout God's Big Lightning and Jesus callin, or 'bout the stork and Buddy's Maw, nor even where hell is. Cant be fun makin much over everything and non a-tall over things that count. Dont wanna grow up too blind to things around me that everybody sees day-in, day-out, but dont never look at. Sure dont wanna hafta drink coffee or like girls or eat Jesus in church; and hafta tell lies too. Let Buddy do the growin-up then, being champeen in so many ways. Worst-a all, dont wanna turn queer as Effie Stone, or odd and limping as Ol' Gundy or work up fevers over everything like you, Ma, but none now with Buddy bein late and no worry in yer voice fer him …).

Johannes didn't mind listening to grown-ups (when I'm not s'posed to), but he could never figure out why they jabbered so.

Desperate to chase away her "disappointment," he grabbed at Ma's smock when she came back to the kitchen: -Am I pure Norwegian, Ma?

-Namen fee da! He stopped her cold: -Whatta question, Jonas. Course you are. What else wouldcha be?

-Buddy too? Kids at school say Buddy's somethin else, cause his Maw's ...

-Johannes Berg! Ma's voice unsettled the clock: -You become the snoopiest lil gossip I ever seen. Wanna grow into some ole maid. Better git this straight, Buddy's Maw – mother's what she is. She's got ... well, got troubles you cant know of, like you cant unnerstan yer teacher yet.

-Wanted to be sure is all. He tried to smile wide at her puzzled look. Buddy didn't look Norske at all, any more than Singing White Wolf would. Hard to think of people not being Norske though, even with all the funny-looking ones in that movie show and in his books at school. That made everything more exciting (and so much more "mysterious," ahhh ...).

Johannes turned his tablet over when she came near.

-You sure beena actin strange all day. Hope you aint turnin odd. She brushed his cheek, then broke away from his Dagwood smile: -Lets see what we can do 'fore Dad gits home with Buddy.

Johannes almost left the chair. WITH BUDDY! Buddy had to be with Dad if Ma said so. Almost every time she sounded sure of things, they turned out that way. Too relieved to say a thing, he listened to her from the windows, where she watched:

-Sure hope they beat the storm. Didja ever see such a sky. No wonder mournin doves sounded sick. Been no cyclones yet this year, thanks God; lets hope hard this storm wont be one, or a-nother hail like the last one. Why, Jonas, that' somethin else fer yer story, the hail that cut the Hansons' threshing short; made you and Buddy miss yer supper too, after all day pickin cucumbers like that. Hail the size-a small potatoes.

She took a jar of shirt buttons from the window sill and left him to himself.

*   *   *

IT'S MIDSUMMER THRESHING TIME with all of Anderegg Corners gathered at Hanson farm to help; all, that is, but Buddy and Johannes (and Buddy's Maw of course, and Ol' Gundy who'd offered to watch us work). They'd escaped their cucumber picking the minute Ol' Gundy trotted off to the backhouse. Now Johannes stands guard at his regular post on the Bluff. Though he doubts he can be seen so high, he keeps low, glancing now and again over his left shoulder to see if he can find Ol' Gundy looking for them in the yards. Happy, too, to be too far away to hear her calls. He forgets her as his eyes run over the Hanson fields where they roll up beyond the wooded slope that separates the graveyard from the benchland farm. "A fancy location," Ma always said, "But kinda spooky too!"

He swears he can make out Solly and Sig with Dad's wagon stacked with sheaves. Dad never took the tractor for exchange-work. It could break down at any time. Besides, Ma said: "It makes you like a kid showin off some toy." But Dad didn't mind showing off the team, the best-matched dappled grays people said they'd ever seen. When Uncle Snorri-Bjorn on a visit saw for the first time (before the stork dropped me on Ma), he named them "Solveig" and "Sigrud," to honor the Old Country, he said. But Ma thought that sounded too high-falutin for a pair of animals, so Dad nick-named them "Solly" and "Sig," and they'd been family ever since. Dad promised to let them die in their own barn when they couldn't work no more. But they could nip the grass around the buildings; "lots cheaper, too," Ma said, "than buyin new-fangled cutters from the hardware store downtown."

Too big to ride and too slow to be dangerous, the horses knew their special place and grew so tame their mangers because a favorite hide-out for the boys when they needed to get away from grown-ups but hadn't time to run off far. The horses never gave them away. There, too, if alone with them, Johannes practiced Norwegian words out loud which he'd heard but didn't have meanings for, while Solly and Sig chomped away, nodding their manes this way and that in agreement or not. Their winter coats had tufted patches of hair sticking out that reminded Johannes of worn-out quilts in the attic. Every time the tractor went on the blinks, they stood ready to carry on. But nothing made their noses twitch so much as Ol' Gundy's store-bought scent whenever she came by. How he loved Solly and Sig, as much as Buddy ever could (trying to be a curryin champeen too).

Now and again winds lifted the puffing pain of the steam engine his way. How it throbbed as it powered the threshing rig that gobbled the sheaves rolling endlessly in on its belts. Lots of business down there, with horses, men, and wagons everywhere. From where he watched (a hundred miles away), it even looked like fun, 'specially the strawstacks behind the cowyard which older boys had been assigned to build. Think of all the excitement when this happened at their farm soon (Dad half-promised he could ride the grain sacks); he pooped. Already he saw Ma ordering ladies around where they packed the kitchen to help with food enough for high noon dinner, morning and afternoon coffee times, and supper at the end of day; everybody by that time hungry, tired, sweaty, but feeling good as darkness came.

Before she left home with Dad today, after the cheese factory truck picked up the milk and left Ol' Gundy to watch him, Ma warned against being late tonight, when him and Buddy had to bring Miss Gunderson to Hansons and they'd eat together after the menfolk finished. The memory of thresher food (bettern any picnic) made Johannes squirm with anticipation: in each of their times to serve, farm ladies tried to out-do one-another with the tastiest dishes, the fanciest desserts, but it rarely worked. Though The Widow Peterson no longer had crews of her own, she always brought her famous graham cracker pies whenever neighbors had occasions ("cant fergit her better times," Ma said, "'fore her man fell down the well."). His mouth watered at the thought of what might await them, only half a day away.

Johannes, too nosey about what he could see at Hanson Farm, hadn't noticed at first how storm banks huddled on the Minnesota bluffs, dark, with faraway thunder he began to hear, only after lightning exploded the insides of distant clouds. He scanned for possible cyclone funnels lurking there. It came from the direction of Eye-Away. Yes, Buddy reminded him when he looked out several times, coming from where Aunt Min lived. And Johannes suddenly wisht that Aunt Min wouldn't get home till 1936 at least.

Whenever the threshing noise shifted with the breeze, the steady hum of it brought more concerns than what the weather planned for them. Maybe this would be the day Buddy called for him to help clear out that mound, where he had to believe the bones of Singing White Wolf slept (and what will we do with em, huh?).

A glint of sunlight on metal struck the corner of his face and disappeared. He swerved and looked down on The Sheriff-Almighty's car-with-the-star far below. It glided slick as a snake along the elderberry brush between the road and Blood Brothers Crick and stopped before it reached the bridge. He's out to catch Town kids or strangers fishing out of season, Johannes thought, but the white star, the black door, brought back the mangled face of Ol' Odin, and with it that twinge of The Winter-Lonely. Almost nothing else could scare him like that (but bats that swallowed yer blood, and God's Big Lightning with power people couldn't hold off ... and maybe trolls ugly enuff to eat small kids). Worst of all, The Sheriff-Almighty had a gun! And a wild car for gallavantin in. Johannes backed away to the wall beneath the overhang. What would he do if he saw them on the Bluff?

Safe in the shadows, he heard Buddy whistling away, but he dared not bust in on him, any more than he'd stand and wave at the car-with-the-star. It had to be time soon to dig into that mound. Although he'd accepted his role as guard, maybe that wouldn't matter today if they found the bones real quick; it'd mean they'd finished their cave, too. And if the bones ARE in that corner ... (it's my right to uncover em!).

With Sheriff and threshers out of mind, Johannes began to fret over their vacation plans, and how the trip to see Aunt Min seemed more important than their waiting in the cave for ghosts or looking for magic flints. With vacation moving on so fast would there be time for anything else before they started down Squaw River for the Miss'ippi? And what about that? Would Eye-Away look the same as it did at home, or like the Minnesota bluffs last fall? And how long would it take The Sheriff-Almighty Strutt to find them and bring them back and put them in jail with the kind of furry rats Uncle Snorri said he found on many boats? Maybe Sheriff Strutt would shoot them instead (easiest thing to do), or worst of all, turn them over to Mrs Preacher's Woman and her orphanage in Many-apples-less. Johannes wanted to sleep away all thoughts.

A low rumble, more a chain of thuds than the faraway thunder coming closer, then a shriek from Buddy burst through a hail of stones that rained against the metal of the spade. Johannes rushed for the cave and crashed into Buddy, who staggered onto the ledge, laughing, and draped an arm around Johannes:

-Whisperin Jesus!

-Whatsa matter? You drunk? And all that racket?

Buddy sparkled with sweat and silt: -Have I gotta s'prise fer you. Wait'll you see!

Suspicious, Johannes refused to be dragged forward without a reason told: -Betcha finished the cave without me, that's what. And you promised I'd be the one to dig into that corner first.

-Only dug to git you started is all. Buddy mopped his cheeks: -Then the damndest thing. Everything caved in, jist came down. You wont hardly b'lieve it!

Johannes shook off Buddy's arm: -But you PROMISED me ... whatta 'bout them bones then?

-Oh, hell, Gramps, you coddled-molly you. Whatsa differnce to you when you see. Now we REALLY got a hidin place!

He booted Johannes across the backside and, with a sweep of his hand, stepped away. Johannes moved through the entrance, stiff as a stick, and stopped inside, daring not to go deeper. (Buddy's stolen my cave and makin me a trespasser ...)

Except for fresh chunks of shale and stones piled around the corner where the mound had been, the rest of the floor lay mostly buried under smoothed-out sand which showed whirls of the spade. The walls had been squared, creating a ceiling now cleared of bats and cobwebs. Johannes could even stand up straight. He recognized nothing but the grain-bin smell in the dampness and that rolled over him in a convulsion of disgust. He'd hoped for weeks Buddy couldn't finish the cave without his help, and now he'd done it all alone (and with no a thought left over for The Ghosts neither, I'm sure). And yet, what a thing to see! He dug at his eyes (it dont belong to me a-tall).

-NOW, whatcha matter with you, Gramps? Buddy croaked and shook his head: -Anyway, there's what I found. Least take-a look at it.

By the nape of the neck, he pushed Johannes into the far corner. Johannes tripped over himself, but saw from the new stones around him, a sliver of light that rose upwards across the wall and faded into rock overhead; the kind of lightning streak, he thought, that stayed in your eyes after the flash had died.

-Dammit it, Hansy, you gotta look up, way UP. Now dont that grab yer balls! A goddam hole right through the insides to the top. Can you b'lieve it ... a secret way, through the rock and all!

"Whispering Jesus!" Johannes echoed Buddy but breathlessly subdued. He could only stare but couldn't poop at the wonder of it. He'd never heard Buddy so excited about anything before, not even on their first day on the Bluff.

-It happened fast, Buddy gulped: -Stones and mud musta washed down and packed that corner so we couldn't see nuttin at first. Soon's I dug, everything loosened and ... and you thought the mound only covered bones. Look careful now; even got places cut out fer yer feet so you can climb up through ... whattaya know.

A way up to the very roof of the Point, all right, but not a tunnel; more of a chimney flue barely the size for a grown-up to squeeze through, and set at the angle of a ladder leaning all the way into the sky. A bend near the top caught sunbeams and hurled them down into his face. Nothing Uncle Snorri-Bjorn described ever prepared him for this (did God's Big Lightning split this open one summer long ago?). Before he could say another thing, Buddy pushed past him and crawled into the shaft, counting off uneven footholds as he climbed. He absorbed what light came down.

Afraid of missing something else, Johannes felt around for a notch, lifted one leg over the other, reached for another step, testing spaces till he'd set a pace, then climbed sideways. When he struck Buddy's knee, Buddy straddled over him, reached for an arm, and pulled him into the sun.

-Wheweee! Must be a million notches. Buddy'd taken on the sky-blue tint of the rock.

Johannes, blank with astonishment, stood on the flat floor on the top of Walking Sorrows Point and blinked at the reflections that darted his way from shallow puddles that pitted the surface. But for two thin roundish rocks like covers that lay beside the hole, not a twig or blade of grass disturbed the smoothness. To Johannes this looked to be about twice the size of Dad's main hayloft, and just about as squared-off. Still too stunned to wallow in exclamations, the boys brushed dust and bits of moss from each other, while they twisted naked inside their overalls.

Finally, Buddy broke open: -Jist think, Hansy. First our cave had a porch, now we got a attic. And a stairway to boot. We can even sleep up here. Sometime. If we wants. Under the stars and all ... if we wants.

Johannes had never heard Buddy take on like this: mentionin stars, much less sleepin with em. And he'd never seen him look like this before; his face glowed like lamplight. He didn't know what to say.

-If there's a storm, Buddy went on, -we'd be dry down there. The crook in the hole would keep the rain off, and lightning couldn't reach down that far (bet God's Big Lightning could). Ever seen a thing this swell? Even if somebody found the cave, they'd never find our attic if we moved them flat stones over. Gee willigers, aint this the swellest thing you ever seen now?

Johannes didn't want to talk and spoil the magic of the moment. He lowered his face to the glassy pool beside him and his smoothness came back to him in shards, and behind them reflected clouds bubbled, ready to kiss the Point (and me, ahhh).

-Hey, Hansy, LOOK!

Johannes turned to Buddy, once again defeated.

-Not at me, Gramps. Where my finger's at! Buddy pulled at him and pointed west: -There it is. What you jawed 'bout all winter. Aint that a bull's titty now!

Johannes didn't have to look, yet. He knew already what he'd see because he'd hoped so hard; that's why he didn't turn to the west when he came out of the chute. But he'd been right all the time, from their first day when they came upon that special clump of birch shoots. His voice too full for words, he hardly dare lift his eyes for fear his heart might stop.

Off on the Minnesota horizon, where the sun burned off the haze beneath the bluffs, a sliver of crystal glittered against the underbelly of the storm, and everything surrounding it hid in shades of purple-blue, as a blackness moved slowly towards them.

He covered his face. His dream come true could blind him. Ever since that day Uncle Snorri-Bjorn showed him the Miss'ippi, the size of it troubled him with doubts about how Broken Thunderhawk escaped, yet lived, being on top like this, with enemies below whooping for his life, and the Ghost of Singing White Wolf keeping his cave a secret, and … ahhh. But where had he jumped into the Squaw from here?

His legs folded under him and he slid to Buddy's feet, but when he saw Buddy struck silent by the view, he quietly set off on all fours to the farthest rim, and let one foot dangle over as he'd done on the ledge below. And wow! Over his knee he looked straight down the cliff into the big black bend of Squaw River. Goose pimples erupted (everything Uncle Snorri ever said is true).

His eyes blurred and he watched the Great Chief hit the water, then drift to a floating log, before the current whisked them downstream. Johannes pinched himself again. How did Uncle Snorri know so much if he hadn't been up here, or had he listened hard to Effie Stone?

In danger again of being scolded for his daring, he slid away from the edge and began to crawl around the perimeter of the Point. He hoped Buddy stayed still where he now lay on his back, out-stretched to the sun, eyes closed, alone with himself too (and safe in the middle of the floor). A rustle of hawks overhead haunted the scene the way whispers did in church. (I'm caught on an island in the sky, as high as the hovering cloud that's strayed in from the stormbank and maybe wants to kiss me … ahhh …).

Johannes couldn't believe how different everything became from such a height: the Howling Grief Ridges fanned out, rib-like, from the backbone of Walking Sorrows Bluff and fell away into coulees, north and south, thick with shadows; places people didn't know about maybe. When he crawled back towards the west again, more of Anderegg's Corners unfolded: farms to the south he'd never seen before, everybody's place together on this wide flat map.

Halfway to the schoolhouse, farm lanes leading out of the hills and benchlands east of the river flats met together at Township Road in a space large enough for turning around and parking cars. In the middle of this circle, the biggest elm in all the world spread shade, behind which the country store once stood until that cyclone blew it to kingdom come, but left the tree and the mailboxes around it untouched. In the middle distance beyond, the chimney of the cheese factory stuck out of a clump of pines, where , people said, Blood Brothers Crick sprang out of rocks. Johannes couldn't soak in everything at once:

Why, from this height he could even trace parts of the graveyard's iron fence, still standing from the time of Grampa but leaning now in all directions. Tall pointy trees ("arber vitas" Ol' Gundy called em) stood straight as exclamation points and marked the boundary corners where all the Anderegg family menfolk in North Ameddica slept (with room enuff fer us, too, Ma reminded him every Decoration Day, and fer yer intended, uff da!).

Those who've gone ahead must be satisfied, Johannes thought, lookin down from heaven on such a purty plot. But how could they be down there and up in heaven at the same time? He dint 'member Grampa's funeral inside the church, but he'd never fergit his face in the box in the parler, or how deep his grave looked when he stood beside it between Dad and Ma; the deepest hole he'd ever seen. How did it feel when they shoveled all that dirt on you? He liked much better what some Indians did, according to Uncle Snorri-Bjorn; they put their dead ones in the trees or on some platforms under open sky where departed spirits became part of the air without having to fight their way through all that hard-packed ground. And he'd never fergit neither how when Ma and Dad picked up clods to drop on the box in the hole and tried to give him one, he broke away from them and ran into the woods on Hanson's slope, where a gathering of fawns with their mothers watched. Ma never let him near a funeral since.

Oh, Johannes warned himself, I'm too excited today thinking so many things and making such noise inside my head. The Ghosts won't have a chance to get to us. He turned at the faint sound behind him (maybe Singing White Wolf in spite of all?). There stood Buddy, peeing in an arc as he tried to hit the outer rim without moving closer to it. To prove himself much braver, Johannes went to the edge and peed straight down into the Squaw. Out of the corner of his eye over his left shoulder, that glint on metal again, and a million feet below, he saw the car-with-the-star slip out of the roadside shade.

Too alarmed to compare dinks as they usually did if they had time like this, Johannes screamed: -Buddy, git down! The Sheriff'll see us.

-Sheriff? Piss on the sheriff! On Ol' Gundy, too. Buddy swung around, waving his peter as pee sprayed tiny rainbows.

-See fer yerself then. He's still down by the bridge and he sure aint pickin buttercups (wonder if anybody's with him).

Buddy fell to his knees and Johannes pushed himself away from the rim to lie near him, breathless:

-Think he saw us, huh? High against the sky like Broken Thunderhawk? Think the threshers see us all the way from Hanson Farm? We gotta stay low after this.

Buddy looked at Johannes for a long minute: -You know, Hansy, you really stood guard real good jist now. All the time I thought you had only Injuns in yer head. But you really warned 'bout the Sheriff. That's sure hunky-dory! He patted Johannes on the knee : -Yer right too. We gotta stay down low. Better not climb up here in daylight, I guess; better save it fer nighttime ... 'less yer scared-a the dark ... or somethin (ME scared-a the dark? Know fer sure now yer the one's scared, trying to push it off on me like that).

Buddy, in a crouch, tossed a pebble at Johannes, then with a whoop dived for him, but Johannes rolled over and scrambled like a spider to the flat rocks near the hole.

-Dont pester me, Bud Trigger, or I'll ... I'll send you over the side.

-You'll WHAT? Buddy came at him like a mother badger.

-Will do what we oughta done to Ol' Gundy if we coulda got her up here. Johannes yelled back and slid into the chute.

Halfway through, before he had time to gauge proper footholds, his feet pulled him forward and he sailed the rest of the way down the washboard. Terrified but unhurt, he landed facedown on the floor of the cave, the front of him well-spanked. When he tried to get up, Buddy crashed down upon him:

-Jesus Willigers, Hansy. Now that's one helluva slide!

It took but seconds to realize they hadn't been killed dead. But Johannes clawed at Buddy who sat on him and kept pushing his face back into the sand. Johannes finally wrenched around and hooked his legs around Buddy's waist, then dug his fingers into his ribs, his only weapon ever since he discovered how skittish Buddy turned when tickled. Sometimes Buddy laughed so helplessly when caught off-guard like that, he wilted. Forgetting theirs bumps and burns, they wrestled back and forth across the cave till they wore themselves down to giggles and broke apart, their overalls and hair encrusted.

All seriousness again, and once more the boss, Buddy shook off the debris he'd rolled in (jist like Ol' Odin sheddin water after wadin Blood Brothers Crick): -Now doncha be yappin to nobody bout what we found. Gotta be special-careful and not be draggin sand back on our clothes and shoes. Got notions, Hansy?

While Buddy brushed him and pulled bits of shale from his hair, Johannes dreamed on: -Jist think, Buddy – Bud. The River dont show 'cept from the top. Wait'll Uncle Snorri-Bjorn hears that.

-I know what we'll do, Hansy. Ever time we're up here, we'll take off our shoes and leave em by the door. Sound good?

-Our shoes?

-Yeah, cant risk bringin home giveaway sand which aint like the dirt around the barnyard or the house.

Buddy unlaced his black high-tops and shook them out: -We been lucky so far, but what if yer Maw finds our shoes in the corncrib by accident and them covered with sand from up here? Besides, if we wear our shoes in here, we'll spoil the floor I worked so hard on. Unnerstand?

-Whatta 'bout the rips we got today, huh? Johannes looked up worried from his shoes.

After lining up their shoes beside the spade just inside the entrance, Buddy inspected their clothes in silence. One knee of his overalls hung tattered, and Johannes felt air pass through the seat of his pants, lightly kissing his hinder (sure feels giggly-good though).

Buddy wrinkled his forehead: -We'll say ... I know, we'll say we got careless and climbed outta the tree house onto the corncrib roof and slid off like we done before; only we fergot them roofin nails agin. How's that sound (Buddy's lies always sound right; mine never do, ohhh ...)? Lets catch our wind.

They dropped to the floor and stretched out side by side, both weary-silent. Johannes marveled at how Buddy found ways out of everything they did, but he couldn't feel jealousy any more, not after

Buddy praised him for warning him about The Sheriff-Almighty. And the cave belonged to him now, too; he almost forgot the doubts he'd had. The time had come at last (with vacation flying by so fast) when they could settle in and wait in peace for The Ghosts to come. If Buddy ever felt the presence of Great Chief Broken Thunderhawk, Johannes bet that his excitement would flare even higher than it had when he first saw the River from up there (maybe make him fergit 'bout goin down the rivers to Eye-Away after that).

Johannes couldn't take his eyes from the slit through the rock. Such awful magic (sure must-a been made by God's Big Lightning). He reached towards the splinter of light that streaked down the wall. Buddy caught his arm, straightened it back, and lay his head upon it; his neck and hair gritty, wet.

-Calls for celebratin dont it. He pulled a wrinkled cigarette from his bib: -Shoulda snuck some-a Maw's homebrew. Too bad yer Maw dont make beer. I dont like it though.

Drained by the day's excitement, Johannes inhaled the whiff of sulphur from the match and gave himself to the moment. The sultry stillness outside rolled into the cave with the heaviness of a summer Sunday noon in church. For Johannes, only waiting for Singing White Wolf filled his heart, not Jesus now.

Buddy puffed and made much smoke: -Sure lucky yer Maw's tied up with threshers. We dont hafta hurry then. The wimmens always work later'n the men. Think-a all them left-overs; hope The Widow Peterson hid some graham cracker pie fer us. We'll jist let Ol' Gundy find her own way there. And when we pull out the sacks of cukes we stashed away last night, sure'll look like we picked em all today. Ol' Gundy wont know differnt, nor nobody else fer sure.

He passed the cigarette to Johannes. Too bad this couldn't make them Blood Brothers, he thought, when he touched it to his lips. He took special care not to breathe in as he'd learned to do at school the times they'd smoked on the backhouse roofs (but how can you be REAL Blood Brothers if yer scared-a blood?).

Johannes cleared his throat, knowing that if he didn't face the problem now, he'd never have such a proper chance: -Guess this is the time we made ourselves Blood Brothers then. What with the cave and the inside steps and the sight-a the Miss'ippi (ahh ...). Still got yer pen-knife in yer pants?

Buddy said nothing, but grabbed the cigarette and tried several times to blow a smoke ring, before giving up: -You say somethin crazy, Hansy?

When Johannes repeated himself, this time with a feeble voice, Buddy rolled his eyes, but didn't call him the nasty names he braced himself to hear:

-Now what'd yer Maw say if we showed up with cuts on us ... and blood? But aint our cave good though. Buddy switched the topic off: -Maybe yer Maw'll have lots-a funerals to sing at. More time fer us up here then. But donchee ever git tired of them funerals?

He finished the cigarette and settled back, quiet. Johannes, defeated again, lay still and listened (maybe if we're silent for awhile, there'll be some ... some tiny sign fer us). Before long, while facing the entrance to the cave, Johannes realized that the storm bank had crept closer, but Buddy jarred him out of his concern when he turned and studied his face:

-Aint that somethin, Hansy, seeing the Miss'ippi from up there. You wont be scared-a the rivers now?

For an instant Ma's face stared at him from the ceiling overhead and his soul did a jig at the thought of her finding his empty bed. He couldn't get over what had happened today much less having to think about Aunt Min and Eye-Away too. And the darkness coming closer (maybe making them miss all that food).

-Betcha scared-a the rivers, that's what.

-Aint neither. Only like to know when we go, is all.

-Not till Aunt Min gits home. How many times I gotta tell you. When she sends that card, we'll know. Gotta be here any time now.

-I'm sick and tired hearin bout Aunt Min's card. Johannes burst with sudden boldness: -Where she gone anyway, stayin away so long. Ever time I ask, you wont say. He waited before offering his far-fetched joke: -Must be in jail, I guess, huh?

Buddy didn't fall for that at all. His mouth tightened: -Aint you the lil fart blossom. And you dont know nuttin bout anything. He forced a cold smile and turned away.

Bats darted past the entrance. The whirr of their wings scratched at the walls of the cave. Johannes heard his insides struggle, but he had to play brave and bring good feelings back:

-I 'member what you said 'bout the rivers, Buddy – Bud. But where'll we build our raft?

-Raft? Whatcha mean, raft?

-Yeah, where'll we …

-Shitfits, Gramps, who you think we are, that Huck or Tom? They're only kids. We cant take no raft down any river; first thing anybody'd see.

Relieved of that concern, another filled its place: -How we gonna go then? Do what you call "hitch-hike"; like you went before?

-Who tole you that?

-YOU tole me. Talkin in yer sleep, you think? And walkin in yer sleep too?

-God-amighty you rile me some. Guess you heard nuttin straight all winter long (and you dint listen straight neither, bout The Ghosts and all).

Johannes held his breath and waited for Ma's face to fade again. He wanted Buddy to come back, not mad.

-One last time I'm tellin you; nuttin to worry for, Hansy. Yer Uncle S.B.'s loony stories sure did give me coupla good ideas though. This here cave fer one; and followin the rivers 'stead-a roads. Buddy's voice sounded smooth as the plush on the parlor chairs looked: -Jist think. We'll shake the posse by waitin up here, then we'll follow beside the Squaw where nobody's think to look (maybe?). By daylight we'll keep to river brush and cross some Miss'ippi bridge at night (what if we hafta sleep unner some bridge; would trolls be there, maybe, and could Buddy save me from em, JIST IN CASE they are).

-Where'd that bridge be, huh? Johannes mumbled as he saw Broken Thunderhawk ride that log across the Miss'ippi.

-Dunno. South-a La Crosse, prob'ly. On the other bank we'll still stick to the brush and a mile this side-a Dee-bjuke Aunt Min sits right on the water. Easy stop fer boats. Maybe we'll pick up a stray boat on the way; not like flat rafts ... (after I git Ma's letter done, will Ma's eyes look so dark and sad).

-And there'll be ponies there to ride. Buddy softened at the size of joys to come (Solly and Sig will miss us, Buddy!): -Wont we s'prise the pants off Aunt Min then? 'tween me and you and the four German husbands, dont think she wears none anyway.

More bats joined the whirligig outside, waiting, Johannes feared for a signal that would send them swooping in upon them. He tried not to swallow his tongue: -Guess we better head for Hansons.

-Oh we got time. Now's yer chance to be still awhile, like you say you wanna be.

When the bat squeaks multiplied, Johannes tried to free his arm: -Betcha you cant wait to eat, huh?

-Sure cant, Hansy, but this is SPECIAL. Whatta you say we stay here all night and see the sun come up on our attic? If we miss the food tonight, we'll make up fer it when you git the threshing rig.

Johannes sprang to his feet: -Stay here? All night? What'd we say at home? How come you aint hungry no more, sick or something, huh?

-C'mon, yer Maw wont care. Least she never whups you.

Befuddled more by another new idea than from the cigarette smoke in the air, Johannes shook his head, exhausted from so many surprises in one day ("You wont worry me now will you boys?"). He moved to his shoes.

-I'm stayin anyway; you can go home alone. Yer only a baby-troll is what; -fraid-a the dark to boot.

Johannes stiffened at the taunts. They stung worse than bees. They brought back those weeks of shame for only standing guard. When the sting threatened to turn nasty again, that overpowering affection of his swept in and anger fled. He hunkered beside Buddy and flattened his hand on Buddy's heart. It beat like mischief.

(Gee, Buddy, I think our cave's the BEST one in the world. And you picked the right one, too, jist like I – WE – planned. And all the work you put into it. I LOVE the cave, almost as much as I love … but …)

-BOYS!

Ma's voice through the megaphone stretched out longer than a monstrous slingshot band, rode the spiral wind into their faces and snapped:

-Wont call you agin. If you dont answer now, it's the woodshed for you (with all them bats, ohhh …). Her voice cut off sharply, as if it hadn't been.

-Holy Jennifer! Buddy leaped right off the ground: -Betcha we missed supper. He grabbed his shoes and ran.

It all happened too fast for Johannes to react at first, and besides, he'd begun to smart all over from the afternoon ride down the chute. His head felt like scrambled eggs. He groveled for his shoes, then sat to rest some more. Ah, that chance to be alone, and if he didn't breathe too hard, maybe The Ghosts would come and honor his invitation.

What would you know when you became a ghost? What would you eat, huh? And how would it feel to be able to see everything and not be seen by no one (ahhh …). Out of nowhere a bat swooped in and Johannes bolted through the entrance right into a furious Buddy:

-Where you been, goddamit? Thought I had you behind me. He dropped to the ground and forced Johannes into his shoes: -you shoulda been listenin. And watchin. Like I tole you. We missed supper too. And with this big storm on us. Jeez how black its got so fast.

Buddy dragged him off the ledge as contrary winds hurled against them (Buddy's scared to death, but I aint though; jist wonder if ghosts would fade forever if they got wet and blown around).

Before they picked their way down to the high field, the bottom fell out of the sky. Hail big as shooting marbles pelleted them from shifting directions. Johannes loved the fury, but he wanted to sink to the dirt and join the screams of surprised leaves being stripped from towering corn.

He'd not forgotten a minute of that day, the most important day of all vacation. And such a hailstorm too. Did Buddy remember it that way? Buddy bucking the winds and pale as buttermilk?

* * *

-SNOOZIN AGIN? HE HEARD Ma lug in his bath tub from the porch. She stood it on end behind the stove and came back to look over his pages. –Why, Johannes, you still aint done a thing. You want Miss Gunderson to think yer Mother's a liar, makin them promises I did. Is that what's in yer head now, makin me a liar?

Her sigh made him sigh, too. He felt constipated all over (dam Ol' Gundy; wisht I had some boogers on a string to hang around her neck).

Ma lingered at his chair; he couldn't stand it when she studied him: -Imagine Buddy actin up this way. And she waited (only reason Buddy does schoolwork, Ma, is to keep Mrs Preacher's Woman outa his hair, and he wont let Ol' Gundy git a handle on him neither).

-Cant stand school , Ma. I HATE it, I HATE it; and now its already back agin. He hadn't meant to yell, but he had to say something to break her silence.

-You gotta go to school, Jonas. You sure know that. Some day you'll amount to something special maybe (like Dad? Like Uncle Snorri-Bjorn?); why, might be County Agent even. How's that sound! Besides, what'll Uncle Snorri think if you wont study?

Johannes took up his pencil again, but nearly bit off its eraser (Uncle Snorri said you had to go to school, of course, even if you only pertended to study, but when you grew up you had to unlearn everything youd learnt and start all over from scratch, whatever all that meant).

Ma went back to the screendoor and pulled it tighter, after shaking off the flies: -Sure smells like a early fall. Still swear I heard wild geese a-callin; kinda soon for goin south I say (couldn't be Buddy though; he'd never been wild geese before). He watched her return to the kettle of stew on the stove.

After sipping its contents, she nodded, satisfied, then spread out the two new shirts on the kitchen table and sat down with the jar of buttons. She glanced his way. Their eyes met in unintended collusion, hers brimming with affection (my, but her eyes are purtier than violets). Emboldened, Johannes released his frustrations again:

-Gee, Ma, this gotta be the longest day I ever lived; its longer than vacation, and now that over too (and, Ma, this is the longest time I ever talked with you all summer).

-Yes indeedy, sweetheart. You been sittin a long time, but you had to be punished fer Thursday, doncha see? What will Uncle Snorri say 'bout that? Miss Gunderson's an ole ... friend of his, 'member; and she's yer godmother too (whatever that had to do with anything).

-Dont say nuttin to Uncle Snorri, Ma; please dont (he'd laugh so hard you'd git mad and that'd spoil his stay and everything).

-All right, Jonas. Dont YOU brag then. I'll tell Dad we'll keep last Thursday secret; between us three (you can betcha boots Ol' Gundy wont breathe a word!).

-Lets try to finish one page before we eat. Fer Uncle Snorri's sake; fer mine too. We'll s'prise Dad (will Buddy care, huh?). Lemme see ... first-a all, make a list of the best times we – you – had. Then you can pick out three or four-a them to write on. Main thing's to git goin now; we'll finish up tomorrow morning fore Sunday School's off and runnin agin.

Her patience undid him more than if she got hopping mad, but he leaned over the tablet in hopeless quandary. If he could stall long enough and look busy at the same time ... and now her reminder about tomorrow burned a new hole in his belly. He hated Sunday

School worse than regular school: everybody stiff and holy and sad and stuffed with "DO" and "DON'T," and punishments fer nuttin and Mrs Preacher's Woman gloomier than Ol' Gundy even when she came in from Town like the first cousin of Jesus Christ himself (he'd heard Dad say), and chirping "tsk, tsk" so much she must be cousin to the chipmunks too. Ma wouldn't let Johannes say nuttin 'gainst church or Sunday School, but if he still had The Widow Peterson for Bible class, he'd prob'ly make it through:

The Widow Peterson knew so many funny-peculiar things and not 'fraid to tell em. Even Buddy dint mind her, 'specially since the time he delivered Ma's butter with him and heard 'bout the tape worm she once carried ("Longest in all-a Wisconsin"), and saw how she kept her gallstones in a fruit jar on a front room shelf (so "mysterious," ahhh …). Said she dint favor birds; ever time one flew against a window, someone's soul flew out out fer sure (a messenger before Jesus called, huh?).

He had to think of something fast to stall Ma off till Dad got home, and there'd be no more lessons for the night. His fingers tightened on the pencil as he began to list some of the times she'd mentioned earlier, the easiest to spell too. Uncle Snorri's clock quivered twice and chimed late for another half-hour gone. Out of nowhere a sudden zing and his mind did a jig:

-Oh, Ma, you think Uncle Snorri'll have some new tattoos?

-Sure as heaven hope not, Jonas. Fee da! Makes his skin look snakey.

She draped their shirts over a chair and began to take down supper dishes from the cupboard.

-Dad's got tattoos.

-Thanks God, Dad's dont show so loud. Now see here, Jonas, if you dont stop wastin time like this, you'll have to go to bed with no funnies; that's all there's to it!

Johannes crouched over his list for possible other delays. But honestly, he couldn't wait to see Uncle Snorri's tattoos again, or to see if he had new ones somewhere else: already he had knots on both elbows like giant bachelor buttons, and when he straightened one elbow it turned into a Viking shield all blue and red; and from the other a Viking boat sailed out; on one shoulder, a smoking dragon, and the flag of Norway on the other. And last year, the most "mysterious" tattoo of all, a streak of lightning right there underneath the fur on his chest (he'd heard Dad tell downtown how he even had a mermaid on his hinder , ahhh …).

Uncle Snorri had lots of face hair, too, but it changed style every year. He had a droopy mustache like Dad wore on those snapshots taken before The Great War (long ago), and after that beards with all kinds of shapes ("Changes looks every time I see him," he'd heard Ol' Gundy complain to Ma).

-What kind-a whiskers you think Uncle Snorri'll have this time?

-Hard to say, Jonas. Dont take to hairy faces, you know that. Cant see what's unnerneath all that scrub, or what they're hidin from. You wanna look like that someday?

-Guess not (nobody in Anderegg Community had face hair on a-tall; not even Dad who said he liked it). –Sure makes you look special though, like havin a differnt car ever so often. Hope Uncle Snorri's got the same car (Love that run-about and the noise it makes with the rumble-seat right over the cut-out and yer bones rattlin all over the place).

-Fer cramps sake, Jonas. You startin on that car agin? Now why wouldn't he have …

-Heard downtown that ever time Uncle Snorri changed girlfriends he changed cars too (still cant b'lieve he's got anything to do with GIRLS).

-What's come over you now? All this jabber 'bout tattoos, whiskers, cars, and now … friendly girls.

She crossed the kitchen and slowed the rocker. She looked over his scribbles. He felt her eyes pierce into his brain.

-You sure caught me up for a minit, you lil … lil somethin or other. Thought youd keep me gabbin till Dad got home, dincha? And youd have no more work to do then. Well, Jonas, you got a-nother think a-comin.

He bit off a sob. Ma lifted his head and examined him like she did the time when chicken pox popped out all over him, or that time he brought home head lice from school one winter day. He liked Ma's face when he put questions there ... (how purty it looked when she dont know what to say and how proud I am that she dont paint herself to look like Halloween the way Buddy's Maw and Ol' Gundy did).

-And you still done nuttin. Well, then, we wont decorate Uncle Snorri's cake. You aint earned the right to lick the frostin bowl today, thats fer sure.

She let him fall back on the cushions, but took away the tablet, pulled the pencil from his mouth, and placed them on the counter.

-Now if we dont finish our sentences, s'pose you'll be tellin Miss Gunderson I worked you as hard as she wanted me to, so you had no left-over time to study.

He heard her add under her breath – wonder if that'd satisfy her.

-What you say, Ma?

-Nuttin Jonas. Guess its thinkin out loud. Bad habit to pick up.

She bustled back to the shirts: -while we wait for Dad (and Buddy dont you dare fergit), might as well work on yer shirt. Finished Buddy's; maybe hafta shorten tail and sleeves. We'll see. You two'll be the same size 'fore we know it.

She came with tape measure and made him stand straight while she poked at him and marked with chalk, all the while talking a streak as if to hold off questions of his for which she had no answers:

-Cant b'lieve it, Jonas. A new school year in two more days. Fall peekin round the corner early: 'fore we know it, silo fillers and corn shredders and packin potatoes; then Halloween. Blink an eye, there goes Thanksgivin; another blink fer Christmas. Then its goodbye to '35! How fast a year's gone, lookin back on it: a few words and its over. And you growin bigger all the while, as it should be too. Then ... another winter waitin ... uff da!

(Ma, yer fussin over Time again)! What did it mean? He didn't understand Time anyway. You can't see Time, so why fret about it, when it's always NOW anyway, even without names for days and months and years they had to remember to use (Uncle Snorri-Bjorn said that some Indians had no names for Time and they're still alive … ahhh). NOW is always, so why fuss?

Only when she held pins between her lips did she stop talking about how fast Time fled; instead, she began to hum "Abide With Me" deep in her throat. Johannes stood alone inside Buddy's shirt, near-sick at what would Time be like if Buddy didn't come back at all. His anxiety crumbled at the thought of the soothing certainty in Ma's voice; of course, Buddy HAD to be with Dad.

Even so, he dreaded winter (jist as she does in her way). He dreaded Christmas when Dad tried hard to play Santa Claus at school and everybody knew him right off by his size and voice. And Ma worked hard to make everything look special, even if the Christmas tree in the sitting room had little under it but spruce and pine cones she'd touched with silver paint. Anyway, last year him and Buddy had been able to hunt for the best tree on the slopes and it tickled Buddy silly to string and wrap ropes of popcorn all over it (Ma even let him handle Gramma's old-time balls and angels and other tinselly decorations). Johannes also dreaded pretending that Santa brought the things that Ma had knitted secretly all year; things for him to wear (last year for Buddy, too): new mittens, winter socks, a dress-up sweater maybe, or a long scarf, and last year's stocking caps that made him and Buddy look so fancy at school the kids called them The Blue Trolls. He never had money to buy Ma a present, but Dad'd help him make wreaths for the outside doors or bouquets of strawflowers and cattails which Ma dropped tears over and placed in the middle of the dining room table for all the world to see (and cluck about) And Ma'd wrap up a plug or two of tobacco in colored paper for him to drop into Dad's sock where it hung with the rest of their Christmas stockings on the indoor laundry line behind the stove. Last year she sent Buddy home on Christmas Eve with the fruit cake she'd saved for Buddy's Maw and family. And she still wouldn't let Johannes join the julebukk which looked so funny-ha-ha, and she'd do the same thing this year, too, he knew.

Sad to recall the holidays, yes, but much sadder afterwards when winter hung on into spring. He feared The Winter-Lonely forever lurking. He feared the chimney fires that always happened at night, usually in the middle of a blizzard; how exciting Buddy found them last winter when they stood outdoors in snow to their knees while Ma indoors poured salt into the cookstove or the furnace (wind in winter chimneys sang sadder songs than Ma's funeral ones, sadder than moans of summer doves). He liked winter nights best when he burrowed into Ma's old-time quilts (which The Widow Peterson exclaimed should be decoratin some wall instead of coverin a bed).

Sometimes, snow came with Easter and they'd have to ski through drifts to church or hitch Solly or Sig to the sleigh. Easter upset him in a stranger way than Christmas. It baffled him to watch grown-ups eat Jesus and afterwards they looked the same as they did before they marched to the altar. Nobody ever had answers for him; not Ma nor The Widow Peterson (and what did Jesus think, huh?). No wonder Buddy dint like church, all that drinkin blood, and eatin people too (like trolls?).

Ma took the pins from her mouth and inspected him: -Gee willigers, I swear yer sleepin on yer feet too. Its been a long day fer you I know. Tell you what: why doncha rest till supper. Cant be long 'fore theyre back (THEYRE back, ahhh …).

She removed the shirts and began to set the table, laying his and Buddy's places at each oval end with hers and Dad's looking at each other from the middle; separated like this, he suspected, to keep him and Buddy from fooling with the food.

-Wont Buddy be s'prised when he sees the water you carried fer his bath too. Wont know what to say. But dont you bring up the shirts, will you. She carried them out of the room.

Again her voice assured him that nothing could be wrong with Buddy, or she'd be acting strange. Why had HE been so bothered then, thinking The Sheriff-Almighty'd run Buddy down while he gallivanted off in opposite directions ... thinking that Aunt Min had come for Buddy after she'd warned him why she'd never visit ... and how could Mrs Preacher's Woman put her hands on Buddy when she wouldn't know where to look ... (all my bein riled up sick and spoilin most the day, ohhh ...).

Johannes sank deeper into the chair, and tried to rock in the lazy way he used to do before supper when he had no school or chores to think about. How "mysterious" that peace, with the heat from the cookstove rising in clouds of left-over cooking and baking reminders that crawled into his nose (and my bed upstairs) and wrapped themselves around his tongue. And memories (that made him poop). When Uncle Snorri's clock rattled five times straight without coughing, the chirpings of summer and the grain-bin heaviness of the cave swept over him.

Eyes half-hooded, he watched Ma pull down and light the hanging-lamp above the supper table. He waited for its feeble glow to expand in the windows of the nook, where behind the glass in daytime trees stood, and now reflections from the kitchen gleamed instead, marking the worn, still-shiny oilcloth that covered the table. There a jelly glass filled with pewter spoons sparkled beside the bowl of sugar lumps, alongside a pair of salt and pepper shakers in the shape of trolls that squatted back to back. Johannes emptied his mind. Renewed, he let the rocker drift on its own.

-Oh, Jonas, Ma called from the pantry door: -jist thought, where you put yer barnshoes? Dint find em in yer room. Soon be kinda late for runnin round barefoot-ed.

Shoes? He reared up and pulled back his bare feet as if he'd stumbled again into a patch of sandburrs.

-Dunno Ma.

-Wherecha say? She came to the counter with corn relish and lefse in her hands.

-Dont 'member. Must be … must be in our tree house (why do lies stink like they do, huh?). Face hot, he struggled to get out of the chair and almost tipped it over.

-No, no, Jonas. Dont need em now. But dont fergit em later. Hafta grease em good for chores 'fore the cold sets in.

-Yeah, Ma.

His head spun stars at this something-else to give attention to, but relief came too (couldnt leave now fer sure; how could they go down the rivers to Eye-Away without my heavy barnshoes too). With Uncle Snorri coming, Ma might forget his shoes.

Light flickered against the lower boughs of the kitchen pines, then sprayed wider across the backyard as Dad's feedtruck screeched dead beside the back porch steps. Johannes stiffened when the truck doors slammed and heels struck a rumpus on the planks. He leaped from the rocker and squeezed behind the door standing ajar against the cove wall, set to pounce on Buddy. The screendoor flew open on a gust of wind and Johannes jumped out with a resounding WHOOP! How huge Dad looked. He filled half the nook; his face bristled with stubble golden as fresh straw in the kitchen light. But …

-DAD CAME HOME ALONE!

-What the sam hill you tryin to do, Gramps, Dad roared, kicking the door shut behind him: -scare the farts outa yer ole man?

-Thor! Ma ran to meet him: -In fronta the boy, too! Sounds like you stopped by the tavern?

-Dont burn yerself, Kari, Hansy knows what a fart is, doncha, Gramps (has Dad been listenin to me and Buddy, ohhh …).

Dad blew into Ma's face, winked at Johannes, shifted his tobacco quid to the other cheek, and strode to the counter with bags of groceries in each arm:

-Great weather. 'Nuff to curdle the balls on a troll!

Johannes held his breath when he saw Ma reach for the funnies under Dad's arm, but Dad, with a nod at him, tossed them into the rocker, followed by a pack of Black Jack gum. He slapped his big hand on Ma's hinder and pushed her ahead of him to the pantry door and into the dining room where the phone hung high and handy. He barely heard Ma say when she got her voice back: Jonas been good today but we dint git schoolwork done. And his ears perked more when he heard Dad say: -shouldn't be doin schoolwork on vacation anyhow. Then the swinging doors shut Johannes out.

Must be frightful news if he couldn't hear it, like when they talked Norwegian about secrets he shouldn't know or of things Buddy tried to tell him meanings for sometimes. Sure that the news had to do with Buddy, Johannes crept along the cupboards into the pantry next to the dining room door. The more he strained to grasp their mumble, the faster the weather blew away their words.

-Jonas, stop bein a pest now. Know yer in there. No pickin at them pies neither. Theyre fer company, 'member. So scoot!

Stuck to the floor, he stretched his ears till they tickled and his lips gaped so wide he began to dry up inside and had to shut his mouth. Disconnected words and phrases trickled out: something about Aunt Min's escape (escape? From WHAT, huh?) and something else about The Sheriff-Almighty, then Buddy's Maw by name, and when Ma asked about Buddy, only one word from Dad's reply made it through the thunder: "Jail." JAIL! Every nerve Johannes ever felt stood up at the sound of "jail" … (The Sheriff-Almighty Strutt has Buddy then, whatever else Ma said or thought).

Though he didn't know what to do, he had to save Buddy somehow. In his panic he skidded across the waxed linoleum for the back porch. The door wouldn't move. He kicked it, coaxed it, tugged at it from several angles, and he only managed to rattle the glass in its frames. He could have been battering the alcove wall for all his success. Then, without warning, the door flung inward with a blast, and a damp rag of a wind slapped Johannes across the eyes, blew out the lamp, and with a crash sucked itself back into the wall, tighter than ever, before Johannes could get away.

Winds hooted down chimneys and rolled through the furnace pipes, spreading dust through registers. Johannes cowered in the nook. He braced himself for Ma to rush in and maybe blame him for fooling with the lamp.

-Good thing you got the door shut, Jonas, she said instead as she carried another lamp which Dad held high while she relit the hanging one (wwhewww! Another "close call," Buddy; dint catch me tryin to run off).

Squalls attacked the porch head-on. He saw through foggy panes the outraged dinner bell perform a total somersault; wash tubs jumped their hooks and rolled out of sight.

-Hoped the storms had ended fer the year, and after last month's hailstones too. Ma came from the stove and ladled stew on each plate: -storm or not, we gotta eat. Cows wont wait neither.

When she returned to table, she buttered lefse for Johannes and put a glass of buttermilk at his place: -Cause you been sitting good most-a the day and bein scared-a storms besides, Dad says no chores fer you tonight. Lets eat now and we'll be safe together.

Ma sat and waited for Dad to take off his glasses and shove away the mail he'd been looking over: -We'll have yer bath and haircut early. Then to bed. If the storm gits worse, we'll hit the cellar if we hafta, how's that by you (I AINT scared-a storms, Ma; it's the only excitement we ever git; I'm scared for Buddy, that's what; if The Sheriff-Almighty shoots him down, or God's Big Lightning splits him in two, ohhh ...)?

-Let's say grace, son.

Johannes stumbled through the familiar Norwegian words (the only ones I unnerstand too), unable to think of what he said with winds rattling the lightning rods. And how could he dig out more about Buddy if they caught him bein nosey. They'd hide bad news if he asked. He'd have to figure from their faces the Meanings they'd flash back and forth. His insides danced. Ma didn't even scold him for fumbling the prayer when they said together a loud AY-MEN!

-Gettin it heavy in the coulees. Dad passed the salt and pepper: -Shoulda seen the sky along the Howlin Griefs. Blackern a witch's tit (right back-a Buddy's house, too; why dint you pick him up then like we would done maybe if I'd been along).

Deaf to Dad's weather report, Ma took over with her ordinary voice: -Only hope we're spared this time. Worst-a all, it could come back on itself like its done before. Cant worry though; nuttin to do but jist hold tight. Right, Jonas (Doncha ever see how I LOVE storms, so wild, so "mysterious" with all the lightning sometimes showin things you dint know before)?

Terrified for Buddy, Johannes leaned back as far as he could into the shadows around his chair, while Ma began to ask a slew of questions about Town and Dad had lots to tell that Johannes cared not a slug about. If they switched to Norwegian, he bristled; it unsettled him when their everyday voices changed fast into words he didn't know and with new expression, too. He knew bad things had happened then: accidents, sicknesses, and who had troubles, who'd done nasty things, and (always) which ones Jesus called on since the last time.

Eyes glued to Dad, who could barely make him out, Johannes toyed with his food enough to show he had an appetite. If anybody could save Buddy from The Sheriff-Almighty, it had to be Dad, but he didn't know Buddy's plans any more then he knew. This time when the Norwegian stopped, Dad's big hand buttered and rolled another piece of lefse and brought it to his mouth where it paused a moment before it disappeared behind his smile. If Great Chief Broken Thunderhawk had come from Norway, he probably looked like Dad, only quieter; but Johannes had no image of Singing White Wolf other than his name which made him think of how a weeping willow cried, or how a tender birch touched the tenderness he had for Buddy if Buddy didn't make him mad or jealous. Johannes thought that God would be more like Ma; Dad couldn't be strict enough to be like God, but there Dad sat, strong as Walking Sorrows Bluff, built all over and covered with kitten fur like Uncle Snorri-Bjorn. Yes, only Dad could rescue Buddy from anything ... but how? Johannes lashed out at him suddenly for knowing not the very things he'd kept from Ma before.

-Almost fergot yer here, Jonas, Ma said, -must be tired. When her eyes found him listening in the shadows, he bent over his food again, but her face, leaning towards him, soft with patience didn't scold. The graham crackers and peanut butter, bought just for him he realized, tasted like sileage now, but he forced a mouthful down. Ma and Dad kept exchanging those Looks that scared him more than words. He shot glances back and forth at each of them. Maybe they'd forget he existed if he continued to sit still enough and let the thunder walk.

-Helluva weather fer Sheriff Strutt, Dad paused for a sip of buttermilk: -said he had to keep a look-out at the County Line till daylight. You think them Ioway jailbirds can git this far? Anyway, Strutt'll earn his buck today fer sure.

Johannes grabbed the table edge. Why, The Sheriff-Almighty couldn't have Buddy then, any more than he had him this afternoon. Now's the time to ask Dad if he'd seen him anywheres downtown, but Ma cut in ahead of him with a busy voice:

-Hear em talkin war agin? She sounded anxious.

-Well, they say at the Post Office dont look good in Spain. And the Eye-talians got their eyes on Ethyopia. Accordin to Post Office Charlie, none of it looks bright.

-Shame we cant git radio batteries and hear from the rest-a the world. Better not to know maybe. Aint it funny, Jonas, you think places like Ethyopia belong to Sunday School, not real for nowadays.

-Sure as hell hope them black bastards give that Mussolini man a real run fer his dollar.

-Ma interrupted: -s'pose Snorri's boat'll git caught up when it goes out agin?

-Hard telling. Think it might be fun, Hansy, ridin the waves in some rusty tub, bein chased by God-knows-what? Betcha it'd beat anything yer Indians could cook up.

-No more-a THAT stuff now, Ma said as she got up to answer the phone.

Dad, leaning toward Johannes, sounded gentle: -Well, Hansy, a Viking belongs on water, not behind a plough. You can see yer Ma dont dream like us men do. Like lotsa wimmens that way, so dont be rough on her. Someday you'll see how wimmens are not like us … us men a-tall.

Johannes had no time to say anything to Dad when Ma came back, complaining about another funeral she had promised to sing at ("Sing for one, must sing for all," she always said): -And now another old one taken (Jesus makin up for summer slack, huh?).

Before settling down, she refilled their plates. On her way from the stove, the phone jangled again. Dad shook his head with a smile after she'd hurried off through the pantry:

-Nobody on God's green earth's busy as yer Ma. She dont even know it; dont show it neither. I swear yer Ma sees three sides to everything; sometimes more.

Dad leaned farther into the circle of light: -Missed you in Town, Hansy. But you had to obey Ma first; had her reasons. You know why.

The roar of Dad's laugh from last Thursday when he heard about Ol' Gundy echoed through Johannes and brought back a secret smile. Now, when he gazed on Dad by lamplight, he didn't know if he loved him more than Ma, or both the same; the same, he guessed, but different. If he could reach Dad like he touched Uncle Snorri-Bjorn … yet, Dad captured his heart by never making jokes of Johannes when he talked Ghosts or ndians, and he always used the names Uncle Snorri had put on all of their everyday places. Dad swallowed several times.

-I say again, Hansy, dont pester yer Ma with daydreams. Like many wimmens she riles herself into a fit for nuttin if things dont sound fer real. Unnerstand?

Johannes nodded as Dad reached for the lefse, flipped a sheet at him and let him work with it himself. The serious business of eating resumed (he's sure the spittin image of Uncle Snorri-Bjorn tonight, without the hair-face though …).

Bearded, tattooed, and browner than Dad, who wore long shirtsleeves (to hide his own tattoos, maybe?), Uncle Snorri looked tallern anybody 'cept The Sheriff-Almighty. Must-a been one powerful lumberjack accordin to Dad, but Uncle Snorri had tales on Dad, too, that made Johannes wonder why they had to live so quiet on a farm when adventures waited fer em all over the world. And when Dad looked far away at times, what did he see, or hear (them oceans Uncle Snorri raved about)? Bein twins, Johannes knew theyre s'posed to look alike, though Dad moved slower and everybody liked him, while the same people called Uncle Snorri "S.B." and said behind his back that he "farted through his hat too much" and passed out wooden nickels (huh?).

But bein twins dint mean you hadta be the same inside, too, did it?

-You know, Dad said softly, -wasnt jokin last Fourth-a-July bout goin to the Dakotas. Meant it in a way, but how in all the world could I go off without you now? And you not wantin to leave school (not SCHOOL, Dad, but Buddy … ohhh).

Dad's eyes twinkled when he leaned in again: -'member one thing, Hansy, there aint no wimmens like yer Ma. Anywheres. Always treat her good. Nobody else like her on God's green earth.

Johannes felt safer than ever when he watched Dad go back to his food, and Ma returned to table, wringing her hands: -Uff da! Poor dear. Thats the third time Borgny's called today; still wantin to know when Snorri's getting here after I've tole her over and over; in time fer supper Sunday night. Finally had to invite her too. Course that's what she's been workin all day. Johannes winced.

-So, yer playin matchmaker now? Dad winked at Johannes.

-Snorri dont know she's still a-kickin. Poor thing, carryin the torch like that (what for's a torch, Ma?). And him all tied up with the last flame of his; even havin her keep his car.

How long'll that last you think?

Johannes squeezed tighter inside himself and hunched over his plate like Buddy did when he followed Dad and the three of them would imitate each other like threshers till Ma'd order them to straighten up and eat right. Tonight she didn't notice him. He had to hear about everything he could, but if they had to talk about Uncle Snorri's girls again, he wouldn't believe , no matter who said what. His ears buzzed, waiting.

-Face the facts, Kari, Dad put down his fork, -Who'd wanta be saddled with Borgny Gunderson and her purple ways (saddled? like on-a horse, huh?)? She's not the only heifer in the county, she's the heifer with the mostest airs for sure (Ma, what airs? Bein stuck-up maybe? Like the way she says "Eye-Away" and "Miss'ippi" and other things, makin us try to say "th" or "t" ...).

-Thorwald-Jon! How can Johannes ever respect his teacher if you call her a cow.

-No harm done; a way of speakin is all. Now lemme ask you this, Kari, what's more respectable than a cow?

Ma tried to hide the smile that puckered her lips, but finally turned and dug into her own supper fast.

He remembered hearing Uncle Snorri explain to Ma how Dad had named their cows after members of her Ladies Aid Society: Cora, Hazel, Mabel, Gladys, Emma, and so on. Wilda already had her name, but last fall, Uncle Snorri called her heifer (HIS heifer) "Sweet LaVon" (said we needed something Frenchy on the farm ... as a reminder; how "mysterious," ahhh ...).

Ma soon came back to life, needing to protect Ol' Gundy more; -Will say this fer her: Borgny's one to settle down a man (now what's this "settle-down," Ma, and WHY?). -Dont see nuttin wrong with that do you?

-Still say she's tryin to slip a ring on him ... in the nose I mean (Dad, men dont wear no rings in Anderegg's Corners but The Widow Peterson say if wimmens take off their weddin bands they lose their marriages; cant unnerstand a thing!).

-Wisht Borgny behaved more common though, Ma said, -She scared the farm ladies tongue-tied; seems to know they say behind her back she acts like her folks came from uppity Bergen, 'stead-a the farm hills of Hallingdal.

-She's still a blown-up heifer to me, Dad teased.

-You menfolks, all alike! S'pose you want yer twin – if he already aint – mixed up with he likes-a Hester Tryg … Ma choked. –Oh, Johannes dear, more buttermilk?

He let her fuss around him. He tried to look as if his ears had fallen off a week ago; he got so fed up with grown-up talk of Uncle Snorri-Bjorn and girls (how could Uncle Snorri care for em when they took too much time away from everything else important). And now, even Ma talkin like that. Alarmed, Johannes piped out:

-When's Uncle Snorri gonna hitch up with Ol' Gundy then?

-Johannes Berg!

-Thats what they always wanna know downtown. Says he sparks with squaws too. He got a Indian sweetie somewheres, you s'pose and wants it secret? Johannes felt tears bubbling to the surface.

-Jonas, what's goin on inside you? Uncle Snorri's business is his own, that's what. Sure as sin aint yers! He'll tell what he wants us to know; maybe you'll be first. Now clean up yer plate before dessert. I'm lettin you and Dad sample rhubarb pie.

Raindrops still fell through the chimney and sizzled underneath the stove top lids, as lightning flashes weakened and thunder sounded farther off. Ma, lost in what she had to finish, paid no attention to the weather.

-With respect fer yer twin, Thor, you know well as me he's the worst disease any woman could catch. ME play matchmaker then? Go soak yer head! Do give him credit though; he's never dragged his flames along when comin here. Hope for Borgny's sake, he comes alone tomorrow, too.

-Dont fergit, Kari, me and S.B.'s outa the same mold.

-So be it, husband mine. You at least got both shoes on the ground. You came outa the same lumbercamps, same sawmills, same war, but you left yer itchy tracks behind. She grinned: -dint you?

While Ma tried to catch up with her supper, Dad served himself at the stove and brought coffee to the table. Johannes eyed them with a rush of overwhelming affection, and brought to mind again his favorite story about them: how Uncle Snorri-Bjorn and Dad, after leaving the woods on their way to a boat for Norway, stopped at the County Fair, and there in a cattle shed beside her prize-winning steer, they ran across Ma, trying to sign up hired men, and Uncle Snorri-Bjorn went off to sea alone (nuttin sounds so "mysterious" each time I 'member it).

Fresh thunder rushed back, cracked a pane in the kitchen door, and brought Johannes upright. What could he do about Buddy, but let Ma and Dad believe he feared the storm as much as he pretended; would that give time to think of what to do? Anyway, they sure couldn't start for Eye-Away tonight, and maybe not tomorrow neither when Buddy heard his news. He tried to make some sense in the Looks still passing back and forth. Unable to understand anything, he only nibbled at the pie Ma'd set before him, much as he loved rhubarb.

-Great pie, Kari, Dad said, pouring himself another cup of coffee before heading for the barns: -hope there'll be some left for Snorri when he gits here.

-Whattaya mean ... Thor, yer the limit! You know Rev Flogge eats Sunday dinner with us ever month when he comes out to preach; and her comin ever week fer Sunday School. Someone gotta feed em.

-Dont mind feedin the suckers. 'tis our lot, I guess (sure sounds like Uncle Snorri, whatever Dad means now). Cant b'lieve that Preacher's Woman's appa-tite. Biggern mine.

-So what if they fill up like pigs. He makes some people feel real good and fancy; 'specially at funerals.

-And all that food afterwards, no wonder.

-Now Thor, stop callin her a preacher's woman! You know well as me she's a respectable wife of a respectable Lutheran minister. AND, she thinks Great Granddad's a reg'laer saint; leavin land like he did fer church and school (and graveyard, too?), as well as lumber off the upper fields fer buildins. You seem to fergit all that.

Ma feigned a hurt look while she sipped her coffee, then got up to check the bath water in the boiler on the stove.

-She sure acts a lowdown preacher's woman to us, donchee, Hansy? Jist a nuisance, right? Hang tight to the table when she's here so she cant kidnap you and mail you off to them missionaries in Africa she's always squawkin fer (would I see them Katzenjammer Kids that tickle me so much?).

-Aint easy wedded to a minister, Ma said from the stove: -everybody watchin every breath you take, ever step, ever word.

-Why they do that, Ma?

-Thatsa way some people are. Can you 'magine Anderegg Corners with no minister though?

-Not if you wimmens say so, Kari. But guess we'd make it somehow.

-I say, Thor, Ma came up to him, hands on hips, with pretended scolding in her voice: -first, you make a joke-a Borgny in front of Jonas, then you laugh at his Sunday School leader, even her husband. Why, Jonas wont respect a soul.

-You gotta earn respect, Kari, not jist expect it. Right, Hansy?

Ma turned her back on them as Dad pushed back his chair, reached for his cap on the rack of deer horns by the door, and swatted Ma across the rump again. It always puzzled Johannes how Ma lost her voice for a minute or so every time Dad did that, and that never happened to Ma otherwise: losing her voice and sometimes turning red too (ahhh ...).

Before going out the door, Dad came back and patted Johannes on the head: -Have a good bath and early bed. See, the storm's already peterin out.

When he noticed Ma testing bath water some more, Dad bent to his ear: -I'll never fergit last Thursday, you ole lady-killer you. And what if Uncle Snorri comes tomorrow early and catches Preacher Flogge here. Fireworks fer sure!

Johannes pooped at the notion. Dad went off into the thunder.

While Ma set out his tub in front of the cookstove and began to fill it from the boiler, Johannes cleared the table and dumped the dishes into the washstand sink.

-Dont needta be stingy now, she said, -if Buddy comes this late, there's water in the reservoir. You can stay in yer tub long's you want. Wont that be nice?

Ma never allowed him or Buddy to work with boiling water, so it would take some time before she filled his tub. Starting to undress, he sank down on a low stool to wait. Every Saturday night him and Buddy took long soakings in those copper tubs left from Olden Times when Grampa Anderegg's sons and hired men bathed and frolicked (ma said) in the horse barn before Solly and Sig moved in. Nowadays, they hauled water every Saturday morning from the pump house or used rainwater from the barrels under the eaves. Every night in the summer before going to bed, Ma read to them while they soaked the day's dirt from their feet. They had to do that because Johannes loved to squish his toes deep into fresh cow flop (like walkin through my fav'rit blueberry pie), and Buddy'd kick at horse turds that he said reminded him of the croquet balls he saw on lawns downtown (cow pies and horse apples are summer treats here, Uncle Snorri said last fall when Ma reported to him). Sometimes, Ma had them sponge off their all-together if they looked too sticky for her spotless sheets.

But the best baths of all they sneaked in the spring-fed horse tank with its oaken walls lined with stringy moss that reached for their sunburnt skins and gave them the heebie-jee-bies. Then always the surprised fun of turning around to find Solly and Sig sucking up water and gawking at their naked hinders.

For regular Saturday night baths, they undressed with their backs to Ma, as if she'd never seen before what they had to hide. After she'd picked up their clothes and laid out fresh ones, she'd go into the sitting room to the pump organ (which Ol' Gundy called a "harmony-um"). While she played and sang, she let them believe that she'd forgotten them, but they knew otherwise, and when she'd turn to ask about the water, they sometimes stood up and flashed their backsides at her, giggling. –Now, boys, she'd laugh, –no takin pitchers of me now. Git real clean now; lotsa dirty work next week.

Sunday would be their only CLEAN day during summer, not counting barn chores, unless (with Dad on special harvesting or haying) they fooled around trying to ride the manure carrier to its dumping point and jumping out before it tipped and buried them.

-you ready, Jonas? Ma asked beside his steaming tub. She draped a big towel on his shoulders where he sat, still half-dressed: -Aint you lucky? Most kids dont git a bath ever week like you (and Buddy, too); summer same's winter, think-a that.

-Yeah, Ma. Thats why I dont like playin round them dam school kids neither; some of em stink ("to heaven and to hell and back").

-Johannes Berg, what did I hear you say?

-Said some stink.

-'Fore that. Ditcha git that word from Buddy?

-No. No, Ma! Uncle says it; say it dont mean a "dam," like inna "tinker's dam"; sure dont mean nuttin nasty ...

-Sounds nasty comin outa you. Never wanta hear that from now on. Will hafta talk to Uncle Snorri.

-Dont do that, Ma. He'll think me a sissy-boy. And Buddy too.

-Foul-mouthed men are one thing. But cussin lil boys, to be sure that's something else.

-Yeah, Ma. Dint mean nuttin nasty. Jist a bad habit I picked up (but what's a "tinker's dam," Ma, and where the hell's hell anyways?).

-Awright then; only 'member what I said. She hung up her smock: -we'll clip yer hair in the morning; saved lotsa cracked eggs to wash yer head with. No use riskin catchin cold in these here storm chills now.

On her way to the sitting room, she paused at the open double doors: -Now soak yerself real good. Git rid-a yer vacation dirt. And you'll be nice and fresh fer Sunday School (uff da! Not THAT agin too!).

His tub faced the pump organ where Ma in heavy shadow settled on the revolving stool, ready to play and sing favorites she needed no lamp for. Most other times, this made the end of day so cozy he (they) slept like dead cats later. But not tonight (how funny-peculiar that Ma's voice aint even worried yet).

Only after he sank to the bottom of the tub with his knees pulled partway to his chin did Ma's Sunday School reminder sink in deep. Zinging flints all but knocked him flat (of course, no wonder Buddy aint here yet). Buddy seldom slept over on Saturday nights if they had Sunday School the next day, except in winter when Ma kept him home with Dad, saying he had no proper clothes for church. Buddy didn't tease when he watched Johannes climb into his Sunday best. Sometimes he'd ask Johannes to do him a favor: "Say 'Hi' to The Widow Peterson fer me, Hansy. Ask her how her gallstones are." "You know, Hansy," Dad told him once when they talked alone, "yer Ma sure does a job keepin Buddy outa Mrs Preacher's Woman's claws. Got nuttin to do with what to wear to church." Ma never wore religion like a party dress, he heard Dad tell someone else, and she never tried to drag Dad or Buddy off with her to church. Instead, she explained to Johannes, Buddy couldn't be away from his house all the time in case his mother and big sister had things for him to do. Once at Community Club, Johannes overheard Ma scold some ladies who fussed too much over Preacher Flogge: "Religion aint much use if you can talk bout it easy (all that church stuff so funny-peculiar, ahhh ...)."

Sunday School again; that's what did it fer sure: that's what's keeping Buddy away. Johannes exploded with such relief, he almost drownd-ed in the purple stars that bubbled from the tub. The knots of this Saturday-everlasting untangled as panic for Buddy shifted. And he'd never let on to Ma that he knew how good she pertected Buddy ... and him.

He stretched as far as he could reach to curl his toes against the end of the tub. Ma commanded him to be respectful to all grown-ups; ones like Mrs Preacher's Woman who vexed him more than Ol' Gundy did (and that's sayin something!), but scared too, almost bad as God's Big Lightning. Whatever she done, she walked with Jesus at her sad side (she said). Why didn't Jesus call HER home then, instead of all the others (huh?); and that man of hers, fat Rev Flogge (as Ma insisted he be called), nodding up and down at everything his sad wife said.

He'd never forget the first time he ever saw them and the memory of it chilled him, sitting in hot water as he did now: Ma'd invited them for Sunday noontime dinner and he had to sit all dressed-up in the dining room, while Mrs Preacher's Woman looked him over like something on the bargain counter in the Farmers Store. She had tiny eyes (to see so much!) set close together with a narrow nose pointing out between, and her voice reminded him of Dad's scythe fighting with the grindstone. Later he heard Dad warn Uncle Snorri that she wore religion like a pair of longjohns on the outside.

She peered at him through eyelids without lashes: -And what are you going to be, little boy, when YOU grow up (why dont she say my name?).

-Jonas is gonna be the best farmer in the land, Ma replied before he understood the question: -might even become County Agent when that time's right. Aint that so, Jonas, dear?

-I'm sure that's nice. How nice, too, that your mother is so proud of you. Yes, this certainly is the nicest ... one of the nicest ... could be the nicest farm around ... well, it would be if ... You see the dear Reverend and I don't have a boy like you, but for our little girls, we'll want them to marry ministers someday.

-How nice, Ma said at once: -how proper, too. More pickled beets, Mrs. Flogge?

Preacher Flogge only snuffled; Johannes thought he dozed. Absolute stillness settled on them for a moment. In the buffet mirror against the opposite wall, Johannes saw Ma beam at Dad, with himself trapped between them.

-Yes, Jonas is gonna be a bigger farmer than even Grampa Anderegg. He'll show everybody how to keep up such a place as good as his dad's a-doin. Wont that be nice now?

Another moment of unbearable stillness and Johannes knew he'd burst wide open if he kept silent any longer: -Dont wanna be a farmer, Ma!

-Gonna be a ship-mate like yer ... Dad tried to rescue him.

-No! Johannes cut him off and sounded louder before he heard himself.

-Betcha I know yer secret, Dad came on, trying to make it all a joke: -gonna be a lady-killer like yer Uncle S.B. then?

That crossed the line. Johannes turned and shouted: -NO no no. I wanna be a INDIAN!

In the mirror he saw Dad flinch and Ma throw back her head.

-Like Singing White Wolf, doncha see? A ghost-singer is what ... he lowered his eyes and slumped against the chair, spent.

Mrs. Preacher's Woman's lavender lips, which hardly parted when she spoke, opened wide enough to reveal a purple tongue: -Why, little Johanny, if not for your Mother being such an upright Christian lady, I'd say she had a little heathen on her hands (oh, what's a "hee-thin," Ma? And doncha dare call me "lil Johanny" neither).

The Preacher Flogge, round as a woodchuck and smelling of mothballs, muttered: -Let us pray.

Johannes heard Dad's feet fidget with the legs of his chair. By the time Johannes had been prayed over in muffled exclamations, Ma knew what to do:

-How nice, how nice-a you. Thank you, Rev Flogge. But you sure must see Johannes is jist a lil mischief. Likes-ta show off at his age is all (dont neither, Ma). Dont git much attention out here, you unnerstand? She pulled back from the table: -Know what, whynt you finish colorin yer Bible pitchers 'fore yer after-dinner nap (WHAT Bible pitchers, huh?). And dont fergit to say yer prayers. Now scoot!

She pointed him to the backstairs entry and smiled on the company: -Good-ta say a prayer before a nap; never can tell if you'll see the light-a day agin. More coffee now? Ready fer some chocolate cake? Dont know if its proper serving devil's food on Sunday, but ... its all I got.

Released, Johannes raced for his room, but tripped over Rev Flogge's flat feet, planted alongside his chair since he couldn't get his gut to the table (must weigh as much as Solly or Sig!). He picked himself up fast and fled.

Johannes tittered at the onrush of such memories riding around his head, still taking space.

He pooped. Bubbles floated up to smack his hinder. Later, when it became a habit for the pair to come often and stay long ("Always a free meal," Dad would snort), Dad sounded just like Uncle Snorri-Bjorn: "Dont ever let them hypo-crits spoil yer fun. And he hoped to learn someday what "fun" Dad meant, and what he meant by "hypo-critts").

The thought of Sunday School again almost invited The Winter-Lonely's presence ... unless ... unless The Widow Peterson still had him in her class. He slid deeper into the tub until the water reached his chest again. He tried to hold down the bar of Ivory soap which bobbed back to the surface each time he almost sat on it. He liked this crazy soap he couldn't control; softer than that sandy Lava they used on knees and elbows during summer, or that Lifebuoy Ma made them wash all over whenever they came from the barns and had to be off somewheres later. He always hoped the soap didn't stink too much then (maybe The Ghosts can SMELL us, like those Uncle Snorri had heard about on other voyages – "all over hell and back"?). He took the deepest breath he could and let it seep out in little gasps. For the first time since Thursday noon, his fears and tears began to float away, as if to promise no return.

He studied Ma at the organ. Her haunches while she pumped away, slowly or faster, moved in time with whatever the music needed. The strains of "Now the Day is Over" filled the downstairs:

> Now the day is over,
> Night is drawing nigh,
> Shadows of the ev'ning
> Steal across the sky.

He saw Buddy leaning over her, asking for his favorite song about John Brown doing something in the grave. Sometimes the organ wheezed like Solly and Sig after chomping too much fresh grass. When Ma struck a wrong key, she'd shake her head and take up some easier Sunday School hymn she thought he liked. He could never tell her how blue they made him instead, cause they carried the smell of church. The music mixed with the steam rising around him. He hoped Ma wouldn't shift to her usual funeral songs, 'specially the spooky one about Jesus calling ("callin fer you and fer me"). Many people wanted that or "Abide With Me," which sounded sadder on the pump organ; though it didn't hang on the air so long as it did from the piano, it went away faster, before he could think of graves. Still there, Buddy's eyes darted over Ma' fingers. He wanted her to show him how to play like that himself. She promised that when winter came, she'd try to teach them both. Buddy said he'd never seen a pump organ that worked before, and Ma said that she liked hers better than the pianos anywhere (in the front room or at school and church); had enough piano-playing, she said, or funerals and other doings. The organ sounded holier (but how, Ma?). Johannes stared so hard from his tub that Buddy "vanished."

(Best-a all, we cant leave fer Eye-Away tonight, cause Buddy's 'fraid-a the dark I'm sure. Maybe if I close my eyes and think hard, like Uncle Snorri taught me, I could BE there anyway, but without going, ahhh ...).

-Jonas, you sleepy-head, been noddin all day long. Guess you dont need no more hot water. Musta soaked yerself dry by this time. She handed him his towel and wrapped another one around his shoulders: -Storm's dyin out. Jist pull the sheets over yer face and you wont hear what's left. Jesus will watch. As he always does (dont scare me with Jesus, Ma; and what's Jesus got to do with it anyway; he'd blow off like a kite in this wind. At least I know why Buddy aint here now).

Drained of his concerns, Johannes needed to be with himself alone in the peace which darkness usually lay upon him. He let Ma guide him up the backstairs after she'd wiped his back and dropped the long nightshirt over his head. The small lamp she carried lit the way, but echoes of "Abide With Me" darkened his path. He tried to jump into his bed as fast as he could and hide beneath the covers, but her arm caught him and held him back:

-Better say yer prayers, doncha think?

-Gee, why Ma?

-Dont know WHY, Jonas. Jesus would favor it, that's what.

-But WHY, huh?

-Cause … cause He'd think it proper is WHY.

He dropped to his knees. Of course he didn't hate Jesus; he loved him cause he had to (but He sure gives me the creeps; whenever Ma mentions His name, seems somebody's dead or goin to be: "Jesus is callin fer you and fer me," ohhh …). And he didn't want any part of Mrs Preacher's Woman's Jesus-talk wrapped around him neither. And it prickled him when Ma gave Jesus as excuses for everything she had no answers for. What Jesus had to do with Grampa leaving in his sleep, or with The Sheriff-Almighty running down Ol' Odin, he'd never understand. So he ended his "Now I Lay Me" with a loud "Ay-men" into the sheets and let Ma tuck him in, something he'd not permitted her to do since Buddy shared his bed.

She bent to kiss his cheek, but he began to quiver when her attention lingered on his face (what does she see? Somethin I dont know about; something bout Buddy, maybe?). When she found no fever on his brow, she lowered the lamp wick: -Gotta leave some light fer you; dont want you falling down the stairs if you git up to pee (dont need light, Ma; I hear better, see much better, in the dark; honest I do, and it more peaceful that way too).

-Sleep good, Jonas. Ma stopped at the stair rail as if waiting for something yet unsaid: -jist think, tomorrow night at this time, you'll be back in Uncle Snorri's room. Where's this year gone? Who can b'lieve that '35s soon over.

-Ma, he called after her, with a sudden urge that she remain: -think Uncle Snorri'll climb the Bluff this time like he always promises to do?

-Hush, now. Go to sleep. Some day when yer bigger, even stronger, 'fore the snakes come out, we'll hafta climb the bluff and have a look up there. Some day. Somebody said if its clear you can even …

-Yes, YES, you can see the Miss'ippi.

-Now who tole you that?

-Uncle Snorri, a-course. 'member, always says its so.

-Oh, Uncle Snorri … yes. Well, you better git yer rest if yer gonna be ready fer him tomorrow. He's got lotsa pep; will wear you out fer sure if you dont git yer sleep (why do grown-ups think us kids can sleep jist cause they tell us too, ohhh …).

He still tried to keep her back as she started down the steps: -Think he'll take us somewheres special this year too?

-Who knows. Maybe to the County Fair next week. That's where Dad met me, you know.

-And that's where there's real Indians, Buddy says.

-Johannes, I declare! You still got Indians on the brain? She grasped the rail: -What's wrong with you? You and Buddy are fine lil Norwegian boys, now that Indian stuff comes up today agin. Hope we're not raisin a heathen (but you never tole me yet: what's a hee-then, Ma?). All right Jonas, say yer prayers. That's what you should be doin.

-Already said my "Now I Lay Me."

She stopped dead: -course you did, dear. Thank Jesus again anyway.

As she hurried down, he swore he heard her mumble to herself about tomorrow being an "uff da day": with Mrs Preacher's Woman in the morning, Uncle Snorri-Bjorn at night, and Ol' Gundy in between. When he heard her shut the stairway door, he got up, blew out the lamp, and shed the nightshirt. He felt safer in the dark being naked and liked most of all the light rising from the kitchen through his grate to make patterns on his ceiling shimmer.

After a few moments, things tonight seemed different. He'd never felt alone before up there; his room had always been his hideaway, his nest, his secret place for dreams. Now his insides itched with invisible things to dread that had no names. And a spooky emptiness creeping into him. Last night, tuckered out from helping Ma with the schoolhouse, he didn't feel odd, cause he knew that Buddy'd be back today (he'd never stayed away but two nights before). Now with Saturday over and no Buddy, whatever explanations he found in the tub, he didn't know where to turn. Or where to look for him in his head, until everything spun circles and settled back on THURSDAY: hours ago before yesterday.

Last Thursday had to be the worst day he'd ever lived. The harder he tried to get it out of his head, the sharper it bounced back at him. If he couldn't tell anybody about Buddy, maybe he COULD let Uncle Snorri-Bjorn hear about Ol' Gundy (but what if he dont laugh as hard as I think he would?). None on earth could tell what Uncle Snorri might say or do (nor Buddy either).

* * *

THURSDAY MORNING, WITH DAYLIGHT seeping into his bed, Johannes shoots up out of sleep, awakened by a scream. Too dazed to know what's happened, he looked around him for a clue; it must have come from him. He scrambles into the empty space beside him, huddles against the farthest corner of the bedstead, ready to face Ma (what can I tell her when I dont know myself). When she doesn't hurry up the stairs, it perplexes him that she could miss his cry. It had shriveled every part of him. He waits, tense, his eyes widening as details of a dream begin to replay themselves, making clear what for a moment had been forgotten: he'd sneaked into the parlor for a look at Grampa in the box (as real as that time Ma wouldn't let him touch) and … and there sat Ma at the piano playing and singing "Abide With Me" with tears all over her face, and leaning against the sawhorses that held up the shiny box, Ol' Odin, black as a cyclone with his pink tongue slobbering loose, whimpered like a pup, and when Johannes inched in to see how close he could get to Grampa's face, a violent force pulled him out of himself and right up against the ceiling where he looked straight down upon the box and saw Buddy there instead. Buddy! With two deep holes where his eyes had been and a black hole for a mouth, which opened wide and quite suddenly into that scream. And the scream vibrated all around him.

When he realized then why Ma hadn't appeared, he fell apart. A good thing, though, that he hadn't made a sound for her to hear (couldn't make one if I died), but he wanted to run off and wrap himself with space and push off the coldness climbing up his legs and get as far away as he could from the tightness hugging his ribs. The echo circled round and round. He couldn't move.

From the chickenyard, a rooster woke up the dawn and set off a chain of challenges throughout the whole community. Johannes slapped at his numb knee and bit into the hem of the sheet. Morning birds began to mock the cock-a-doodle-doos. The rosier the sky became, the sweeter the summer air pushing through his window screens. And with it a weakening relief that he hadn't had to lie again to Ma. The Widow Peterson said that is you told about bad dreams, the telling made them happen. Who could he ever tell about seeing Buddy in Grampa's box like that (sure as sugar daren't breathe a word to Buddy, even if he makes me mad).

-Jonas, Ma yelled from the kitchen, -Wake up now!

He heard her snap kindling for the stove, but he didn't answer her. He dared not say a thing until that echo in him "vanished" and his ordinary self got back. Bacon sizzled on the griddle and the smell of it crept through his grate and around his room until it found his nose. The clack of the wooden spoon against a bowl of batter promised his belly a feasting to come on favorite flap-jacks (which Uncle Snorri called Ma's special pancakes). The instant Dad stomped in from the chores, Uncle Snorri's clock ding-donged six uncertain times. They sounded busy downstairs. When daylight began to slide off Walking Sorrows along the crests of the Howling Grief Ridges into the tree-tops beyond his dormer, the terror that gripped Johannes softened, and he faced the brightening windows with a funny-peculiar gnawing in his chest.

-Jonas? Aint you up yet? 'Member we gotta be gone right after breakfast. Cant keep the Olsons waitin can we now, and with all the things to do today! Jonas?

-Yeah, Ma, I'm up! He shouted, loud enough to be heard through the grille.

The moan of a mourning dove, muffled by the kitchen pines, met an answering sob from the front gate spruces. The Widow Peterson also reminded them that ghosts turned into mourning doves sometimes when they wanted reunion with each other, and maybe that's why Buddy liked to imitate them to confuse him (what if he needs my help, ohhh ...).

Johannes hit the floor with a bounce, dragging the bedclothes with him from one dormer to the other before reaching the west windows, where he rolled the shades. How could Buddy be coming from more than one direction, and why, when he didn't need to tease now; besides he always stole up the backstairs whenever he got back too early or too late.

Hoping to find clouds near or over the Point, Johannes scanned the sky, then dropped his gaze on Grampa's sugar maple. He wiped his eyes fast as the morning dream popped back at him. Sure as sin, there lay Buddy propped against the tree, and in such a position nobody could see him from either the kitchen or the back porch (what if I hadnt come to this window, I'd-a missed him for sure; whatta close call, whewww ...). Before anything else, he had to see if Buddy had holes in his face instead of his regular eyes and mouth.

He rattled one of the windows and sent a 'Psst!' through the screen. No movement, no response. His heart raced. He banged down the sash. Slowly, Buddy turned at the sound: -Shhhh, he ordered with finger against his lips, before he rolled behind the trunk. Seconds later, he poked his face out and scowled at Johannes, finger to lips again.

(Betcha Aunt Min's card's come! Musta got it yesterday; that's why he's down there 'stead-a runnin up to me, case he bumped into Ma or Dad – he's never shied from em before. That meant ... that meant they'd leave fer Eye-Away today fer sure ... but, OHHH ...).

Johannes fought a way into his overalls and when, in his excitement, he found he had them backwards, he tumbled to the floor in a fury.

-Jonas! Jonas?

-Yeah, Ma, he yelled back, getting into his clothes the right way. It came over him as he snapped his suspenders, that there'd be no time for writing letters. Maybe he could scribble something and leave it on Ma's bed after the Olsons drove away. Would that make their journey right (and what will Uncle Snorri say when I'm not here to welcome him?) ... That pesky icicle melted into his backbone and the familiar finger tickled the insides behind his belly button. He pooped like a champeen and ran down to breakfast. He took the last three steps in a leap.

-My stars, Jonas. Droppin outa the sky are you? She pointed him to the washstand: -Miss Gunderson'll be here on the milk truck soon. After you finish yer pancakes, why not start yer 'rithmetic; make her think you been studying hard.

The orders continued while she cleared the table around him: -Be sure you answer when she calls you now. Like I promised her youd do. Dont wantcha missin meals I put up fer you; somethin you'll like too. If we're late tonight, her brothers will start milkin, like before. So you got nuttin to be worryin 'bout, 'cept … bein good.

Johannes studied Ma to make sure he'd remember how she looked when he got to Eye-Away. When would he set eyes on her again and her without a notion of what lay ahead for him and Buddy. Oh, how purty she looked in her black funeral dress as she moved around getting ready to leave. No decorations on her neither, not even her fav'rit beads (the ones Uncle Snorri brought her once and she dint even know came from Indians).

And how long before he saw Dad again … and Uncle Snorri, too?

She carried steaming pancakes to his plate and waited for him to butter them: -Whatta busy time-a year to have Jesus call on Great-Gramps Olson. And him wantin to be laid in his first homestead beside his first young wife. Miles outa the County Seat too. Think of it, Jonas came to North Ameddica a lil boy on the same boat as Great-Granddad Anderegg; 'members him good with his rockin chair. Then later on, moves down the road as Grampa Anderegg's new neighbor. Now aint that somethin? So we gotta honor the wishes of the Old Ones. Anyway, graves aint far from the cabin. All them relatives and visitin and eatin, that's what takes the time.

Listening to her (for the last time, Ma?), he buried his excitement in his food so she wouldn't grow suspicious. If his face looked feverish or worried, she'd stay home and that'd spoil the day for ever-one. Tears welled up when he saw her at the washstand mirror, working with her hair.

Ma had lots of soft brown hair and when she unpinned her pug, it fell all the way to her apron strings, a reg'lar waterfall (Ol' Gundy cut her hair short, pasted spit-curls to her cheekbones beside each ear, and kept it black as a crow, which he'd heard Ma tell someone she dyed (dead hair?), and that made her face as whitewashed as the pumphouse walls; what if ghosts looked like that (huh?). Ma never powdered her face neither. It glowed by itself sometimes with such a light, Johannes hurt with love. He watched her wrap her hair around the back of her head, making the pug tight and small.

-Ooops, she said, -cant fergit a hat now, and she hurried off to her bedroom to choose a proper one.

They'd only heard about Great-Gramps Olson's funeral after Buddy went home for mail, so he knew nothing about the free time in store for them today. If Aunt Min's card hadn't come (hope it dint git here; hope it never comes), they'd have all day on the Bluff. At last. Ever since the hailstorm that cut-off Hanson's threshing, him and Buddy got to their cave twice, and each time too short for doin much of anything. Afterwards, their own threshers and summer flu and cucumbers and new chores kept them jumping every hour (if we dont leave for Eye-Away today, its time we got to be Blood-Brothers, ahhh ...). If Ol' Gundy tried to head them off, they'd drag her along and ... and (maybe) shove her right off the top into the big black bend of Squaw River. He pooped at the picture of it, then stung with horror as he did each time he remembered Ma's explanation for the limp and how she'd gotten it at his age when she came down with some spooky sickness.

Back at the washstand mirror, with a stiff round black hat set smack on the top of her head, Ma leaned into her reflection. Johannes missed being too big now to sit in her lap and trace the lines in her face, which used to make them both laugh when she'd ask if he knew where the roads on her map went, and the lines rolled down her neck and jiggled into her bosom. He watched her cock the hat from one side of her head to the other, then frown, then chuckle (grown-ups laugh at things that never seem funny-ha-ha). She turned to him, surprised, and turned serious suddenly:

-Thorwald-Jon, whatever's holdin you? Theyll be here any minit.

-Keep yer skirt on, Kari. Be right there. Want me to go with no pants on?

She replaced her hat where it sat before, stuck a long pin into the crown, and came to Johannes: -Hope we git home 'fore dark, Jonas. Aint good fer cows when strangers milk em. But the Gunderson boys, like their sister, are so helpful. She hugged him to her breast, kissed the top of his head, and went to wait on the back porch. Tears sprayed down his face.

After the Olsons drove away, Johannes held his breath until the sound of their Essex died in the pass, in case they had to come back for something.

-Hey, Buddy, he called through the kitchen screens, -come and eat now while I git my shoes. Flap-jack's in the warmer and got sorghum too, fresh from Thompson's mill. Hurry, Fore Ol' Gundy gits here.

Before he headed for the corncrib, he snatched a plug of Dad's "Day's Work" from a cupboard drawer and pocketed it. When he got back to the kitchen and found it empty, he panicked. He dashed around the house to Grampa's maple, terrified that the Buddy's he'd seen from upstairs might have been a left-over part of that dream. But the real Buddy lay against the tree as before, his face hidden. Too relieved to notice anything wrong, Johannes threw himself down, breathless:

-Got Aunt Min's card, huh?

Silence.

-Nuttin from Aunt Min fer sure?

More silence.

-No chance to let you know 'bout today. We're free. Ma's singin fer Great-Gramps Olson; Dad's helping with the box; and they wont be home till night. Johannes prattled on while he worked himself into his shoes as fast as he could, seeing that Buddy already wore his high-tops for coming through the short-cut: -If you hurry up and eat, we'll git away 'fore Ol' Gundy gits here. We'll take food Ma left fer us and find apples on the way. We'll make a picnic on the Point and nobody'll know the difference.

Only when Buddy staggered to his feet and started to limp away did Johannes notice how odd he looked, all torn and dirty too, with his face out of shape and looking fat. Johannes tugged at his shirt to hold him back:

-Ohhh, whattsa matter, huh? Why you look so ... so differnt now? In a accident? Tears boiled up but he held them in.

Buddy set off in uneven strides for the climb to the ridges, still without a word, but he moved ahead faster each time Johannes caught up to him:

-Dont tell me you slept outside last night? Whynt you come upstairs then? And still no card from Aunt Min? What's happened? Why you mad at me, huh?

With each of his questions unanswered, Johannes felt the pounding in his head race faster than his heart. Finally, he let Buddy go ahead. He had to be alone for fear his tears might break wide open at this sight of Buddy being mad (I aint tole no one bout the cave if thats what you think; honest, Buddy, honest to God, and double honest too).

By the time Johannes reached the cave, Buddy had started a small fire inside, and stood fanning it with a bough until it smoked more, but he paid Johannes no attention. With great care he bent to blow on the sparks until they flared (why, he aint even taken off his high-tops and that's his own strict rule for us bein up here!). Johannes slid carefully inside and carefully untied his laces, set the shoes carefully beside the spade at the entrance, the way Buddy had ordered them to do, and squatted ever so carefully behind the flames, careful to make no mistake to upset Buddy more. He even tried to hold his breath as long as he could.

Smoke soon filled the cave but mingled so well with the fog outside no fire would show on the face of Walking Sorrows. The smoke didn't feel so clean as the mist beyond it, mist that began to make his morning dream come back alive. Johannes couldn't hold back any longer:

-Honest, Bud ... nobody knows bout the cave. And we dont know if we'll ever have a chance like this again this year. We should celebrate.

He pulled the tobacco from his pocket and offered it to Buddy, who didn't bother to look his way. He bit off a chunk from the plug, looked crooked for a moment, then spit it out fast (Uff da! dam thing tastes like The Sheriff-Almighty looks!). He tossed it over his shoulder into the tree-tops beyond.

Hunkered near the blaze, Buddy showed few signs of being present until after a few minutes of stoney silence, he stood up without a word, unsnapped the bib and let his overalls fall to the ground. He stepped out of them bare-assed, but with his shoes still on and scooted around to Johannes. He turned his back on him and bent double (like when they took Ma's "pitcher" during bath times).

-See that? Buddy snarled, -took the horsewhip to me last night. Goddam em. Goddam em both.

Johannes, startled but relieved to hear a voice at last, tingled at the forbidden curse, then gasped: firelight traced a pattern of welts turned greenish-blue that wiggled across Buddy's ribs down to a swelling above his butt and along one leg, where a wrinkled trail of blood had dried deep brown.

-Yer MAW? Johannes choked on shock.

-Not her, but she let the Sheriff do it. Goddam em both to hell!

Johannes pooped at the repeated curse, but it brought words pouring out of Buddy's clenched jaws:

-And her all drunk and slobbery. Said I dint love her and all that stuff. Buddy gagged on a sob, but went on: -and if I dint wanna stay home more and stop bein "shamed-a her, the Sheriff'd really give it to me ... and he's one mean sonnuvabitch. I aint 'SHAMED-a her. Dont like her much is all; cant help that, but not 'shamed though.

Johannes tried to close his ears against such ugly news. To think of anybody not "liking" their maw and saying so. It ran away beyond him. He didn't even know how to think about it, not "mysterious" any more, but funny-peculiar. Unable to speak, he reached out to touch the welts, but caught his breath as Buddy straightened himself and the raw wounds on his arms, not noticed before, quivered like that dying rattler in the swamp last fall.

Buddy picked up the clothes he'd stepped out of: -If she ever pulls a stunt like that agin, the both-a them, I swear to God ... I swear

I'll … I'll run away fer good. Same day too. You betcha life. That turd-snapper's never gonna touch ME agin, ever. EVER.

Buddy croaked the last words, then slumped by the fire. He toyed with the branch and fanned the smoke away.

When Johannes found his voice, he edged closer: -Doncha see then, you can REALLY live with us fer good. Fer keeps …

-Nope.

-But honest, Buddy – Bud. It'd be okay with Ma, you know that. And Dad says yer the brother takin the place-a the one Jesus called on.

-How long you think that'd last? Maw'd keep sickin the Sheriff on me. Must be mad cause I seen what foolin round they do. Makes me wanna puke.

Johannes blushed, but didn't know why, as he repeated his offer.

-And Ol' Gundy and that Mrs Preacher's Woman jist-adying to do me good by putting me off somewheres bad.

-Wait'll Ma hears-a this. Ma wont stand nobody touchin you.

-Dont tell yer Maw; she cant do nuttin now. Aunt Min'll take me though. Said she wanted to adopt me if ever things got bad. Buddy pulled on his overalls and forced his chin out high, somehow revived by thoughts of such a possible future.

Johannes refused to listen to anything else. He jumped up scared: -Whatta bout our plan, huh? He hid his face behind a gust of smoke.

-We gotta change it, maybe?

-CHANGE IT?

-Yeah, maybe you cant go if I hafta go real quick.

-Cant go!

-If school's started, you cant go. Maybe I hafta run ahead, cant make it fast if you aint by yerself.

-But Buddy … Johannes knew better than to beg for understanding.

-Dont pester me, Gramps. Cancha see, if I hafta run first, they'll think I'm at yer place and that'll gimme a head start, cause nobody'd miss me for a coupla days. But if we CAN run away together, we'll come up here first and hide like I said. Could use a extra day or two if the Sheriff's on my – our – tail. Understand now?

Of course Johannes couldn't see that. Ever since Aunt Min came into their plans on his birthday night in June, and for all their weeks of plans, he'd never thought of THEM as "running away." Why, running away from home looked as bad as telling lies or even killing people maybe (wouldn't that bring down God's Big Lightning?). In his wildest dreams, he never imagined missing school of Sunday School neither, hard as he hated em both. But, "runnin away"? Him and Buddy'd only been planning a summertime visit, he thought, like some folks downtown took what they called "excursions (x-cer-shuns?)." Why, they'd make it to Aunt Min's and when the fuss blew over and everybody knew and nobody felt mad no more, they'd be back for school like they hadta be. Now Buddy made their plans sound wrong.

-Unnerstand what I said, Hansy? You dont say nuttin.

Buddy's ghost of a shape came at him through the smoke, and Johannes, failing to fight off his suspicions, struck Buddy's face so hard they both went down.

-Fer Chris sake, Gramps, stop actin loony, Buddy roared.

He grabbed Johannes by the front of his shirt and held him tight till his neck wobbled inside his collar: -All I want is make you promise you wont squeal … that's IF I hafta go alone … sometime … or first.

-Cant we go on top and see if the Miss'ippi shows above the fog?

-Promise? Buddy's grip tightened and Johannes made out his own face, tiny and gaping, shining back at him twice from the blackness of Buddy's eyes.

-Whatta 'bout the magic flints and the Ghost of Broken Thunderhawk. Whatta 'bout the bones of Singing White Wolf, huh?

-You still aint promised, Gramps. Buddy's face had never looked so cold: -You can even come and see me sometime if you promise not to tell a soul. That's if I hafta go first. If you dont promise, never wanta see you any more! Buddy twisted the collar; -So ... promise?

The words bounced off the walls of the cave, echoing yoyos in his mind; not only their sound ("never") but their meanings ("any more"). Johannes opened his mouth to promise but nothing came out. After trying to speak again, he simply nodded, then nodded more, and still more, until Buddy dropped him, this time gently to the ground and covered the fire with sand.

-Thats more like it, Hansy. Now I gotta git back and see if Aunt Min's card got here today. Sure cant tell what's holdin her up; shoulda been home weeks ago.

Buddy brushed his clothes in a bent-over way and headed for the ledge: -Be careful wontcha when you go home. You know the way real good and 'member yer promise. 'Member yer promise Hansy and dont git caught.

When Johannes nodded, still weak and dizzy, Buddy reminded him again not to fall off the rocks, and he went away (like a ghost?). Stranded, Johannes went blank, too bushed to stir at first. Never had he ever expected to be alone in the cave like this. First, he had to get used to such luck. Clouds had been kissing the Point since daylight so The Ghosts must be ready to move in on him. His heart sang even as a chill welled up behind his song:

And when he felt their presence, even if he couldn't tell if they had shapes or faces (or wore braids), everything would turn out right. He'd ask Singing White Wolf for a ghost song against The Winter-Lonely, and where to find his sleeping bones; he'd ask Great Chief Broken Thunderhawk if the flints still worked their magic, or if he'd turn into a juniper if one that zinged by him struck him by accident. Think of telling this to Buddy later (and what would Uncle Snorri say?).

How TERRIBLE to be alone, how AWFUL in such stillness all around him. Unafraid, he lay back and fastened his eyes on the streak of light that throbbed inside the chute. Such a ton of silence weighed him down. He rested patiently. What if nothing happened, nothing at all? He pooped softly not wanting his excitement to be too loud. He waited and waited some more (seems like days, ohhh …). Instead of The Ghosts, the smell of The Winter-Lonely came out of the walls and crawled into the campfire ashes. Overhead, Buddy's face emerged from the rock, bigger than the morning dream, his curls snarled, with black holes for eyes and mouth. And outdoors the creaking of bat wings (flyin right fer my blood, I bet). Johannes bolted upright and listened.

A shadow exploded across his face and Buddy the dream slipped into the real Buddy himself, who blackened the entrance. Without a word, he kicked through the sand, reached down for Johannes, took his hand and pulled him quietly along the ledge and down the shelves. On the slope where the high field ended, Buddy stopped, patted Johannes once on the back, and without a word limped towards his short-cut through the woods.

Johannes followed (I'll git to see the tops of the Howling Grief Ridges, and the inside of Buddy's house, ahhh …). After a few yards, Buddy turned, surprised, and motioned Johannes back. He stood his ground and Johannes didn't move. When Buddy turned to go on, Johannes followed as before (I'll save you from The Sheriff-Almighty, Buddy. I will. I will even if I hafta … hafta KILL the … the "one mean sonnuvabitch"; I'll stop him; I hafta …). His blistering determination restored some energy. After a short distance, Buddy looked back and, finding Johannes still on his track, thrust a fist at him as he ran forward shaking it (the way I used to scold Ol' Odin when he tried to follow me down Township Road to school). When Johannes stopped, but refused to turn for home, Buddy began walking backwards, and Johannes, stilled by the message he read at last, stood numb as Buddy grew smaller and "vanished," no bigger than a tick, into the brush.

Long after shadows had eaten Buddy, Johannes remained barefooted in a patch of sandburrs that didn't even hurt yet while he continued to stare at the spot where Buddy'd been (maybe he's jist teasin me some more and he'll come runnin back fer sure).

-Johannes. Where are you, Johannes? Time to eat. Ol' Gundy's call became a shriek through Ma's megaphone. It took away his appetite for any of the specials Ma had left.

Undiscovered on the lower edge of the high field, Johannes watched her cross Township Road to the farmyards. She tripped along on her high heels to the side of the cow barn and stopped to call again. He ducked and saw her step out of her purple shoes, snap their straps together and hang them around her neck, all the while making sounds he barely heard. She paused at the base of the silo to fill her arms with the tiger lilies mingled there with flowering weeds, and she screeched back at the bluejays that darted and swooped in circles around her (does it hurt to be so loony? does it hurt to limp like that?). His dash of tenderness got swallowed in the siren blast of his name again sent forth:

-Johannes Berg! You hear me now? If you don't answer, I'll … I'll have to flush you out of your tree house by myself.

(How does she know 'bout the tree house, huh? Betcha Ma tole her, or Uncle Snorri-Bjorn? And jist think, we aint done nuttin on it since last year and Ma dont know that yet.).

He slumped behind a clump of birch, eyes not daring to stray.

She carried the lilies, her pocketbook and the dangling shoes back to the house. Before he could rush down the orchard and garden to the backstairs stoop (she'll never think-a lookin fer me in my room), she stepped back into his view, still in stockingfeet, and headed towards the corn crib, her head and voice rotating like an owl almost. He hoped she'd step on sandburrs (betcha that would make her squeal all the way to hell and back).

When she caught sight of Solly and Sig coming around the kitchen nook, she started to move backwards (like Buddy's done), trying to shoo them off, and the more she hurried, the faster they clopped on as they sniffed the air and whinnied. She swung about-face and ran for the backhouse, where she locked herself inside. The puzzled horses stopped in the shade of the lilacs and glanced at each other, but (like jailers, huh) didn't go on.

Johannes buried his face against the tender birch bark and laughed so hard he pooped into a fart. He loved Solly and Sig more than ever and they didn't even know how much they'd helped him shed Ol' Gundy. On the way to the back stoop, his laughter turned to sudden sobs when he remembered how Buddy looked, bending over in the cave, and how he limped away into the leaves. The idea that anybody on earth could hurt him at all didn't seem real (who could ever HATE Buddy like that and make him run away, maybe ...). Tears streamed from all the way to his room, where nobody would ever know how hard he'd cried.

Last Thursday had to be the worst day he'd ever lived. Would he ever fergit it? With Ol' Gundy actin so funny-peculiar and dear Solly and Sig so funny-ha-ha, too? None of this made sense a-tall as his sorrow welled and spread.

*   *   *

RELIEVED THAT THE EVERLASTING Saturday had come to an end, Johannes tried to erase all thoughts of Thursday. He lay and listened to the silence until Uncle Snorri's clock broke in. He counted off eleven strokes (there'd been only nine jist a few minits ago; I musta slept). The storm had blown itself away but after the chimes, the earlier emptiness sneaked back into his room like something unknown waiting to declare itself, he thought: maybe this is the time for The Ghosts to come out since they don't seem to be around in daylight, or maybe they won't come for another hour. He liked the notion of "midnight," a ghostly word that lightning or the moon when they lit his room couldn't brighten away. He sighed and listened. Maybe the promise of a ghost song if not the song itself yet. He heard his heart against his ribs instead.

Flash!

A beacon shot along the pine boughs beyond the south dormer, made a loop of itself, then slid across his sheets. A car out of nowhere skidded to the back steps, sounding like it rammed Dad's truck.

Johannes jumped from his bed and, unable to see anything from his windows, threw himself beside the grate. He saw nothing there either, but he heard Dad and Ma stumble into each other on their way to the pounding on the kitchen door.

Then voices.

One of them reminded him of how Buddy's Maw had looked that picnic day. Another growled: -Is Buddy Trygrud here?

The presence of The Sheriff-Almighty burst upon Johannes as real as if he stood at the foot of his bed: thin as the flagpole at school with a watermelon belly hanging over his rattlesnake belt, and the skin on his bald head covered with musk melon bumps and those stoney eyes daring Johannes to breathe. His voice sliced into the night.

Johannes rushed to the rail at the top of his stairs, ready to race down when he heard Ma speak loud and clear: -Like I said already Sheriff Strutt, he aint here.

-You musta seem him somewheres. The woman's voice this time, dripping tears.

-Not since Tuesday, Hester. Stayed over like he does and the next noon, Wednesday noon yes, thats the last I seen him. Tell you the truth, said he hadda hurry home to help you and git set fer school too.

-If he shows up, Thor, gimme a call. Gotta keep a eye on the County Line till morning, but I'll be back and forth at the hotel.

The voice took off in another direction which Johannes felt nobody else should have heard: -whatta I tell you bout chasin that worthless kid all over hell and back, when you only s'posed you knew where he'd be at. And I s'posed to keep on look-out fer them Ioway jailbirds too.

-Wait a minit, Sheriff Strutt, Ma called after him, -jist thoughta something; be right back.

When Johannes heard Ma open his stairway door, he couldn't move. Instead, he tightened an arm around the rail and hung on till she ran into him in the dark:

-Stars in heaven, Johannes Berg! Whatcha doing up this hour? Naked as all git-out too. Wanna walk home dead from chills now? She pushed him ahead of her to his bed: -Or couldnt you find the pot. First, git under the covers. Now tell me when YOU seen Buddy last.

She didn't scold him for blowing out the lamp or for shedding his nightshirt, but, fighting his resistance to be tucked in, she bundled the sheets around him tight.

-Did he act kinda funny-peculiar when you seen him Tuesday night? Or Wednesday in the morning? Like he had secrets? Like somethin wrong? 'Member what he said?

Not expecting answers, she patted his bare shoulders and sat on the edge of his bed, pinning him fast. Her warm hand touched his forehead as it always did when she sounded too quiet to be normal. He felt her eyes digging at him in the dark:

-He dint come by on Thursday did he, with me and Dad away? No, guess not. Miss Gunderson dint mention him a-tall when we got home. So late (oh, Ma, stop askin me bout Thursday or I'll hafta tell more lies, and lies are so much trouble, Ma).

Talking more to herself than to him, she pressed a firm hand on his legs to calm him. -Know fer sure he dint come by yesterday with us cleanin school till dark. Her voice began to lose its patience and he wondered what she'd do if she knew what happened every time she held him down like this: why, he jist left his scrawny body behind and went to the Bluff to wait.

-You hear me, Jonas? ANYTHIN you recall? You see, the Sheriff's downstairs with Buddy's Maw – Mother, and theyre trying hard to find him. Dunno where to look. Seen him last they said on Wednesday night sometime. 'Fraid he mighta run away and in this awful storm too.

If all the enemies of Singing White Wolf stood around his bed with killer flints, Johannes couldn't have opened his mouth; he couldn't even say his name now if he had to. Ma's words raked through his alarms, churning them over fresh inside of him like night crawlers

174

brought out after a rain. He stretched as far as he could and kicked the bedclothes loose, forcing her to stand (cant tell no Sheriff nuttin, but how long did it take to go down to Eye-Away with the cricks runnin over and the sloughs fulla mud?).

Johannes stared where the shape of Ma in her tattered robe looked more solid in the dark than any ghost could be. With tiny breaths he waited until she went away. Where she paused against the rail before going down, Buddy now leaned towards him with a scowl. Sand clung to his legs and cheeks and the dried-up welts on his sides and back slipped in and out of the reflections of fire which filled Johannes and revived his fears (see Buddy, I dint tell a thing, did I? And now you got a long head start like you said you needed if … hear me, Buddy, dont go … dont go yet).

In spite of fighting to keep it out of mind, Thursday's memory of sandburns left him stunned again; that Buddy would WANT to take off without him, even if what he said in the cave made sense … then. Now that the first had happened, pain came back in places he couldn't rub away cause he didn't know where to begin when it hurt everywhere else so much.

He no longer strained to hear the voices raised downstairs, nor cared when the car-with-the-star sped off. It took some time to realize that in all the commotion and pressure from Ma, he hadn't broken his promise to Buddy. Pride in his behavior brought little comfort, but it forced whispers of The Winter-Lonely back into the walls. (And to think that by the time they give up lookin fer him, Buddy'll be down the River with Aunt Min and nobody'll fuss any more maybe. THEN I'll go there and bring him home fer sure. Oh, Buddy, guess I did know this when you dint show today, but couldn't b'lieve, dint dare even think, that anything like this would happen … ever.)

Johannes shut his eyes, pretending to sleep, in case Dad came up to try to talk things out of him where Ma had failed. Though Dad had to be a million times stronger than her, Ma behaved in more secret powerful ways (Uncle Snorri explained once). When Dad didn't appear, he wiped the sand from his eyes and drifted off, floating down Squaw River on a log with Great Chief Broken Thunderhawk riding beside him (oh, fer sure, hafta go down the rivers now to bring my Buddy back; and I wont stop near no bridges neither ... if maybe trolls are real).

Without a rumble of warning, thunder ploughed into the house and lifted Johannes out of sleep. Renewing Ma's yearly worries about Time and the weather, the earlier evening storm had indeed turned back on itself (to pester her fer her perdictions, huh?). And it came without mercy.

Johannes couldn't remember if his room had ever danced like this before (or so it seems), nor how one thunderous outburst on another rolled into a continuous roar that lasted without spaces in between (sure seems so), and God's Big Lightning blinding him blue when he tried to find things in his room he hadn't seen before. He needed to pee, thunder rattled the cover on the pot (I'm sure). He pooped with strained anxiety instead, for branches scraping the north dormer threatened to smash in and pull him apart (ahhh ... aint it awful, aint it terrible, and not ways to tell this in words). He climbed behind his pillows, holding them in front of him as shields against the wonderment of God's Big Lightning, which recharged itself without a pause (or so it seems) and flashed white-hot throughout the room and left reflections multiplied behind his eyes. The Indian on the feed-store calendar stepped lightly off the wall, and in each renewing flash, a dozen Big Chiefs marched to his bed, each bearing a Singing White Wolf on outstretched arms, but never showing faces. And then the world went black ... (Oh, Buddy, what a "helluva" storm yer missin; gotta be the best one ever, right outa Great Granddad's Bible with God splitten open the sky).

Somewhere out of the rafters, Ma's left-over voice in the left-over words sifted down: -"fraid he mighta run away and in this awful storm too." And in THIS awful storm now with God's Big Lightning lose ready to stroke somethin dead. A dullness filled his heart, the kind he remembered from the graveyard after a body'd been put under. Dead! Dead? What's "dead"? ("dead's only a word, Buddy; only a word. But how long DID it take to go down the rivers with the cricks runnin over and covered in green scum and the sloughs fulla snakes, which you hate so?).

It thundered with the sound of a pile of logs rolling apart and lightning answered. Johannes opened his eyes wide to force the sight of "dead" from his brain where its disconnected letters skittered around like mice in his bedroom walls. Anyway, only old people died and too-many kittens when they had to be drown-ed and soldier uncles of course and people with sickness or when Jesus called kids right out of school sometimes if they got scarlet fever or somethin worse. But God's Big Lightning spared no favorites, Uncle Snorri said. Yet The Widow Peterson reminded them in Sunday School that nobody died if you loved them strong and solid (so that made Buddy safe, ahhh …).

The next explosion brought Johannes to his knees and wiped out his ears. And through the west windows, right before his eyes, a flaming spear split Grampa's sugar maple tree clean down the middle; each side lurched into the air, then settled side by side across the backyard fence. Gramma's apple tree from Norway looked on, bend double. The stink of sulpher filled the air (or so it seems, ohhh …).

-MOMMY!

-On my way, Jonas, Ma called from his stairs, -dont be a-scared. We're gonna be all right.

Before she reached his side, in the hours it took for her to get there, he shouted at her above the tinkling window panes: -Buddy's run away Ma! Buddy's run … (Uff da!).

-Dont worry, sweetheart; storm's passin on hard's it can, not like at supper, or we'd go to the cellar. What … what'd you say now, Jonas?

She loomed over him taller than Dad or Uncle Snorri-Bjorn: -Did my ears hear right? Tell me what you said before, child.

The winds slowed down to give him a hearing, but his tongue filled all of his mouth and started down his throat.

-C'mon, Ma prodded.

-He ... he ... he's run ... AWAY (and in that awful storm too and in this ...).

-Jonas, dont be so mixed up. See how fast the storm's a-movin. Tell Ma how you found out what you jist said.

As she sank beside him in the darkness, the storm sounded farther away. After the Fourth-of-July commotion of the past minutes (must be hours), the house became quiet too suddenly, unreal, as if it and his bed waited for him to give up the rest of his secret; even the flapping windowshades stopped to listen.

-Tell me how you know all this 'bout Buddy.

Unable to escape by holding his tongue, he tried to pick the safest words: -He TOLE me. And that's all I know.

-You mean he's run off agin? Gone to see his ... his Aunt Min maybe? Blessed Jesus (Oh, dont say "Jesus," Ma!).

Johannes nodded once, then crumbled. His words had turned to a wad of oatmeal stuck in his throat. He coughed and quivered.

-I see, Ma whispered, but asked nothing more. She waited for his shaking to stop, for breathing to slow, but her voice to herself, and later, sounded miles away. He closed his eyes and pretended to sleep, but behind his lids, his ears trailed her to the phone. He covered his head. No use. The windowshades began to flap again, but couldn't snuff out Ma's news as it rode the wires over Township Pass into The Sheriff's hairy ears downtown.

("Promise, Gramps, promise? If you dont promise, I NEVER wants ..."). -Oh Buddy! Johannes wailed to himself, -lemme be, lemme be (you one mean sonnuvabitch, OHHH ...).

He curled into a ball. He didn't want to hear or see anything, nor fight with Buddy's presence for space and air. He'd broken his promise; could do nothing about that. And Ma'd already used the phone. Wouldn't Buddy see he'd only tried to save him: not giving up to The Sheriff-Almighty, but sparing him God's Big Lightning, that's if he hadn't got to Aunt Min's yet. (When Buddy hears this from me, face to face, wont bein a "squealer" now be as forgotten as my bein "lazy" all summer at the cave? Wont it, Buddy, huh?). He wouldn't let The Winter-Lonely play hop-scotch in his head anymore and he'd KILL The Sheriff-Almighty if he had to (ohhh ...), but nobody, nobody, could fool around with God's Big Lightning. His confusion soaked up shame. Then, a small glow in the dark: Yes, YES, to be sure. He hadn't said a thing about their cave.

Beyond all else, THAT Buddy had to know. But how? Another letter, uff da! But different from the ones for Ma and Uncle Snorri. If he let Buddy know their cave remained a secret, his broken promise wouldn't matter then (would it?), and he'd let him know that Dad would save him from The Sheriff-Almighty, and when he hears what I did to Ol' Gundy Thursday noon, he'll maybe even hug me. But how to tell all this on paper ...

Wider awake than before with this and another solution, he left his bed, grabbed the home-made candle in its fruit jar on the dresser, and scurried down the main upstairs hall to Uncle Snorri's room, open now and aired.

He set the candle on the window sill. While he worked on a new letter in his head, he'd signal same as Paul Revere done in that poem, case Buddy dint git to Aunt Min's yet and still hid somewhere near (ahhh ...). Jist think, doin two things at the same time, but then he saw that he'd forgotten matches and he sure couldn't fetch none from downstairs with all them open doors. He slapped himself. But he'd do his best to watch and stay alert.

Uncle Snorri's front window looked up Township Road to where the pass began and it ran two miles down hill afterwards, right past Buddy's house. When Buddy came here late, he used the road, even in moonlight (too hard to follow the short-cut by night, he said, but thats cause yer scared-a the dark I know).

On his knees, Johannes leaned against the hump-back lid on the mermaid chest and peered through the glass. What if Buddy needed to come back for something (maybe even come back fer me, ahhh ...). Goose pimples covered him.

Now that The Sheriff-Almighty knew he'd run away, Johannes had to warn Buddy that Dad would form a posse with the Sheriff as soon as daylight broke. He pressed his face against a pane until his eyes adjusted to the dark. Once, several deer scampered across his vision into the windbreak which hid the barns. If Buddy took shape, Johannes would climb onto the upstairs porch and whistle him around to the backstairs stoop (though we'd hafta hide with Solly and Sig till Ma straightened my bed in the mornin). For now, he could only keep awake and alert (like The Sheriff-Almighty watched at the County Line, huh?).

He felt more secure with the smell of Uncle Snorri-Bjorn in this room. No Buddy yet (or at all, I hope), nor The Ghosts, not even a sigh from The Winter-Lonely. The thumping in his ears came from his chest, its rhythm reminding him of the way summer Holsteins swayed down their pasture lane, their bags about to bust with milk.

Without light, he couldn't write Buddy's letter, but he'd make it in his head and put it on paper in the backhouse, now that he didn't have to write to Ma or Uncle Snorri. He'd tell everything so good Buddy'd never be mad at him again.

Then a problem crept in: how to send the letter. Would he get it if he wrote: TO Buddy Trigger, Aunt Min's House, Dee-bjuke, Eye-Away? Maybe a P.S.: house sits on the River bank. And what about a stamp? Would the mailman leave it if he put it in the mailbox with the red flag up, but without a stamp? Maybe there'd be a loose one in Ma's letterbox, like the one he found when Buddy wrote Aunt Min about The Sheriff-Almighty.

Tuckered out from so much fiddling in his head, a tiny smile hesitated on his lips before it burst into the widest grin. What will Buddy say when hears what I did Thursday noon: How he, Johannes (yes!), put a dead jay in Ol' Gundy's purple pocketbook ... how he hung her purple high heels from the peak of the corncrib roof ... and ahhh yes, how while she fretted in the backhouse with Solly and Sig on guard outside, he sneaked around the woodshed, crawled underneath the horses, and flipped the outer latch that locked her tight inside and there she had to stay till the folks got home that night. Late. All the tom cats in twenty coulees couldn't have raised such a racket (SEE, Bud Trigger, I showed you dint I. Now whose a champeen, huh? I aint a baby no more AND I dint tell about yer – OUR – cave at all). His face lit up at the thought of Buddy's glee, at the laughter in his eyes when he crossed them silly (maybe he'll hug me fer sure).

He wouldn't tell Buddy what puzzled him the most: when the folks came late and Johannes pretended to be asleep up in his room, Ol' Gundy didn't tattle. She tried to laugh off what she called a "funny accident" when one of the horses rubbed its nose against the backhouse latch and trapped her in. Then through the grille in the floor, Johannes heard Ma say that neither Solly nor Sig would do such a nasty thing.

TWO

Sudden Sunday

For a long time, half-asleep Johannes listened to roosters bring on the day. Without opening his eyes, he let the sun nibble on his ear, before the crease in his cheek began to smart from his lying so long against the mermaid chest. He didn't remember when he left his room; during the night sometime, but that didn't matter now. Uncle Snorri-Bjorn filled the space around him and made it easier to mourn for Buddy's taking off alone.

Each time he heard the phone downstairs, it came to him from far away, muffled, and no longer filled him with dread or curiosity, just as the sounds of Ma at work barely reached his ears. Buddy's disappearance remained less real if he kept his eyes shut; he hoped that would hold Ma off as well or send her on to Sunday School without him (imagine such a funny-peculiar thing!). If he lay still like this, maybe he'd find a way to make sentences of his befuddled thoughts for that unwritten letter to Buddy. He tried to wipe everything else out of his head (like erasing the blackboard at school), but he strained too hard to think straight (ohh …). He couldn't even return to the refuge of sleep. And the morning growing "mysterious" …

Johannes opened one eye, then the other, but closed each fast against the brightness, then repeated the routine, one eye at a time, and both shut together fast, before he settled for a squint. The outdoors glistened (had Ma been up all night varnishing the world with the left-over cleaning stuff from Friday?). He jerked his head back and gasped:

Between the window sill and the black Norwegian spruces puddles of sky pock-marked the whole front yard. Across Township Road in the windbreak, familiar old-timers lay toppled and uprooted in crazy positions the way kindling fell when he dropped it in a hurry in the woodbox. The sight of Grampa's maple being split flashed across his eyes. He pinched his leg and hoped he woke up from such dream scenes as these.

-So, here you are. Ma stood in the bedroom door with his nightshirt in hand: -See you cant even wait fer Uncle Snorri but you must have a stiff neck, sleepin all cramped up like that. You gave me a flutter when I found yer empty bed and yer empty nightie too. Thought some troll'd reached through the roof and hustled you away.

When she crossed the room, he buried his face in her arms, and braced himself to be scolded for sleeping bare-assed, and draped over Uncle Snorri's trunk to boot.

-Worst storm we ever had, Ma said instead: -We been spared, Jonas, 'cept for them trees out there and Grampa's sugar maple. Looked out this morning and had to cry when I saw it split down the middle like a butchered hog. No more syrup from now on we know.

She dropped the nightshirt over his head and leaned into the window for a closer inspection: -Aren't we lucky. Sheriff says everything's flooded from the flats to Minnesota. Dint you hear Central's early call? Six rings to warn us that the bridge is gone; jist floated off (would any troll there get drown-ed then?). Think-a that. Sheriff said he 'most got left on the other side. Now the church and schoolhouse are sittin in a lake (ready to float off, too, maybe?). No Sunday School today fer sure. Maybe no school neither fer a week or more. Uff da, we'll hafta clean it all over agin. Cant b'lieve the storm came back so fast I hardly heard you call. Thanks God, it went on jist as fast.

From inside the nightshirt tent, he listened to her seriousness and hoped she wouldn't ask more at last night (wouldn't seem like it had happened then).

-Sheriff Strutt says most our Anderegg roads been spared all the way to Town, 'cept fer some trees down and some fallen rocks, easy to git around. A marvel the phone aint dead; that's usually the first thing to go. Sure no tellin how storms behave; this one bad as any cyclone.

He pushed his head out of the nightshirt and met her smile as she turned from the window: -'fraid Uncle Snorri'll be hung up. Called early from La Crosse to say his train got there on time. Dint know 'bout the roads up here. Says he's startin out anyway, soon's his run-about's gassed up. Says he 'members lotsa back ways. That's yer Uncle Snorri fer you.

She examined his face and mussed his hair, then opened the windows to let the morning in: -You aint said nutting, Jonas. Feel all right? Up half the night and naked as all git-out too. She led him back to his room and started to make his bed to keep him from crawling back into it: -Git dressed now and have yer breakfast with me. Dad ate hours ago, but I'm waitin fer you; wanted you to sleep late today. And while I waited to hear some sound-a life up here, frosted Uncle Snorri's cake and saved the bowl fer you to lick. But breakfast first. Put on yer second-best today, she called from the stairs: -dont know who'll be comin by. Miss Gunderson, a-course; sure to be some Townfolk snoopin fer some damage. Maybe even Uncle Snorri.

Who can tell. Ooops, guess what else I did? Finished embroiderin Buddy's shirt and you snoozing in the other end-a the house. Hope you like it; will make yers a different color if you want ... And her words faded in the stairway.

It stirred him to be treated like a grown-up and be asked to eat with her alone like that, but he couldn't understand her unworried quietness about the news he'd dropped last night. He hurried into his clothes and ran down to the washstand. He tried to avoid the window there; if he didn't see Grampa's tree split like that, he could pretend it hadn't happened, but if he looked real fast he'd maybe see the schoolhouse floating off to join the church (ahhh ...).

-Know what, Ma said, handing him a fresh towel (and not a word 'bout clippin and washin my hair), -winds knocked over the toilet too. Dad's got it right-side up agin, but you should see ... that Sears Rowbock catlog's all over this side-a creation, pages hangin in the trees. Whatta sight. And company comin too (wisht Ol' Gundy'd been inside, her and them limpin shoes).

Blushing from such naughty thoughts, Johannes settled into Dad's armchair across from Ma. He tried to sit as proper as he'd seen grown-up visitors do. While his waffle baked in the iron on the stove, Ma brought the bottle of iodine and dripped a drop into his glass, as she did every morning (keeps goiters off, she assured him; sure dont wanna end up like Mrs Kittleson with an extra chin as thick as the bull's and as wobbly too). He waited for her to ask more about Buddy and dreaded the idea. Buddy, too special to talk about till he got his letter down, now had a good head start and nobody could find or stop him (not even storms, and he's far ahead of any posse). It soothed his spirit some more at the thought of not squealing about their cave, even if his spirit hadn't time yet to figure anything else. When Ma mentioned Buddy, he'd only repeat what he'd already said, then ask about Uncle Snorri's plans instead (maybe I can git HIM to take me to Eye-Away to bring Buddy home, ahhh …).

Ma set a dish of his favorite blueberry sauce beside the steaming round waffle she forked onto his plate, and sat down. Still uneasy as to what she might say next, he glanced past her through the screendoor to the porch. His knee struck a table leg and he knocked over his glass of buttermilk. He almost croaked. The white star on The Sheriff-Almighty's car blinked at him from the restless shade of the pines.

-Jonas, dear, whatcha so jumpy fer? Cut worms in yer pants again? She turned to see what troubled him: -oh, that! The Sheriff's out with Dad and the neighbor men. After they raised the toilet, they've been combin the fields and woods for Buddy, case he got tired or hurt now we know he's run away. Dont know how far anybody'd git going west though. Ma chattered on while cleaning away the mess he'd made: -Men think he might be hidin some place close; jist to rile em. You ask me, I say he's already to where he headed. The time before they found him in Dee-bjuke, said he'd been gone from the County Seat only three days.

(Thursday morning, Friday and Saturday all day, and now, Sunday in the morning agin ... he's gotta be there by now. But Ma, how long does it take to go down the rivers with the cricks runnin over and the sloughs ...)

Johannes looked up and out in the pine shade saw Buddy beside the car-with-the-star, grappling with The Sheriff-Almighty, cussing him out, kicking him in the balls, before he broke free and raced down the slope and across the road for the barns, and, unable to scream, Johannes saw the Sheriff reach for the rifle he kept inside his car and point it after Buddy and he fired it again and again and again with empty shells jumping out like popcorn and the lead passed right through Buddy who wouldn't drop like a pheasant but ran on faster and faster around the barnyards with big holes clear through him but with no blood a-squirting. Johannes had to save Buddy from more bullets but he couldn't move any more than that drugstore Indian could. He finally blinked away the horror.

-Whatsa matter with you, Jonas? Ma's voice still made everything sound ordinary: -You gotta eat. Made them waffles jist fer you and me, and yesterday Dad brought the wheaties only fer you. She poured sorghum on her plate and passed the jug: -Tole Mr Olson to pick up Buddy's Maw – Mother – and bring her here to rest, after he's picked up the other ladies who wanna help me feed the menfolks. When I'm through eatin now, gotta finish housework, but if you eat yer breakfast you dont hafta dust fer me this time.

He separated the waffle into its wedges and nibbled on one quietly, waiting for her to leave him. Before she hauled out dust pan and dusters, she set a cup of cocoa beside the untouched cereal in his Shirley Temple bowl: -Now there's nuttin to worry for, Jonas. Buddy's safe. Besides, Jesus will watch (dont scare me with Jesus, Ma, when I got The Sheriff-Almighty on my hands too!).

When Ma moved to the front of the house, Johannes gripped the edge of the table, hoisted himself out of Dad's chair, and ran to his room. He threw up his breakfast in the thunder-mug, dropped the cover on it, and fell back on the floor beneath his gable windows before Ma reached him to find out what he'd done.

She came with his writing tablet: -That's right, Jonas, take a nap; dint sleep much last night I s'pose. Nap as long as you can and you'll be rested for Uncle Snorri, case he comes. Otherwise, you can work on sentences up here where its quiet.

He loved her so much that it hurt when she smiled on him with her warm eyes smiling, too. Ol' Gundy and Mrs Preacher's Woman never smiled with their eyes and their mouth at the same time, and their eyes chilly as fish. Ma looked around the room, sniffed the air, then backed away and left.

The letter begun in his head for Buddy had disappeared. He lifted himself and opened the tablet. Each time words almost returned, he'd glance down on Grampa's butchered maple and his mind blanked out, or if he looked over at Gramma's apple tree, he saw Buddy there as he looked Thursday morning. He turned off his memory as much as he could and shifted to the north dormer. He rested his arms on his desk and waited for Buddy's letter to write itself. Each time he heard Ma on the stairs, he pretended to doze, or if she surprised him, he got busy with the pencil on his open tablet. That kept her from speaking and he didn't have to make new lies. Most of the time alone, he searched through the tree-tops for the Bluff. Sometimes, frolicking squirrels fell from the branches, but after hitting the ground, if they did, they'd shimmy in circles before scampering up another trunk (did The Ghosts really visit with such critters and what would they say, huh?).

Morning crept along being always NOW. He didn't listen for Uncle Snorri's clock, nor when the men came in for coffee or for news exchanged. When Ma brought him down for the noontime meal, nobody said a word about Buddy (fer my sake I know). Instead, they ate like threshers from the neighbor ladies' hot dishes and Ma's platters of roasted roosters. When they talked at all, it had to do with storm damage or recollections of other blows, or they laughed too loud at Norwegian jokes he didn't understand, before spreading out in every direction again, even to the flooded flats.

By half-past one, the front room boiled with gossip. When Johannes, wandering around downstairs after eating, saw Ol' Gundy's brothers leave her at the back porch, he tried to hide but bumped into her where she came upon Ma grinding coffee beans in the pantry.

She burst into loud snuffles when Ma told her they still had no signs, no news: -whatever's happened to that poor, poor boy (she cant or wont say Buddy's name)? Do you suppose he'll get here for supper ... the boy I mean? She crinkled her face and wadded her hankie. Not wanting the others to see Ol' Gundy undone like that, Ma directed her up the backstairs and told her to find a bed in one of the spare rooms and to rest there till Ma called.

Back in the front room, the ladies cackled over Uncle Snorri-Bjorn as they always did before and after his visits. He'd heard Dad tell Ma: "Gotta give the wimmens a chance to peck at Snorri before they go a-flutter like setting hens" ... (guess Ma musta hinted that he might be home fer supper). Johannes chuckled when the car driving in turned out to be not the sky-blue runabout they waited for, but someone else:

Mouth agape, Johannes saw Buddy's Maw jump out of Olson's Essex before it braked. She headed for several men she saw out on the slopes to the Bluff, but Ma hurried past him to catch Hester Trygrud and guide her back to the house (how "mysterious"). When they passed him on the back porch, he noticed that Buddy's Maw wore the same dress she had on for the school picnic, the one with birds flying all over when she moved. He trailed them, trying to see how her face looked today under the cotton-candy hair. Ma stopped him at the dining room door and motioned him back:

-Now Johannes, you cant be hanging indoors on sucha nice day. Know what you do? Mrs Hanson wants some dahlias. Whynt you see if any' left standin, and cut her some real nice ones now. She thrust cutters into his hands: -After findin Buddy, we'll celebrate with a picnic ... supper. How's that sound?

He looked at her with an empty face (but how they gonna do that, huh? when you said yerself he's already got where he headed ... unless them storms maybe slowed him down), but she hurried back into the birdsong that filled the front of the house. Anyway, the longer people fooled around the community, the more time for Buddy's trip (even if it aint our vacation visit). And he believed he had saved Buddy by keeping his mouth shut ... almost.

Alive, but less dangerous now, The Sheriff's car-with-the-star snoozed under the pines, its reflections no longer spraying him with terror. Johannes edged towards it with a shudder. Which front wheel had done Ol' Odin in? Revulsion flared for an instant, and he brushed away the whiff of The Winter-Lonely. He moved around to the right front fender, inspected it, then kicked at the tire underneath. The force of the blow knocked the shearers from his hand, but he left no mark on the rubber. Furious, he backed away and struck with greater force. The wheel had turned to concrete and it put such a painful dent in his school shoes it pinched his toes inside (if I had my barnshoes on, I'd show what a kick is like!).

BARNSHOES!

He's completely forgotten that she'd asked about em last night, what with the storms and everything else. But what could he do? She'd find out fer sure where he'd really left them by her way of bringin em up. He saw em clearly, right inside the cave, beside the spade. Right where he'd placed em ever so carefully Thursday morning; ever so carefully so as not to rile Buddy more. His knees weakened and he prickled hot all over, but he wouldn't rest against the car. He forced himself to stand straight and stiff, as he surveyed the Bluff.

Walking Sorrows loomed cornbread yellow against the faded sky. A wispy cloud hovered over the Point. Rattler weather, Dad called this, when snakes came out to dry in warm shade one last time before slithering away for winter. That didn't bother him. But he hesitated to move when he studied the heights until he convinced himself he knew the way even if he hadn't gone the distance himself. He thought of the reward he'd find when The Ghost of Broken Thunderhawk showed himself without a noisy Buddy trying to scare him off (The Ghosts must know how scared Buddy really is). He pooped. Think of writing about that to Buddy too (and think-a Uncle Snorri's face when told, ahhh …).

Zinging arrows whizzed around him when he picked up the cutters and backed away from the-car-with-the-stars. He worked his way around the house to the summer kitchen foundation and into the garden where Ma expected him to be. There, everything lay flat. Where once between every two or three rows of vegetables a row of flowers brightened the patch, not a single flower stood (and all the work I done there not knowing real plants from weeds with purty blooms, ohhh …). Too baffled to dwell on the scene, he hurried on to the orchard. There broken limbs had scattered apples in all directions. In disbelief, he dropped the shearers beside a mound of rotting fruit which Dad left every fall for the deer to nibble ("no sight like that of a drunken buck staggering away on three legs," Uncle Snorri once told his listeners). Around a toppled fence post, wild blue gentians wrestled with purple asters in a tangled mess. Johannes almost forgot his goal.

He raced free through the brush, slipping and tumbling up to the high field, that last safe slope before the hard climb began over the rocky shelves to the wrap-around ledge high above. Rows of corn stalks lay on their sides, ground into the muck. He stopped to catch his breath (had giant trolls marched over everthing with lefse rolling pins?). With Ma's echo about the shoes running circles in his head, his pounding heart pushed him on. At first, he refused to look behind him. Ahead, crowns of oaks and fan-shaped elms, with up-turned roots of hickories, plastered against the slopes between the benches, made such a jumble he worried that he'd lose their path. Soggy pits of sand caught between rocks squirmed like pudding when he stepped near. On hands and knees he scrambled around splintered scrub. Nothing looked the way it should; had he gone wrong?

When he looked back on Dad's silo (a million feet below fer sure), it stood where it always had, at the same angle from which him and

Buddy could draw a line in the air to the flag pole in the schoolyard (must be a hunnert miles to it out there), and when that stood right behind them way down there, a torn hankie tied to a juniper marked the only place where they could make their final climb. What seemed to take hours, and not expecting to find it, he came upon the marker; it drooped, too sodden to signal in the breeze. Way down there behind him, the flag pole seemed to lean a bit as if looking at its reflection in the flooded waters all around it. Whewww! At least he'd found the right way, however unreal the whole world looked.

The more he struggled to move faster, his need to stop increased; not from the lack of energy, but his spirit nagged at him for coming this far by himself. Without Buddy, it felt like cheating. Yet, each time the urge to turn back tempted him, Ma's reminder pushed him on. On a shelf just below the high ledge, he belly-flopped, winded, onto a patch of grass. Drenched in sweat, the bug-bites and scratches on his face and neck and arms stung worse than bees, but he wouldn't let that distract him from the wonder of where he lay. In his panic over his shoes, he'd left no time to prepare for The Ghosts and that sure dint seem right neither, 'specially when this might be his only chance to be alone like this. He rolled over on his back, ready to receive and greet, he hoped, as overhead kissing clouds rode low.

An unbearable silence settled over all, even stopping the breeze (maybe The Ghosts dont like the sun; maybe theyre sick-a being kissed by clouds all-a time). He sat up and hugged his chest. From the corner of his eye he inspected the matted grass around him. He shook the echo of a timber-rattler from his mind, but when The Winter-Lonely slid along instead and blew on his neck, he jumped up and forced himself ahead. No turning back now when he'd almost reached his shoes. Only that last stretch left along the base of Walking Sorrows Point, then around the bend and into his hideaway, where he'd feel safe in its familiar smells; where his eyes couldn't see destruction.

The overhang beckoned as it always did, but the top of the Bluff holding up the sky humbled him. Made him puny beneath all that weight that could crush him as easy as stomping a walnut. Yet, it didn't threaten his sense of "comin home." He paused at the spot where he'd slashed the bushes last May, where Buddy then made him stand guard for the rest of vacation. He drew a deep breath and held it, closed his eyes, calling that moment back, wanting it to last forever as he began to relive the magic of their first day here, then the return in wonder of that July afternoon when Buddy pointed out the steps into the sky. He moved on, one slow step at a time now (like coming down the aisle in church). Suddenly, unable to hold back any longer, he bounded around the bend to dash into the cave.

A howl tore open his face, and Johannes crumpled to the ground. The cave ... the cave had "VANISHED"!

When he could lift his head, Johannes pinched his leg, desperate to wake up and get back into his skin (but how can I wake if I aint already asleep, huh?). He blinked, but closing and opening his eyes changed nothing ("Jist think, Hansy, first our cave had a porch, now we got a attic. And a stairway ..."). Only God's Big Lightning could have done this thing. And God's Big Lightning stabbed him, too (Ohhh, Buddy, that attic-a yers has come down the stairway and filled up our cave and overflowed the porch to flatten the woods below).

Too violated to weep yet, he pinched himself again, then once more to be double-sure. Minutes became hours for him where he lay, the size of the damage too dazzling for words (what if Buddy blames all this on me for breaking my promises?). But Buddy wouldn't have to know of his broken promises in that unwritten letter if he told how God's Big Lightning took away their cave. And with the cave no more, nobody need ever know there'd even been one, or that it once had belonged to them, ohhh ...

If Time ran backwards on itself ... (not like Ma's Time which always runs ahead-a everything) ... if ... He turned away and pretended that nothing had changed, that nothing had happened. If he didn't stare at the destruction, he'd not see it, and nothing would be different. Still dazed, he scanned the world beyond and crushed and muddied woods below him to see what else last night's storms had done.

Flood waters from Blood Brothers Crick and Squaw River spread together into one vast lake that buried everything. Crooked lines of tree-tops marked the normal course of each stream, but the schoolhouse and the church hadn't floated away as he'd hoped they would. (HOW do you git to Eye-Away with ... everything runnin over, and the sloughs ... no longer there?)

He dared one backward glance, still hoping he'd only dreamed about what he'd discovered; then he whipped around and hugged his knees and gave way to wrenching sobs. All the letters in the world couldn't tell of anything this big. Emptied of feeling, he dozed.

("Jonas, where you put yer barnshoes now?") Ma's echo in his head brought Johannes to his knees. Where would his shoes be now; probably underneath all that confusion below (and more lies to tell!). When he rubbed his eyes, he no longer needed to pinch himself. Nothing could be more real than everything around now; only the color of the dirt had changed, which showed how the sun kept moving west (like nuttin's happened a-tall). He surveyed the damage around him, unable to think about climbing back down until he'd thought about his shoes some more. And what would The Ghosts do now (and where will I ever meet em?).

A sunbeam shot into the shadow of the overhang and the flicker of something faintly red hit the corner of his eye. Puzzled, he leaned forward. At first, it looked like a feather from one of the flints (Uncle Snorri-Bjorn said colored feathers often guided arrows to their mark). He moved in closer, but couldn't believe what he found: the worn red grip of the spade's handle. And he saw himself placing his shoes beside it (ever so carefully) last Thursday in the fog.

YES! They should be near the handle then, unless they'd bounced into the trees ahead of the slide, or if the spade itself knocked them about when rocks struck its scoop. He stared at what he saw; could this be real? Stretching as far as he could, one finger touched the wood (real wood!). He worked another finger, then his hand, into the grip, but couldn't dislodge the spade. Energy seeped back into his arms and legs. The harder he worked, the more the handle jiggled until the earth around it cracked. Johannes yanked with all his strength. Without warning the spade popped free, and he landed sideways against the slide, almost slipping over. But excitement pushed him on. He made an arc in the air with the scoop and nearly scared himself when he saw the new stubble he made of blackberry shoots that rested untouched beside the broken birch. Without thought or resistance, he jabbed the spade back into the dirt, set his foot on the top of its blade, and adjusted his hold. It looked easy enough to start work where the spade had been, with the sand drying and so many of the rocks in pieces. His shoes had to be nearby. He paused long enough to unbutton his shirt and roll up his pants. Again he brought his foot down, this time harder, and began to dig as if he'd always made holes; but now, for the first time doing something like this on his own; unbidden, but something that HAD to be done (or else?); had to be done now, as fast as his muscles would help him.

The sand, not so soft as it appeared to be, lay packed in layers beneath the false smoothness left behind by waters washing over it. The deeper he thrust, the more the ground threatened to fold in on itself, and the spade grew heavier with each load. With no work habits of his own to lighten this kind of job, Johannes tried to recall how Buddy'd dug and lifted. And the more he looked back on the past months (seems years ago now), the quicker his sense of summertime failure faded.

Each time the hole collapsed, Johannes started over, no longer discouraged, not entirely winded yet by what he demanded of himself. He insisted that his shoes couldn't be far from his efforts. Beyond that goal, his head buzzed with new promises: he'd remake their cave now that he knew how to dig; he'd dig every day and if he came home late from school he'd tell Ma he had to stay to help Ol' Gundy (uff da, but he'd work to remember his true-sounding lies), and he'd dig on Saturday and Sunday too if he could leave church fast enough and when the days got short, he'd work faster and even after dark too; he'd dig and dig and dig more until he'd made their cave. Doing what Buddy hadn't let him try before. And THEN he'd write to Eye-Away and tell Buddy everything (how nuttin bad had come cause he broke his promises).

When the hole didn't crumble at last, Johannes dug until tears soaked his face. Never had he dared dream that he could work as good as Buddy. And nobody had showed him, nor told him, nor forced him. Nobody could call him weak and lazy now. Maybe he'd turned into Buddy, his hair curly black, and his eyes big as plums. He pinched his leg hard to be sure that he remained Johannes.

He struck shale and see-sawed the spade until the stones crumbled and he tossed the larger pieces behind him. Tears of accomplishment eventually gave way to sobs of impatience which drained him. Sweat dripped like raindrops on the sand. Then, on the verge of giving up, he struck something soft as a rotten melon and from the scoop of the spade a muddied shoe danced out and buried itself so fast he couldn't tell what happened. One of his shoes! The other one had to be nearby. But from the looks of the ground, had he seen anything at all? Couldn't be sure. Why, the shoe might only be a chunk of dirt, what with the sweat in his eyes and shadows crowding in. Yet, if a shoe, why did it look as brown as his own and at the same time as black as Buddy's? He shivered.

At least he knew where to dig to make sure of what he'd seen. He began from scratch, more frantic than before to retrieve what he'd come for. He'd leave the rest of the cave work for later; later when it would be easier on his muscles. Small cyclones of alarm began to remind him of Ma and the dinner bell, of the unpicked dahlias, of the urgency to fetch his shoes without anybody seeing him come back. It never crossed his excitement during the climb to worry about a guard (the guard's s'posed to be me, ohhh ...). He crawled around the bend for a glance at his house below; nothing had changed the commotion he'd left (hours ago?). But he had to work faster.

That something that jumped out at him had to be his shoe and it waited to be recovered beneath this newest cave-in. And what about its mate? Johannes plunged head-first into the new hole he'd begun and he dug deeper with both hands now, throwing dirt into the air behind him like Ol' Odin did the badger mounds. When he pressed against the edge too far and everything began to fold in, he pushed himself away, stammering: Gotta git the shoes . . the shoes . . and the sand came down around him halfway to his waist.

-JOHANNES child! What in heaven's name you DOIN!

Ma's voice shattered the afternoon. But close. CLOSE. He pulled himself loose, rolled over on his back, and looked straight up at her (Ma herself, ohhh ...), crowning the rubble above him. He pinched himself but she didn't "vanish." She braced one hand against the wall of rock, the other clutched her breast. He glanced, terrified, from the narrow ledge between her and the treetops to her face, now white as her smock, which beat the new breeze like a rush of wings.

-Blessed Jesus, baby (dont say "Jesus" ma!), whatever got you clear up here. She gasped: -couldn't b'lieve my eyes when I accidentally looked at the Bluff and saw yer black pants scootin in the rocks.

Breathless, she could only stare at him until he choked (dont git mad, Ma, and scold and even cuss and ... and fall off the cliff!). When her voice came back she still didn't move: -Whatta you gotta say now? Answer me. What you doin anyway?

Trapped by the most important thing he'd ever done, Johannes had no way around her this time. His voice sounded strong: -I'm digging, cancha see. He tried to rise to go to her but fell forward on his knees.

-What loony thing is THIS?

-A cave, Ma, cancha see, a cave! He turned on her as if she already knew what he knew she couldn't know.

-But what cave, Jonas?

Things happening behind her face scared him more than even being found like this. He had to talk her back into her everday self again: -OUR cave, Ma . . got buried in the storm. Gotta try to dig it out 'fore ... OHHHH ... His wail took with it whatever energies remained in him. Terrified, too, that Ma might fall (and helpless to go to her), he lay numb and watched her pick her way through the rubble towards him, using at outstretched arm for balance, and avoiding any look over the rim of the ledge. When she came closer, he turned over and tried to burrow into the ground. His fingernails broke, but he didn't feel a pain.

She touched his ear. He turned to meet her terror. The blackness in her eyes, the whiteness of her cheeks, knocked words right out of him (dint think Ma'd be scared-a high places like this and I cant tell her there's nuttin to worry fer).

-Oh, Jonas, she crooned when she clamped her fingers over his: -Jonas, Jonas. Together they rocked in silence for a timeless moment.

Once more the babe being soothed on a winter's night, he didn't resist her when she lifted him from the base of Walking Sorrows Point. Her breath short, but with strength beyond his wildest dreams, she staggered along the ledge away from the nightmare behind them.

He no longer saw his cave destroyed; he saw only early golden rod brightening their way off the Bluff and the silk of milkweed caught in the corners of brush like mattresses left in the weather, and the reddening of the sumac to remind him of the blood shed by warriors long ago.

She carried him off the Howling Grief Ridges and set him down at the edge of the high field. There she took his hand and dragged him after her, in and out of the flattened corn stalks. Fast they went, then faster. Several times she dropped his wrist and ran ahead, but she soon stopped to coax him to her through gutted orchard and garden rows. Baffled by her "mysterious" strength and silence, he lost what sense of anything he had inside, and felt no pain yet as he limped behind her to the back porch (oh, Buddy, Buddy, I dug in our cave, and now I'm limpin like Ol' Gundy, ohhh ...).

On her way to the kitchen, she rang the dinner bell. When she lifted Johannes into Great-Granddad's rocker, not a word about his torn and dirtied second-best, nothing about his school-shoes caked with mud. She didn't even wash his face after she wrapped warm rags around his blistered hands. Without a word, she hurried back to the porch, rang the bell again, then rushed to the field gate, waving her smock to get further attention (why she's calling, huh? And who? Why dont she use the megaphone?). At the sound of the alarms, the buzzing of ladies spread throughout the downstairs and into the backyard. But Johannes no longer had curiosity, not even when Ol' Gundy tip-toed down the back stairs and limped out after the others without noticing him huddled in the chair. He hoped Ma with her white mask stayed away. He'd never been so bewildered.

He lay crushed, too, from his physical exertions. He felt smaller than ever before: his brain drying up, and the rest of him empty-dead. If he could wipe away Ma's look … if he could tell her how safe Buddy must be now, away from The Sheriff-Almighty and from the posse hunting him; if he could tell her not to worry herself white about a cave and him. He could not more speak about such things than he could hold off last night's agonies coming back on him (this gotta be a-nother bad dream, cant be fer real). He pinched his leg, but the sight of his damaged pants told him the truth.

He couldn't help Buddy yet, but he could excuse hi … excuse him for going on ahead like that; excuse him for the teasing and the naughty names; excuse him for getting mad whenever Johannes got in his way. And he'd excuse him for everything he could think of under the sun if he came back soon after Aunt Min had seen him … (if he came back before he had to go down the rivers to fetch him home, ohhh …).

Too exhausted to fight anything more, Johannes braced himself against the back of the chair, expecting The Winter-Lonely to take him. He waited, helpless. Yet, The Winter-Lonely stood off where he couldn't sense it; he couldn't believe that with his almost-willingness to let go (this first time ever!) The Winter-Lonely didn't seem to give a tinker's dam no more and dint send forth warning whiffs to complicate his sorrows. He shut his eyes tighter and yearned for blessed sleep.

A double-Buddy stared back at him, one behind each lid, each looking worse than Thursday morning's dream, and then Ma's white mask blurred everything and his shoe jumped out at him again but this time black before it disappeared and came back out as brown as mud and everything turned gray (wont Buddy call me "loony" if I tell him I dug up his shoe instead of mine and him needin his high-tops all the way to Dee-bjuke).

The urge to sleep lessened (jist think, Buddy, no needta hide or find our shoes no more; no letters to write, no new lies to 'member neither; no Sheriff-Almighty on yer tail; no Ol' Gundy, no Mrs Preacher's Woman, and everthing else The Winter-Lonely gobbled on, and alla that gone now ... maybe?).

Yet, what if The Winter-Lonely turned back on itself like the storm did last night and caught him when he didn't expect it? Prepared to fight again he snuggled in the rocker, but nothing happened. Instead of choking on it, his breath came back to life in its regular way. He shifted the cheeks of his hinder and warmth began to seep back into his legs and arms, and with it the first awareness of pain as muscles jumped (like Dad's tractor shook after bein turned off). Soon he smarted all over, but couldn't tell at first which places hurt worse. Each finger on each hand twitched separately, each with a sputtering flame beneath it (see, Buddy, I did dig in the cave, I did, and all by myself I dug). He unraveled their wrappings and his hands lay raw and swollen in his lap as shapeless as winter mittens laid to dry behind the stove. Small stabs of pain turned into larger ones as they came and went with the pulse of the rocking. And this carried him away.

Uncle Snorri's clock struck five sharp notes. Johannes opened an eye (must be hours since Ma put me here). Stillness sat on the house as chilly as January ice on Blood Brothers Crick. A stillness greater than ordinary silence with sounds you KNOW rather than HEAR rustling all over inside of you. A ripe tomato of a sun hovered over the bluff tops in the west. Walking Sorrows stood blood-red (what colors had Broken Thunderhawk been wrapped in when he floated down the Squaw to die? Did Buddy see the same colors when he went along the water?).

He heard Solly and Sig tramp alongside the alcove windows and watched them stop at the back fence gate, their necks stretched west, ears perked. Out in the far end of the winter-wheat field, Dad's feed-truck stood beside The Sheriff-Almighty's car (the truck as shabby as Ol' Odin beside a fancy collie). He couldn't understand why people gathered there, at the bottom of the cliffs of Walking Sorrows; looked like potato-picking time (but no potatoes planted there this year). When they melded together into a big shadow of their own, they moved on towards the house, leaving the cars behind. Dad in the lead, barely visible but for a sunbeam that bounced for a second off his face.

Around the oncoming men, the ladies who'd been in the house when Ma sent him for dahlias now flocked and fluttered like chickens come to be fed. He thought he saw Ol' Gundy kneel in the dirt and take off shoes (how loony can you git wearin high heels in the dirt, huh?). He did see Buddy's Maw when she ran against Dad and beat at him with both arms flailing, and when The Sheriff-Almighty (with a differnt sunbeam stabbin at his star) stepped out of nowhere and caught her by the wrists (how "mysterious" ohhh …). Losing his breath, Johannes pinched his leg. He couldn't make sense of anything he saw (must be that posse Buddy'd warned about). Kicking giant shadows ahead of them, the force marched forward down the fall-ploughed field straight for his alcove windows. Johannes tried to stop the rocker. From the corner of his eye he saw Solly and Sig toss their manes. One of the horses winnied.

Without a sound, Ma stepped from behind his chair. Her billowing smock blotted out his view. He froze. How long she'd been in the room he couldn't tell, without so much as a sigh to give her away and now looking into his startled face (dont scare me, Ma, with that white face!). The buzz of voices moved closer, low as the swarming of bees. She kept her silence, but continued to look at him as if seeing him for the first time ever.

When the field gate creaked and he heard Dad order the horses back, Ma stepped from the window and knelt against his knees, pressing him deeper into the rocker. And when the shape of the posse went around the nook and along the kitchen pines to the back porch, she opened her mouth to speak, but only her eyes moved, not the lips, and the eyes full of water didn't run over. She stared at him with a faraway look (why, Ma's turned into somebody else; what can I do, ohhh …).

His blood turned to ice. Of all the meanings Johannes remembered from Ma's changeable faces, he'd never seen this one before, except a bit of it high on the bluff … (how long, how long ago now?). Again she opened her mouth to tell him something, he knew; still nothing came out. Suddenly, he had to escape; out of the chair, out of the room, out of the house, away from the rattlesnakes in his chest; he had to run far, into the sky where it wouldn't look so old. Her hands tightened, holding him in place while the sounds grew muffled on their way to the open alcove door. (Why does it take ferever fer that posse to git here? I'll jist hafta lie some more and tell em I dont know where or why Buddy's gone.)

Johannes strained to listen if Singing White Wolf had sent a ghost song, warning him to hold his tongue. When some voices turned into sobs, Ma pulled him to her bosom, then backed away and took his face between her hands and held it from her, her hands spring-water cold, her eyes blacker than midnight, and when she forced out some words at last, she spoke in a faraway tone. She spoke in broken Norwegian (she dont want me to know whats happenin, ohhh …).

Their eyes locked (MOMMY!).

-Jonas, my baby, she said. She brought his face to hers and touched his forehead with her own; gentler the fingers now, still cold: -Jonas, she struggled, -Johannes sweetheart … Her voice hesitated, once again in Norwegian, then stopped. With sudden resolution, her words came out in regular everyday talk: -Jesus has called fer Buddy.

Johannes whimpered in her embrace (DONT, MA, DONT! Dont scare me with Jesus agin. Aint a baby no more cant you see ... I dug in our cave and I even WAITED for The Winter-Lonely, so dont scare me now with ... Jesus, huh?). She held him tighter and nodded slowly, which made her words sound final:

-Yes, my Johannes, she whispered: -Jesus has called Buddy home. Found him ... sittin in the sand ... alone. Her voice disappeared.

-But Ma, Johannes fought back: -cant be true. Buddy's gone down the river ... down the river to Eye-Away, cancha see nuttin? To his Aunt Min Eye-Away. Cancha see, Ma, huh? (But without his shoes, maybe ...).

Feet rumbled up the back steps. Ma hugged Johannes tighter, squeezing the sound out of him, until his quivering shook her too. Dad's voice said something low. The porch planks vibrated. Somebody tapped the dinner bell (I tell you, Ma, agin: Buddy's gone down ... and I dug ... and the Winter Lonely dont want me no more ... maybe Singing White ... but Buddy's gone down to ... down the river with no shoes?). A mourning dove sobbed behind the front yard spruces.

Johannes twisted out of Ma's arms into a standing position against the back of the rocker. He faced the open outside door laid back against the alcove wall where in each of its eight panes the orange-red sun dipped into the Minnesota bluffs. The thundering footsteps stopped for a moment. Then the screendoor flew open and a purple shadow swept in over everything. In silence. No flashes of God's Big Lightning. No zinging arrows around his head. Time just stopped like in those snapshots.

And Johannes stood in the presence of Great Chief Broken Thunderhawk who carried on his outstretched arms the limp and sandy form of Singing White Wolf!

Paralyzed with wonder, Johannes could only stare at the rays of sunset fading from curls as snarled as any Ol' Odin ever had. (Uncle Snorri-Bjorn! I see em, The Ghosts I do, but . . but Uncle Snorri, their heads aint shaved, and they aint got ... braids).

205

His heart sucked out of him, Johannes floated free of Ma and left her holding fast his legs. He hovered over Singing White Wolf's face. Suddenly its mouth jerked open. Johannes shuddered. And listened. A chirping cricket died behind the cookstove. Johannes waited for the ghost song. For another instant, nothing moved. Johannes listened. Then Time moved on, and still …

… still Johannes listened.

Then heard no more.

1935 came to an early end that year.

(Trygwald-Rol : 9/1999)